ning

And then, as if Gayle D'Angelo's perfume rode on a last drift of dangerous June air and called him forward, my father, at that moment, strode across the park from the parking lot. I remember reading later, in one of the books Ms. Cassaday would give me, about those sirens in mythology. The ones who sat on the rocks and with their singing lured sailors to their deaths. When I read that, I thought of my father then, walking across the park. His hands were in the pockets of his khaki pants, and his face wore this hopeful, uncertain look...

He saw me too. He gave a wave, then poked his finger in the air to indicate where he was headed, a goofy dance-move gesture. It made me worry for him, that gesture. Like when you see a kid walking to school with really short pants and you just say to yourself, *Uh-oh*.

# The Queen of
## Everything

**SCHOLASTIC**

## DEB CALETTI

Scholastic Children's Books,
Commonwealth House, 1–19 New Oxford Street,
London, WC1A 1NU, UK
A division of Scholastic Ltd
London ~ New York ~ Toronto ~ Sydney ~ Auckland
Mexico City ~ New Delhi ~ Hong Kong

First published in the USA by Simon & Schuster, 2002

This edition published by Scholastic Ltd, 2003

ISBN 0 439 97699 5

Printed and bound by Nørhaven Paperback A/S, Denmark

1 2 3 4 5 6 7 8 9 10

The right of Deb Caletti to be identified as the author of this work has been
asserted by her in accordance with the Copyright,
Designs and Patents Act, 1988.

For my roots and branches —

Mom, Dad, Sue, Warren, Sam, and Nick.
With love

# Acknowledgments

Special thanks to Anne Greenberg
and Jennifer Klonsky.
And to Ben Camardi,
gratitude beyond measure.

# Chapter One

People ask me all the time what having Vince MacKenzie for a father was like. What they mean is: Was he always crazy? Did he walk around the kitchen with an ice pick in the pocket of his flannel bathrobe every morning as he poured himself a cup of coffee?

Some ask flat out, as if it's their right to know. Others circle it, talk about the weather first, thinking they're being so sneaky when really they're as obvious as a dog circling a tree.

When they ask I always say the same thing. I say, "He was an *optometrist* for God's sake. You know, the guy who sits you in the big chair and says, 'Better here, or here?' The ones with the little pocket-size flashlights?" And that's all I say. I try to keep it all in the tone of voice. I don't even add a, *If you must know, you insensitive jackass.* Well I did say that once. I don't count it though, because it was to an old man who probably had bad hearing.

What I won't do is tell anyone what he was really like.

I won't say that when I think of him now, I see him outside, at places he can no longer go. I see him mowing the front lawn, wearing his University of Washington Huskies cap, holding his hand to his ear to let me know he can't hear what I'm saying over the mower's engine. I see him dumping the basket of clippings into the garbage can, small bits of grass clinging to his sweatshirt. I see him watering the rhododendrons, his thumb held over the end of the hose to make the spray less harsh.

And I see him—us—in our house. The house we used to live in. I see him with his tie loosened after work, pouring himself a glass of milk and asking how my history test went. I remember sitting next to my father at the kitchen table, him trying to explain my math homework but making it more confusing. And me, saying, *Oh, I see!* when I didn't, because I didn't want to hurt his feelings.

I won't tell anyone his faults either. That he swore when he fixed things and flirted too much with waitresses and swaggered around more than he deserved to when he was wearing a new shirt. Good or bad, I keep those things to myself. I don't want those parts of him, the real him, to turn into something cheap and meaningless. It would make me the kid with no friends, giving out candy on the playground. People would grab up those bits of him like greedy children with a roll of Lifesavers. They'd peel off a piece of him, roll him around in their mouths for a few seconds, and then swallow and forget about him.

Besides, that's not what people want to hear anyway—that my father was just a normal guy whom I loved, *love*, with all my heart. It makes them nervous. Because if he was normal, if he wore Old Spice and liked nacho cheese Doritos, then why not their own fathers? Or themselves? Deep Inner Evil—we like that. It's easier to accept than what Big Mama says, which is that wanting things for the wrong reasons can turn anyone's life into a marshmallow on a stick over a hot fire: impossibly messy and eventually consumed, one way or another. People want to think that I lay in bed awake at night, my heart pounding in fear of him. They don't want to know that I slept just fine, dreaming I'd forgotten my locker combination just like them.

Or that I went to live with Dad because he was the regular one; that it was my mom who I was convinced was nuts. Claire was the one I never wanted my friends to see. She had this shaggy hair under her arms that always made me think of a clump of alfalfa sprouts in a pita pocket. And you never knew when she might suddenly flop out a boob to nurse Max, which she did once during a parent-teacher conference to the shock of my new math teacher, Mr. Fillbrook. By the look on his face I'm positive Mrs. Fillbrook always got dressed in the dark. Or else she did that trick when you slip your bra through your sleeve every night when she put on her nightgown. All Claire had to say about the whole thing was, "If he was *titi*llated, pardon the pun, that's his problem."

God.

When I lived with my mom, it was her house that embarrassed me, never Dad's. Mom had turned our old house into a bed and breakfast, which is one way to make a living on Parrish Island if you don't want to rent kayaks or work the oyster beds. At Mom's house you never knew who was coming or going. And Nathan's metal sculptures were spread all over the yard, spinning like mad in the wind and hanging from the trees like giant Christmas ornaments. Nathan is my mother's husband; he's ten years younger than she is. He's also an "artist." His work is "kinetic art for the outdoors." That's how I thought of their life. Like it all belonged in quotation marks.

When I moved in with my dad, *that's* when

my life got normal. I moved into a regular neighborhood with a regular house. I transferred from that goofy alternative school I hated, where we made quilts and "worked at our own pace" and where the teachers all wore sandals no matter what the weather, to Parrish High where you had to sit in your seat and learn English and the kids weren't weird. I met Melissa Beene, who lived down the block and whose parents had a big black Weber barbecue and electric garage-door openers. Everyone in my dad's neighborhood mowed their lawn and thought breakfast was the most important meal of the day and got upset if their kids missed their curfews.

Anyway, evil. If anyone was truly evil in all this, it was Gayle D'Angelo. She put that gun in his hands. I don't like to think about her. I *hate* thinking about her. But Mom and Nathan and everyone else keep telling me that it's *healthy* to get the feelings out. Big Mama says that even salmon carry their life stories on their scales, the way a tree does with its rings. And my old English teacher, Ms. Cassaday, claims writing this out will be good therapy. "What is therapy after all," she says, "but telling your tale to someone who won't get up in the middle?" So okay, fine. Just so I don't suddenly fall apart one day when I'm thirty-five in an aisle of the grocery store or something. Carried out kicking and screaming while the ladies squeezing lemons pretend they don't notice a thing.

I will think about her. And it will be all right. Because, true, the story starts there, with Gayle D'Angelo. But it does not end there.

I first met Gayle D'Angelo at the True You Health Center. My best friend, Melissa Beene, got me the job at True You. We worked after school, the occasional evening, and more hours in the summer. True You is in a strip mall, in the new part of town that the original Parrish Islanders hate. If you took one of those snoots who say they watch only PBS and dangled a game show in front of their eyes, that's the kind of reaction I'm talking about. I used to think the whole argument was stupid. My mother would go on and on about the yuppies coming from Seattle and Microsoftland with their plastic money, building plastic things, intent on destroying the spirit of the islands. The San Juans had always been an escape from all that, she'd moan.

"And what's with these minivans?" she said once. "I feel like I'm in some sci-fi movie. *Revenge of the Pod People.* Invading the world in Dodge Caravans. You watch, those people are going to wreck everything. I bet even the whales will get wind of what's happening and stop coming around."

"That's what the farmers said when you

hippies started moving out here, Claire," I said. Parrish, and the other large islands of the San Juans, used to be mostly orchards. There were still stretches of sprawling farmland and spots of gnarled apple trees where the deer met up with their friends for garden parties. "And what the Indians said about the farmers."

My mother glared at me. "Jordan," she said.

"I'm sorry," I said. I used to say this a lot, especially when I wasn't in the least. "I just never got that, the way people yelled about trees being cut down as they sat in their own cozy home in front of a blazing fire."

"This is not about selfishness," she snapped. "It's exactly the opposite. It's about having something pure and true, and trying to protect its essence." This is the way my mother talked. She was getting worked up, flushing the shade of a ripe peach. "What's happening is a crime. An abomination. A *bête noire*."

"What's that, a perfume?" I said.

She sighed.

"Sounds like a perfume. 'Purchase a three-ounce bottle of Bête Noire and receive a one-ounce line minimizer and cosmetic tote as our gift to you.'" I chuckled. I was happy with my misbehavior.

My mother stopped glaring. Now she only tilted her head and looked at me oddly, as if I were, say, the produce guy from Albertson's suddenly in her home. It was a look that said, *I know I know you from somewhere, but for the life of me, I can't figure out who you are.*

She gathered up her long hair into a pony-tail, held it in her fist, and set it loose again. Finally she said, "I should send you to your room for the rest of your life."

"Too late," I had said.

I used to think a lot of stupid things. About Parrish Island, about my parents. But Big Mama says thinking we're ever done being stupid is the dumbest thought of all. Being occasionally stupid is just part of the human job description, she says. Big Mama's voice is like molasses pouring from a bottle. When she calls, I press that phone so hard to my ear, it's as if I'm getting her strength right through the wires. And right when that strength seems to be running out, there she is again, filling me back up.

You can imagine how my working at True You got under my mother's skin. I didn't always purposefully try to get under her skin. I didn't. It's just that sometimes things can be too real. Too intensely real. Too honest and bare. Like the way you feel looking into the eyes of some-one who loves you, or someone in pain. Or the way you feel when you hear beautiful music. It can be like looking into the sun. You've just got to close your eyes. Even go inside for a while. Or keep it all at arm's length with words like *crazy*, covering it with a smooth layer of embarrassment. My mother and Nathan were like that. Parrish Island was like that.

As I said, Melissa got me the job at True You, and at the moment Gayle D'Angelo came in, Melissa was in the large weigh-in room with Laylani Waddell. Laylani and her husband, Buddy, owned True You. Anyone who names their kid Laylani is looking for trouble, if you ask me. You had to be careful with Laylani. She and Buddy were Christians with a capital C, the type who think they've got God's secret phone number. If you let so much as a *shit* slip, Laylani would start hiding these little religious bookmarks with prayers and sunsets on them in your lunch bag and in your coat pockets. She wouldn't say a word about them, either. I think she really believed we might be so stumped as to who put them there, we'd start suspecting God himself.

I could hear Laylani's voice coming through the weigh-in room door. Her voice sounds the way a maraschino cherry might sound if it could speak. The door was propped open with a small block of wood, the way Laylani demanded. Large people overheated easily, she always said. She worried about this a lot. I think she had a secret fear one of the fat people might have a heart attack on the premises and sue her and Buddy for the house and the RV with the built-in shower. Melissa liked to get revenge for the bookmarks by hiding this block of wood, which would send Laylani scurrying around in a tizzy, sprayed hair releasing in bunches as she searched for it underneath the furniture. Like a madwoman she'd try other propping devices in the door, like the stapler, which would only slide free and shoot across the floor.

When Laylani's inspiring pre-dinner lesson was over, Melissa and I would do weight and measurement. In the meantime I was copying an article, "Recipe for Success," that would be placed in new "team member" folders. This is what people who joined True You were called, the idea being that they were one enthusiastic group fighting a tough but conquerable opponent—fat—with the help of Coach Laylani. I sat on the edge of the reception desk and read the article as the copy machine flashed and made its *kershunk-kershunk-kershunk* sounds. "It's your total diet over several weeks rather than what you eat in a given meal or even an entire day that determines whether you're eating healthfully and weight consciously," I read aloud.

"No kidding," I said to the paper.

And then there she was in front of me. I'd been so busy being amused by the article's obviousness that I hadn't heard the swish of the door, or her heels, quiet on the carpet Buddy Waddell had installed himself.

"Ah, it's so nice and cool in here," she said.

Which was funny, because my very first thought looking at her was, *I bet this woman never even sweats*. She was lovely, really. The kind of woman you save that word for, lovely. Dark hair swept up in a clip, two perfect tendrils coaxed down. Short, sleeveless black dress. This great shade of nail polish. Expensive earrings, expensive smile. Warm though. It didn't occur to me then that some people could make a smile warm with the same deliberate efficiency other folks use to put wool socks on cold feet. I was not all that well acquainted with manufactured smiles. I hadn't yet bought a car, met a preacher's wife, or been to a PTA meeting. According to my mother, there are more fake smiles at a PTA meeting than in a false-teeth factory.

The woman in front of me fanned the air with a slender hand. A drift of perfume was set free and roamed around the room as if it owned the place.

"They'll be done in there in a few minutes," I said. "If you want, you can sit down." I gestured to the chairs in the waiting area, done in soothing shades of rose and tan.

"Oh, you think . . ." She laughed. "Aren't you sweet. I'm not here to pick anyone up. I'm here for *myself.*" She leaned in as if to tell a secret. "We all need a little help now and then, don't we?" She took a pinch of her side.

This disappointed me. Obviously, there was nothing there to pinch. She probably lived on cups of coffee, doing leg lifts as she poured it. That's what her body looked like. She radiated charm and money and capability; I didn't want her to be a self-pincher of nonexistent body fat. This was the kind of woman I wanted to be someday, who would have considered alfalfa-sprout hair under her arms to be repellent as venereal disease. She would even use words like *repellent*. Unlike my mother, she would not be the type who would pop out her emotions for everyone to see, spraying everyone in the vicinity in the process, same as Grandpa Eugene with his dentures.

"Oh," I said. "Well, in that case I'll have to make you an appointment with our health consultant, Laylani Waddell." I handed her one of Laylani's business cards that sat in a Lucite holder on the reception desk. Laylani loved for us to pass them out. Her name gloated in the corner of those little white cards with the pink stripe across the top. HEALTH CONSULTANT, they read. OWNER. Yep, she was a valid member of the human race. I opened the wide, loose appointment book. "It'll take about an hour."

"Maybe you can just tell me a little about your place here," she said. "Since I'm not even sure what it is you do."

I was actually relieved. Maybe the woman

thought we were a gym. I hoped so. I didn't want her to be one of those diet bimbos we saw so many of, who knew the fat grams in a pretzel stick, and who only wanted to hear how little they needed what they came for. Diet bimbos pissed me off. I couldn't imagine what they did to the truly overweight. On behalf of the real sufferers, I always tried to do what I could during a diet bimbo's Game Plan Consultation. I'd find slices of fat they never knew existed and measure them for long periods of time with my tape. I'd shake my head when I wrote things on the clipboard and mutter "Whew" a lot. I'd be extra cheerful and say things like, *Now, we shouldn't think Fritos are the fifth food group!*

I didn't think I could be mean to this woman. "I have a brochure," I said.

"As long as it covers price. My husband tends to be tight fisted, bless his heart." People tended to say this, I noticed, whenever blessing seemed the last thing on their minds. "The first time he ever went to Costco, I swear he got a hard-on."

It's not too often that someone says *hard-on* when you've just met, I thought, but okay, fine. Besides, her voice had an ever-so-slight Southern lilt, harsh twangs polished smooth; it was the kind of accent that can make even a word like *hard-on* sound harmless and sweet as a mint julep drunk from a porch swing.

"Oh, boy," I said. I mean, what do you say?

"Tell me, do we know each other?" she asked, leaning in to examine me with one eye narrowed. "I never forget a lovely face."

I actually blushed. "I'm not sure," I said. *Lovely.* It was the word I had thought so perfect for her. I wondered if it could actually be true. Me, with my curly brown hair (chestnut, my mother called it), and legs that seemed too long. My mother said I was beautiful, Melissa said she wished she looked like me, but compliments from your mother and your best friend don't count. I'm embarrassed to admit what pleasure that *lovely* gave me.

"You must know my sons," she said. "Markus and Remington D'Angelo? Parrish High? They were new last year."

I did know her sons. At the name Markus an image swam up. Tall blond boy, quiet. Hands stuck into the pockets of a swim team jacket. But more than that, I knew her house. It was the recently built one behind our neighborhood in the Crow Valley. Nothing you could overlook. A huge new faux Tudor with its own airstrip. It dwarfed the quaint house of Little Cranberry Farm on the adjacent property. It was the kind of house that made my mother scream.

"Oh, right," I said.

"I thought you must know them. I'm Gayle." She extended her cool fingers, and I took them for a moment. I hoped she didn't notice the shade of pink on my own nails, which suddenly seemed silly and girlish and was peeling besides. "And you are . . . ?"

"Jordan MacKenzie," I said.

"MacKenzie?" She pointed one ear at me as if offering it a second chance to get it right. "You don't happen to belong to Dr. Vince MacKenzie, do you?"

Normally I would have said that I don't *belong* to anyone, but she was so nice that I only nodded and smiled. At this, she grasped my hand and hushed her voice. "I can't believe meeting you like this. I think your father is just wonderful."

It was the way a middle aged woman would react if she'd just met the daughter of, say, Elvis. I wondered what my father had done to deserve it. Believe me, if you heard my father sing, you'd know no one was going to throw their underwear at him, even those waist-high control-top ones that women my mother's age wear. And I didn't think that a free glaucoma check or sunglasses frames at cost would cause someone's voice to get all breathy like that.

"Thank you," I said, which I was embarrassed for later. It's not as though I could take credit for my choice of the guy.

"You have his eyes," she said. She studied me. "Beautiful deep brown. You must have to fight off the boys with a stick! My goodness, I would kill for that figure of yours. I bet you are your daddy's little girl."

That thought made we want to gag. "I wouldn't say that," I said.

"No? Still, you must be close. The father-daughter bond and all."

"I saw it in a movie once," I said. I don't know why I said that except that maybe I was trying to let her know the daddy's girl crap had no place in my life. After I said it though, I felt my conscience jab me at this small betrayal of my father. I mean, we *were* close in our own way. But if we're being honest here, getting truly close to fathers is like trying to dig out a really old tree stump. You get exhausted with the effort and don't actually get very far.

Not only was my conscience being Goody Two-Shoes, but I also started feeling a little embarrassed about what I'd said. It seemed kind of personal for a first conversation, even with the *hard-on* ice already broken. But Gayle D'Angelo only laughed. I could hear the rustling of bodies in the weigh-in room, papers shuffling, the sudden burst of mixed conversations. Laylani was finished. "Our health consultant should be right out," I said.

"That's all right," Gayle D'Angelo said. "I'm only here for the information." She waved the brochure in the air.

Melissa popped her head out of the weigh-in

room door. "Show time," she said. She looked at Mrs. D'Angelo, caught my eye, and raised one eyebrow, a trick I always wished I could do.

"Nice to meet you," I said to Gayle D'Angelo.

And it was. Afterward I carried around a strange thrill. The kind you get when something seems possible that didn't before, or after you've been truly *seen*. I wondered if she was the "influential person" my horoscope that day said I'd be meeting. I didn't consider, until much later, that maybe what I felt were really the hypervibrations that come with warning; the way your heart pounds when you are playing hide-and-seek and sense someone is about to spring out at you. Even salmon, Big Mama says, can sometimes get caught after their instincts have confused them.

Melissa and I usually walked home together after work. Whiffs of Gayle D'Angelo's perfume had lounged around True You's waiting room the rest of the day, and now it was following along behind us. Though it was early evening, and only the very beginning of June, it was hot out, unusually so for Parrish at that time of year. Normally that kind of weather starts mid-August and ends two weeks later. But, hey, if you can guess the weather in the Northwest, we'll probably crown you ruler of the land.

Outside, the air was stifling; it felt like trying

to breathe through a knitted scarf. "Wanna get doughnuts?" Melissa said in the parking lot, as True You's door shut behind us.

"Maple bar sugar hit," I said.

"Let me see if I've got money," she said. She swung her backpack off her shoulder and rooted around inside.

"How can we even *think* fried food after Laylani's lecture?" I mock-scolded.

"Yeah, they usually make me too sick to eat," Melissa said to the inside of her backpack. Two cars started up in the parking lot, one belonging to one of our team members, another to a customer of the dry cleaner next door, a garment sheathed in thin plastic hanging from her back window. The door to True You opened again, and a girl just a little older than I stepped outside. She squinted and blinked, as if the world was more bright and shocking than she could stand. She had stayed behind for a one-on-one with Laylani, something Laylani required when she felt on the verge of losing a customer. The girl looked down, avoiding our eyes when she passed us, and her huge frame, draped with a floral cotton dress, moved with great effort through the parking lot and toward the sidewalk.

Melissa held up her wallet. "We're covered," she said. She followed my gaze. "Aren't you just entirely sick of fatties?"

Her voice was loud. Too loud. I could see the

girl flinch, her shoulders lifting ever so slightly. And then her purse slid from her arm, dropped to the sidewalk, and spilled. She stopped, stooped down, and balanced on the ball of one foot to gather her things. Sweat was beginning to darken the armpits of her dress. For a second, so quick I couldn't even be sure it happened, she looked up at me and we caught eyes.

And then I did a horrible thing. A cruel thing. I turned away from those thick fingers picking up loose coins and a half-empty pack of gum and a small bottle of hand lotion, and I laughed. Loudly. To show Melissa how much I agreed.

"Entirely sick," I said.

And then Melissa and I walked away. To buy doughnuts to eat before dinner. Me trying to forget what I had just done, trying to forget the coin rolling away on its edge and escaping those fat fingers.

"We'd better be quick," I said. "You know how pissed Dad gets if I'm not there for dinner."

We hurried past Randall and Stein Booksellers, the shop my father's longtime girlfriend owned, waited for a break in traffic, and jogged across the street to Boss Donuts. The doughnut guy was Mel Thurber. His name should have been Mole Thurber, with his bald head, and eyes that were always squinting, as if they still hadn't adjusted to life aboveground. I got a squeamish feeling when I thought of him touching my food, even when he used a square of tissue paper. I was always glad to get out of there, to escape the smell of hot grease and the container of pink lemonade that looked as though it had been there forever, little skin flecks of lemon pulp clinging to the glass sides.

"I can't see how he can stand to drink coffee in this heat," Melissa said. She was referring to Officer Ricky Beaker, whom we called the Tiny Policeman, due to the fact that he was barely five feet tall and had a voice that resembled one of the Lollipop Twins of Munchkin Land. How he had managed to dodge the height requirement for police officers, no one could ever figure out. The Tiny Policeman could usually be found sitting in the corner of Boss Donuts, nursing a cup of coffee as if it were a whiskey in a cowboy-movie saloon instead of a Styrofoam cup on a sticky table set under fluorescent lights. His eyes glanced suspiciously about, as they always did. He was waiting for the bad guys in black to ride up on their horses and step through the swinging doors. You could tell that he desperately wanted some real bad guys around. There wasn't much crime on Parrish. The most serious crime fighting the Tiny Policeman did was taking down the license plates of the high-school boys who shouted,

"You should've eaten your vegetables!" at him from their car windows.

Outside, Melissa held out the waxed bag to me. I took out a maple bar and we ate as we walked. When we reached the entrance to our neighborhood, I looked down the street. "Dad's not home yet if you want to come over," I said.

In our driveway, I had seen only my father's red Triumph, an old one covered by a tarp, which he called his midlife-crisis car. I guess he felt the crisis was over; he never drove that Triumph as long as I could remember, though he started it on occasion to make sure it still ran. The Ford Taurus that he actually drove, and that he washed and vacuumed once a week and wouldn't let you eat in, was not there yet.

"Oh, God, don't look," Melissa said. She grabbed my arm to hurry me along, clasped the collar of her shirt, and raised it to cover half her face. I was sure this strategy had never succeeded in hiding anyone.

"What's he doing?"

"Don't ask," Melissa said. "Probably seeing if the trees are talking to him."

Melissa's older brother, Jackson Beene, lay under the big tree in their front yard, staring up at the branches, hands forming a pillow behind his head. Ever since Jackson got lost in the woods on a hike on Mount Conviction three summers ago, he "hasn't been quite right," as

21

Mrs. Beene put it. He had gone backpacking with a friend, who during the hike fell down a ravine and broke his leg. Jackson tried to get help. The friend was found that night by the searchers, but Jackson had gotten lost and was missing for five days. On the sixth, he appeared at a ranger station. Melissa said he'd lost something like twenty-five pounds and couldn't eat at first without throwing up. What saved him, Jackson had said, was the sound of bagpipes, which he followed to safety. He was sure he had been rescued by a spirit; after that, he mailed away for instructional tapes and took up playing the bagpipes himself. He would play them in the front yard or over at Point Perpetua park or across from the ferry terminal on a busy weekend. The Beenes tried to be supportive (if you looked up Larry and Diane Beene in the dictionary, you'd see that word), but you could tell this embarrassed them as much as it did Melissa.

I sometimes saw Jackson playing his bagpipes at the old oil tank, which sits on its side on a mound of grass at the crossroads of Horseshoe Highway and Deception Loop; a place you must pass to get anywhere on Parrish. Usually the oil tank is a patchwork of messages: HAPPY 40TH WAYNE with a couple of black balloons stuck on, and DISCOUNT CHAKRA READINGS THIS WEEK AT THE THEOSOPHICAL SOCIETY, along with some old stuff painted on, like CLASS OF '79 ROCKS! I would pass on my bike, hearing the music get louder as I got closer, and when I saw Jackson standing on the oil tank with his tasseled instrument, I was glad he wasn't my brother. Strangely though, I was also just plain glad. That music—it was both mysterious and sad at the same time. It could make you feel things you couldn't quite explain.

Melissa and I sat on the step of our front porch and finished our doughnuts. We licked our fingers, then washed the stickiness off under the garden hose. Dad finally arrived home, looking happy. He teased Melissa and me about something I don't remember and carried in a fat bag of groceries with a bunch of celery sticking out the top.

That was the day I met Gayle D'Angelo.

It's funny, but when I think about that day, I don't think much about Gayle D'Angelo herself, or the fact that when I came back out from the weigh-in room, the brochure I had given her was left behind on the counter. No, what I think about is that fat girl. She never came back to True You. I never even saw her again, although I thought I did once, leaving Bonnie Randall's bookstore.

But she's what I think about. The way our eyes met. The way, right then, she seemed more real than me. I think about the way my own laugh had made my insides twist, made the pink polish on my fingers seem hateful, fingers that had so recently touched her skin.

Fingers that had only moments before slipped a tape measure around her fleshy arm.

# Chapter Two

Everyone who lives here knows that in early June some kind of strange tonic floats in the air on Parrish Island. My mother says this is a magic brew, ignited when the first warmth of the year penetrates the fir trees and the saltwater, peels the bark of the red madrona in papery strips, and soaks deep into the ground where the island potters dig their clay. She really talks like that. But those are the smells—she is right about that—earthy, sweet, and warm.

You can see the effects everywhere, something like spring in other places, I guess, but with the volume turned up high. Class size always doubles at the Rufaro School of Marimba, next door to my mother's, the new students playing their instruments with the frenzy of a tropical storm, and Cliff Barton gets dangerous again in his biplane, buzzing the ground and making everyone scream. The Franciscan nuns who work the ramp at the ferry terminal Tuesday through Saturday, guiding the passengers to their destinations, get all red-cheeked from the warmth of their habits; and all the old men on the island get out their nets to try to catch the rabbits that now swagger out of their holes in droves. I think the rabbits and the old guys are a good match, both of them frisky without any-place to put it. When you see the way they stare one another down, those rabbits so sure of themselves and those codgers so fierce with their nets, you can't help but think those old guys are reliving some big battle they fought in World War Two.

As with those bottles of aromatherapy that prune Cora Lee sells at the Theosophical Society, you can be sure June air will affect you, but there is no guarantee just how. Once in June a man went insane and shot himself on the ledge at Point Perpetua, the place that pods of orcas and porpoise have come home to for hundreds of years. You can still see blood on some of the big stones out there, by the lighthouse. I know because I've seen it. And once, a young woman claimed to have felt the effects all the way in Chicago, where she packed up her belongings and suddenly moved west after seeing a postcard of Parrish Island slide across the counter of the post office where she worked. The man who went insane was Big Mama's husband, Clyde Belle; the woman who saw the postcard was my own mother when she was eighteen.

So what I mean to say is, June was not a good time for Gayle D'Angelo to become a part of my father's life.

The windows of my creative-writing class were opened halfway, and I could hear Custodian Bill on the riding lawn mower somewhere out on the football field. Ms. Cassaday should have shut the windows. She couldn't compete with that air—though, if you ask me, she was the only one of my teachers who was right to think she might. I was glad to be there in her class, where I had a chance of putting aside, at least for a while, the uneasy feeling I'd had since that morning when the phone rang at breakfast.

At first I thought it was Melissa. Dad liked to give me a ride to school every morning to "Start the day off on the right foot," as he said. Sometimes Melissa came along.

"You can come if you don't mess with my dad's radio station," I said into the phone. "Peppy Johnson or no ride."

"Jordan?"

It was not Melissa on the phone but Bonnie Randall, who'd been Dad's girlfriend forever. A long time ago, Bonnie had written a book, *The*

*Milkweed Diaries*, which I tried to read once but it was so boring I couldn't get through it. How much can a person stand to hear about the inside of a flower? Other people must have felt that way too, because she hardly sold any. I guess she had a book signing in Seattle and signed only one book, which she later found out had been stolen. So she gave up writing and now had a bookstore, Randall and Stein Booksellers. She was Randall, of course, but Stein was this dog she'd once had, named after Gertrude. That woman was scary looking, if you ask me. Gertrude Stein, not Bonnie. Bonnie is sweet and quiet and has freckles. If you want to look at anything in her store, you've got to step over the two dogs she has now, Daisy and Jay. They always lie right where you want to be, as though they can read your mind.

"Oh, hi, Bonnie," I said. I was on the kitchen phone, and my father was seated at the table with his bowl of Total and mug of coffee and the newspaper propped up in his left hand so he could eat with his right. That was my father. A Total man. A Shredded Wheat and All-Bran guy. At the sound of Bonnie's name, his head shot up.

"Is your dad there?"

He met my eyes, shook his head to say he didn't want to talk to her. This surprised me. Bonnie's voice sounded as propped up as Dad's newspaper. I could tell she was about to cry. It wasn't like my father to be cruel to her, even if they had been fighting. He took after my grandmother Margaret that way. A calm person. His car, a broken toilet, finding a spot on a shirt he thought was clean when he was running late—those were the kind of things he got mad at. Not people.

"Just a minute," I said. I held the phone against my shoulder. "She sounds upset," I whispered.

He set down his paper and locked my eyes in that firm way that is supposed to make me reconsider who is in charge. "I'm. Not. Here," he mouthed.

"Okay, okay," I whispered.

He went back to his paper, to show he was finished with the topic, but I could tell he wasn't. His eyes were focused in one place, not reading a word. His chin tilted up, concentrating on making sure I did as he instructed.

I didn't understand what the hell was happening, why he was suddenly treating her like this. His coldness startled me. "Bonnie? He must have gotten in the shower."

"Oh." She knew I was lying. I've never been a good liar. People always hear my guilty conscience. My stomach felt a little sick.

"He's going to be late." She laughed. The laugh was for my sake, but she shouldn't have bothered. It was that high, forced kind of laugh that walked too close to the edge of something out of control. "Have him call me?" she said.

"I sure will," I said, but she had already hung up. I looked over at my father, who was reading again. I felt terrible, and he didn't look in the least bit disturbed. In fact, who he looked like was Max, whenever Mom or Nathan gave in to one of his tantrums. The-world-is-going-my-way-again-just-as-it-should-be look. It made me mad. Me, I had no problem with anger.

"That was mean," I said to my father. I liked Bonnie. She was plain, and her sweaters sometimes smelled of dog, and she and Dad spent too much time pretending they didn't have sex, but I liked her. And I'm sure she guessed that Dad was on the other side of the phone, waving his hands around so he didn't have to talk to her. Not many things could make you feel worse.

He ignored me, still wearing that cocky look like he could give a shit. Let me tell you, this was just not him. "Mean," I said again, louder.

He kept reading. Or rather, at least his eyes perused the paper oh-so-casually. He threw a few words out at me in the way you'd brush a fly off your shoulder. "Ah, well. If you've declared it, it must be so," he said.

Apparently he'd had a little taste of being an asshole and found it to his liking. A bolt of fury shot through me. I nearly jabbed the back of his paper.

I didn't though. Because in that room I

suddenly felt the barely restrained fury rise between us, the kind you know might just tip to something ugly if you let yourself make that small move. It was the tension of a face-off, animals on the brink of a fight, where violence bubbles up inside and feels so much like a thrill it can be hard to tell the difference. Later that's what bothered me. Never in my life had I been in that place with my father before, though I'd been there with my mother a hundred times. That place where the space between two people is so charged that a flinch can turn into a slap and words can suddenly draw blood; that place where one movement can unleash a viciousness that leaves you feeling awful for days after.

I turned and left the room, shoving my schoolbooks in my backpack. In the car, my father acted like his usual self, though he kept the radio on, loud, so we wouldn't have to talk. During the ride, Peppy Johnson argued the pros and cons of tourism with a caller.

When we got to school, my father turned the radio down. He took my hand for a moment. The self-satisfied look was gone. Now he only looked concerned. I was relieved about that.

"Honey," he said, "some things are my business." With that, it was as if he had taken his two hands and shoved me into the same corner he had shoved Bonnie Randall. I wondered what we were doing there together.

I snatched my hand out of his. "Fine," I said. I slammed the car door. I don't even know what I was so mad about. Of course some things were his business. It's not like he was in the habit of telling me all about his private life anyway.

All day I felt weird. I hoped maybe an hour with Ms. Cassaday might shake off the bad feelings I'd carried around through science and French and PE with that pervert Mr. Bartlett, who I swear was always looking at our butts.

"It's meant to be for children," Melissa told Ms. Cassaday, before reading the story she'd written. It was called "Freddy Fir Visits the Lumberyard." I'm not kidding.

"This is a children's story?" Ms. Cassaday boomed after Melissa finished. Melissa had the little fir getting plucked from the forest, sent to the factory, and made into wood chips. Melissa was my friend, but even I could see that sometimes she was one taco shy of a combination plate. When someone disagreed with her, her best argument was usually, "Yeah huh!"

Ms. Cassaday clutched her heart. "Somebody call the paramedics. *My God!*" I don't think she was supposed to say *God* in school. Ms. Cassaday said things she probably wasn't supposed to all the time.

"It's got an environmental message," Melissa said defensively.

"All right, all right," Ms. Cassaday said.

"Does anyone have a comment on this?"

"I liked it," Chantay West said, which was no surprise.

Chantay was always ready to pucker when it came to Melissa's ass. We always made fun of her name behind her back. Chantay, a drugstore perfume. One of those girl groups from the fifties—the Chantays.

"*You* liked it. Would a child? Think of your audience. This could give a kid nightmares. This could give *me* nightmares." Ms. Cassaday paced, as if her feet and her brain were having an argument about the exact place she should be. "My God, I can see it now!" She slapped her palm against her forehead. With her batik skirts and jiggly arms and numerous half-drunk cups of coffee on her desk, she was a bit like my old teachers at the alternative school, but I found her strange and fascinating. I could watch her all day, the way you can watch and watch someone you could never imagine being. The way you sometimes can't turn the channel when it's those TV preachers with big hair on Sunday mornings.

"Think of this," Ms. Cassaday thundered. "Pop is reading Junior his bedtime story. Here's little Freddy Fir with his nice little family in the forest, then wham! You've got saws buzzing and sparks flying and Freddy in the back of a truck. Freddy is about to be annihilated! Freddy is heading to a *death camp*! Okay, Junior, take your drink of water and go to sleep now."

The class snickered. Melissa looked as though she wanted to send Ms. Cassaday through the chipper next. A lot of people hated Ms. Cassaday. I wouldn't admit it out loud, but I thought she was great. With Ms. Cassaday I felt that secret glee you get when you're with someone who goes around being honest all the time, saying all the things you wished you could.

"This was supposed to be about preserving our forests then?" Ms. Cassaday asked.

"It was my mom's idea," Melissa said. I believed it. Diane always did things like pack Melissa's lunch in that plastic Barnes & Noble bag with Langston Hughes on one side and Tennessee Williams on the other. Larry Beene got it on a trip to Seattle once and bought the canvas version for himself. I think they liked it so much because not only did it show that the Beene family was okay with gays and minorities, but that they recycled, too. I doubted Mr. or Mrs. Beene had had a thought of their own since the seventies, when thinking was safer.

"Well, there's the trouble. *Your* ideas are what we're after here, not your mother's. You did a great story last time about the girl who didn't want to go to college. Here, though, you start with a moral. You lost sight of all the fine points. Didn't see the forest for the trees, we could say." Ms. Cassaday raised her eyebrows up and down.

More snickers. "Okay. Moving along." Her eyes roamed around the room then settled. "Mr. Kramer." Kale Kramer cleared his throat. Kale was one of the guys at school that you were supposed to drool over with desperate wanting. Most girls did; good looks, I guess, have a way of making some people overlook little things like stupidity and cruelty. Kale had perfect features— his nose, mouth, and eyes might have been designed to meet exact factory specifications. He was athletic and muscular, but he was short. Short was the thing that probably gave him the pissed-off air, like somebody had messed up in manufacturing and he wasn't going to forget it. He was popular, and there were always rumors about him: that he once killed a cat in some brutal fashion, that he had a tattoo on his penis that said I GET A RISE OUT OF YOU. For some reason those stories only seemed to add to his allure. Melissa was crazy for him. Kale worked at the Hotel Delgado docks on the far end of the island, where boaters cruising the islands got together for parties and to use the showers. Melissa would walk her dog, Boog, out there to try to get Kale's attention, even if this meant driving way out to the other side of the island and basically carrying poor old Boog around under one arm.

"'The Bad Killers,'" Kale read. He paused and grinned at the class before looking down at his paper again. In his story a couple of guys were walking into a diner, talking. I watched Ms. Cassaday. She stalked to the window, crossed her arms over her chest. She listened to him read, and I could see her cheeks flushing red.

Finally Ms. Cassaday whirled around. "Enough!" she shouted. "'The Bad Killers,' Mr. Kramer?" She stood over his desk. Her ears were turning red now too. I'd never seen anyone's ears turn a color like that before. Kale Kramer peered out from the brim of his hat and shrugged.

"Hey," he said.

"Poor, poor Hemingway. Like he wasn't depressed enough. You think I wouldn't recognize *Hemingway*? Even butchered to hell?"

"Oh man," said Mathew Bukowsky, who sat next to me.

I thought the same thing. I wish she wouldn't say *hell*. I could just see Rosemary Lewis going home and telling her mother, getting Ms. Cassaday in trouble.

"And what exactly is this?" Ms. Cassaday tapped the brim of Kale's painter's cap. "Besides a nice floral? No caps in school, am I right? Even if they're *pretty*?" She looked around the class as if someone might actually speak up. "I begin to understand Hemingway's despair when I think of a kid in a flowered hat stealing his work."

Kale Kramer looked exceedingly pissed off. You got the feeling he and Ms. Cassaday despised each other. For a moment his eyes flashed anger, his jaw muscles clenched. I thought again of my father and me that morning. Kale's fingertips grabbed the edge of the desk as if he might knock it over. Then a smirk returned.

"Hey, this is a fashion statement," he said, stretching the elastic of his hat with his thumb.

"Oh, and what's the statement? How much you like marigolds? You stole from Hemingway. I'd like to send you to jail for theft," Ms. Cassaday said. "Or twist your perfect nose off your pretty little face," she said. She picked up his paper and ripped it in half, made a show of tossing it into the wastebasket. "Since I can't do either, you'll have to give me ten pages by tomorrow. Okay, everyone, pack up."

The class groaned in Kale's behalf. "But I work," he said as we filed out.

"Life is hard," Ms. Cassaday said. "Sometimes the shits," I heard her mumble after her back was turned. She sounded as if she meant it. Behind me I heard her sigh. In the narrow rectangle of glass on the door, I saw her at her desk, lifting coffee cups, trying to figure out which one was still warm.

"Dyke," Melissa said to me outside in the hall. Loudly, and more for Kale's benefit, I guessed, than mine. I thought about seeing Ms. Cassaday and our old typing teacher, Elaine Blackstone, working at the oyster farm last summer. I thought of Ms. Cassaday's troubled sigh.

"What do you expect from a lesbo," Kale Kramer said. "Hey." He nodded his head to me. "Catch."

Before I knew it, I was looking down at his cap, which I held in my hands. He grinned at me. "I'll call you tonight," he said, as if we were Mr. and Mrs. Kramer and he was just leaving to go to the office. He turned and went down the hall with his friends. I was left with this hat in my hands. I could see a dirty ring where his forehead had touched the elastic. I felt odd, as if I was suddenly left holding a bedroom slipper or a cantaloupe or some other strange thing in the middle of school. I didn't know what I was supposed to do with it. Besides, I'm not fond of marigolds.

Afterward that stupid hat was all Melissa wanted to talk about. Lucky me, we had plenty of time for it too, as it was Friday and our day off at True You. "What does this *mean?* He gave you his *hat!* Why'd he give *you* his hat? You don't even like him."

"He's got a hundred girls all following him around with their tongues hanging out. Maybe I'll auction the thing off and make a few bucks."

"You've got to come over," Melissa said. "We've got to talk about this. My *God*."

"Okay, but I can't stay long," I said.

"You want to get back for *the call*," she said. She sounded both mad and interested at the same time, the way she sounded when my mom tried to make peace by taking me to a Jimmie Dix concert in Seattle last summer. Jimmie Dix was one thing Melissa and I were in one hundred percent agreement about. Even though most people we knew listened to those groups with names like Snoop Doggy Doo on Shoe, we both said you had to be made of ice, or dead, if you didn't get the shivers watching Jimmie Dix sing "Battleground of Love" in that video where he's with the woman on the beach.

I was not anxious to get home for Kale Kramer's call. I was anxious to get home to see where things stood between my dad and me, but I wasn't about to tell Melissa that. I'd realized by then that confiding in Melissa about the big things was about as helpful as if I bared my soul to her dog, Boog. Maybe *he* would even get my point, who could tell? Besides that, I felt it was my duty to act at least a little interested in Kale Kramer. Since Kale had thrown me his hat, my stock price had split. Wendy Williams had even said hi to me in the hall. I've known her since the seventh grade, and the only thing she'd ever said to me was "Je-sus!" one time when I bumped into her going around a corner. All afternoon Melissa had been clinging to me like we were trying to escape from a burning building and I was the fireman.

Melissa worked the key into the lock of her front door. It was one of my mother's complaints that before all the people like the Beenes moved onto the island, no one locked their doors. In fact people would just leave their keys in the ignition of their cars in case a neighbor needed to borrow it. But no more.

We took our shoes off before we went inside Melissa's house, as was expected. Diane said it was important to integrate the traditions of other cultures into our own lives, but I suspected she just wanted to keep her carpets clean.

"Mother, have you lost your mind?" Melissa said. The Beene couch sat in the middle of the living room. Diane stood on a chair, wrestling with the end of a long, mossy tree branch.

"Oh, good," she said. "Girls, would you each hold up an end of this? I want to get an idea of how it'll look." Diane hopped down and handed her end of the branch to Melissa. She brushed her hands clean. "I saw this on the Home Decorating Channel. Natural curtain rods. Here, Jordan." She handed me my end. Diane tended to get carried away. The whole house was stenciled: the kitchen with a rim of baskets overflowing with grapes, the laundry room with a smeary line of lemon-colored ducks. Melissa's room was done almost entirely in men's red-and-blue handker-chiefs—curtains and pillows and even the bed-spread. If you had to blow your nose in there you'd have it made.

"Higher girls," Diane said.

"My arm's about to fall off," Melissa said. "Mom, you got crap all in your hair."

Diane absentmindedly brushed at the bits of moss and leaves that had hightailed it out of the forest via the blonde poof on her head. She looked at us, then tilted her head and squinted her eyes. I guess she saw something other than I did, which was two girls power-lifting a log that stank like wet leaves. "Okay," she said, and nodded, pleased.

"Don't tell me you're really going to stick a tree branch on our wall," Melissa said.

"To each his or her own," Diane sang. "Just set it down there on that plastic sheet."

"Oh, God, a spider." Melissa shook the sleeve of her shirt.

"Careful, Melissa." Diane Beene scurried for the television listings, bent down to let it crawl onto the paper. "Quick, open the door."

"I can whack it with my shoe," I said. You should have seen the looks I got.

While they made sure the living being who shared our earth got safely outside, I went to the small guest bathroom to wash my hands. Here the walls were ringed with stenciled seashells. Also, there were little seashell soaps and folded seashell towels that you weren't supposed to really use, and small seashell books you weren't supposed to really read.

"You didn't cut that off a live tree, did you, Diane?" I yelled to her over the running water. I pulled my shirt out of my jeans, dried my hands on the tail, and rejoined her, Melissa, and the branch.

"Oh, my God," she said. "Oh, my God." She sounded just like Melissa. She put her hand to her head like she couldn't believe what her brain had done without her permission. "Do you think people will think that? I found it on the ground. I swear."

"It was *my* first thought," I said.

Diane sat down. "I'm going to have to reconsider this," she said.

"It's fine, Mom," Melissa said. "No one's gonna think that. Jordan hardly represents the entire population." She scowled at me.

"I don't know," Mrs. Beene said.

"Trust me," Melissa said. When she pulled me upstairs to her room, she said, "Real nice, Jordan."

"What?" I said.

"She was excited about that stupid branch. Sometimes you just don't think enough about other people."

Another day, when Kale Kramer hadn't just given me his hat, she would have laughed. It wasn't true, anyway. According to my mother, I thought about other people too much. "Someday you've got to figure out how to belong to yourself," she always said, which sounded like more of that seventies "Find Yourself" nonsense she was so fond of. The idea of having to find yourself always cracked me up. How exactly would this work? You wander away from yourself one day, end up roaming around some small town, until you finally pull up alongside yourself and say, *Hey Jordan, glad I found you. What the heck are you doing here?*

"I'll go down and tell her I love her branch," I said.

"Seriously," Melissa said.

A loud, angry voice doing a bad Texas accent, muffled only slightly by the bedroom wall, stopped all conversation about my behavior. "God, I hate him. Just ignore him," Melissa said.

"What's he doing?"

"He's been calling radio shows. That dumb-ass Peppy Johnson your father likes."

I put my ear to the wall. "All you are is a yellow-bellied snake if you think that cow dung ain't a vi-able natural re-source." Pause. "Why, you can make clo-thing outta cow patties. You should see the shirt I got on."

"You don't want to listen," she said.

But I did. I kept my ear to the wall. I liked Jackson's sense of humor. Melissa let out an exasperated yell, stomped out of her room, and began to pound on Jackson's door. "Would you shut the hell up in there?"

I scooted off the bed and poked my head around the corner. Veins were practically snapping from Melissa's neck. The voice quieted, then stopped. I could hear the clunking of a phone being settled into its receiver. The door opened a crack, and Jackson's head popped out.

"Evening," he drawled.

He smiled at me. I smiled back. There was always something about the way Jackson looked at me that made me feel like he really knew who I was. I didn't know the Beene family very well before Jackson's accident, as I had just moved in with Dad about then, but according to Melissa, Jackson used to be "normal looking." I was glad he wasn't normal looking anymore. His hair was a straggle of colors, dark with dyed streaks of blond. He was unshaven and rumpled; his eyes looked as if he hadn't slept in a while. At least they had that red-rimmed intensity you get when you've stayed up late and talked about things that matter.

"Goddamn it, you freak—" Melissa began, but Jackson had already shut the door. I could hear him moving about in his room, and I wondered what he was doing. I'd never been inside

his room before—the door was usually shut—
and right then I had the strange urge to see what
it was like.

Melissa had given up. "My mother told him
if he wasn't going to go to college he had to get
a job or move out, so at least he won't be around
much after next week. He's getting his own
apartment at the end of the summer. Got it
picked out and everything, but hey, as long as it's
far away from me. Can you believe the Hotel
Delgado hired him? As a *waiter*, as if you want
him touching your food. How desperate can
you get? I swear, I'd like to get him back out on
that mountain and give him a second chance at
getting lost."

I didn't say anything. I didn't want to get in
trouble with her again by pointing out what I've
noticed—that the people who use those expres-
sions like *I Swear* and *Over My Dead Body* are usually weenies who, past their moment of bravery,
crumple at a barking dog. Real tough guys don't
swear, they just do.

Finally I said, "Let's get out Kale Kramer's
hat. We can try it on and make fun of ourselves."

"Are you *kidding?*" she said. You'd have
thought I suggested snatching that little shoulder pad the pope wears on his head and dancing
naked with it on. So instead we just talked about
Kale Kramer for a while, and then Diane called

up the stairs asking Melissa to help her drag the branch back outside until she could discuss the matter with Larry. I sat in Melissa's room, looked at last year's yearbook, and read the message she didn't want me to read from Andrew Houseman, which was no big deal except for the fact he said she was real sweet, which is the same thing he wrote in mine.

Bored, I peeked out into the hallway. Jackson's door was half open, and he seemed to be gone. I pushed open the door with my fingertips. I could hear Melissa and Diane and the bang of the screen door as they struggled to get the branch outside. I went into Jackson's room.

It smelled like a guy's room, if such a thing is possible. At least, it smelled different than my room or Melissa's—thick somehow, steamy. The room had managed to escape Diane's decorating, and so it looked like a real person actually lived there. On the floor, a pair of Jockeys had found their soul mate, a white undershirt, and the two of them were rolled together in an intimate ball. The desktop held a scattering of sheet music and scrawled notes on paper scraps, a book titled *Poets Of The United Kingdom*, a tube of ChapStick, and a chain necklace with a slender silver vial that Jackson usually wore around his neck. Three shelves above the desk held more books, a jar of pennies, and high school soccer trophies. It seemed funny now to think of Jackson playing an organized sport on a high school team, and he must have thought so too: the golden heads of several of the frozen players now sported odd items like a wad of gum and a tiny knit cap that made the player look ready for winter despite his stiff golden shorts. One player had a man's ring dangling from its forever-kicking foot, like it was a halo that had fallen and was about to be flicked back up into place.

I crouched down by the phone and lifted it from its receiver. Where he had held it near his face it smelled like soap. I listened to the dull tone for a minute, then hung up. A floppy phone book was on the floor beside the phone, covered with ink doodlings of trees and plants that looked like part of a child's book of fairy tales. Jackson was a good artist. I stood again. A half-drunk cup of coffee on the floor by the rumpled bed made me think for a moment of Ms. Cassaday and her desk full of cups.

I heard Melissa and Diane bang back inside, their voices becoming loud and clear again. In a moment Melissa would come thunking back up the stairs, and I sure as hell didn't want her to catch me in there.

But in the corner of the room near the window, I noticed the bagpipes. They were set down carefully on a chair; the case with indented felt compartments that usually held its pieces lay open underneath. With its leathery stomachlike bag and jangle of tubes it looked like a skeleton of some huge prehistoric spider. I wanted to hold it. I lifted the contraption off the chair, and the pipes clicked together noisily. I was trying to figure out how to manage its awkwardness, when my slow brain finally registered what it had just seen outside of Jackson's window.

There were no trees to block my vision; there was a clear view of Crow Valley, the several miles of flat, grassy acreage behind our planned neighborhood. From where I stood, I saw Little Cranberry Farm and Osprey Inn, a bed and breakfast that competed with Mom's. I could see part of the Horseshoe Highway, the main inner island road that connected with Deception Loop, the main outer road.

All of this I would have expected to see. What I didn't expect to see, with such sharp clarity, was the faux Tudor D'Angelo home. From Jackson's second-story window the adjacent airstrip was a long gash in the land. The driveway was nearly as long and certainly roomy enough for the blue Ford Taurus parked there.

I wondered what Dad's car was doing at the D'Angelo house.

I stood at the window, my mind helpfully supplying the vision of Mrs. D'Angelo the day she'd come into True You, a visit I'd forgotten about since. I remembered her cool hand stretched out, her voice like a melted caramel: "I can't believe meeting you like this. I think your father is wonderful."

But, God, it wasn't like he was the only one around who drove that kind of car. It was stupid to think it was his, and why would it be? My morning with him had gotten me off balance, was all.

Still, I had a feeling the car was my father's. Even though I couldn't see the flat Christmas tree hanging from the rearview mirror, the one that stank worse than any natural car-smell could. Even though I couldn't see the metal box of Altoids Dad always kept in the half-open ashtray or the dent in the right passenger door, from when I accidentally ran into a shopping cart in the Johnny's Market parking lot the day after I got my license. It was one of those knowings you have with people who you're close to— the way you can tell their car is about to come down the street, or that they are on the other end of the phone you haven't yet picked up. The way you might know their blue knit hat among a hundred others just the same. I'm sure if you asked that prune Cora Lee at the Theosophical Society, she'd have something to say about it, this knowing. Something laughable, no doubt, about energy and crap that would make you forget what you knew was true.

"Jordan!"

Melissa stood in the doorway of Jackson's room, holding Boog in her arms. Poor old Boog.

If the Beenes didn't think to carry him around, he'd probably never move from the rectangle of linoleum in front of his food dish. He was round and fat as a bratwurst and about as smart as one, too.

"What are you doing in here?" Melissa shrieked. Boog looked alarmed too.

"I was just going to the bathroom, and then I saw . . . I thought I saw my father's car," I said. I hooked my thumb at the window.

"Oh, *right*. And that's why you're holding my psycho brother's bagpipes. Right. I get it. Why you are here in his *room*." *Room,* said like it was something worse. Bed, maybe.

I set the bagpipes down. "Oh, I'm sure," I said to what she was implying. Guilt was doing that creeping trick, starting at the toes.

"I don't understand you, Jordan," she said. I followed her back to her room, where she plopped Boog down on the bed. He would stay there, no doubt, until someone remembered to move him again. That dog was doomed to be forever stuck where other people put him. "I mean, since, you know, *Kale*, you've been acting really weird. Is this going to change you? If it is, I swear, you'd better tell me right now."

"Nothing's going to change," I said. Which are about the stupidest four words in the English language.

"Fine," she said. She seemed reluctant to

take her argument further. What did she think, that I was about to dump her? Leave her behind with Chantay West as I went off into the wide world of men?

"I think your brother's totally strange," I said.

She looked relieved. "Kale probably likes you because you're hard to get. And because you're in that *gifted* class together."

This was something that bugged her to no end, my being in that class. "People don't realize," she always said, "that there are school smarts and life smarts."

"You know how much I hate that class," I said. Which was a lie. I liked the class, but also I liked the idea of being in it. I liked the word *gifted*. It sounded like I could sit down at a piano and start to play, music flowing from my fingers. Truthfully, though, if you saw who was in there, you'd wonder. That's the thing about stupid people and smart people. Sometimes it can be hard to tell who is who. "I think Kale's parents bribed the school to get him there," I said.

"You are never going to keep him if you act so flip all the time."

I heard the rumble of the Beenes' garage door, a car door slam, and then the scraping slide of the garbage-can bottom against pavement. A moment later, Larry Beene's voice wafted up. "Swi-ing low, sweet char-i-ot.

Coming for to carry me home! Swi-ing low . . ."

"He sings that whenever he does chores," Melissa said. "I swear, I'm the only normal one in this family."

Sometimes I know when to keep my mouth shut.

"If your dad's home, I'd better go," I said, after I was sure nothing else might pop out. "Grandma and Grandpa are coming over for dinner."

"Well, I want to hear *everything*." She gave me a long look meant to be significant. "*Not* about your grandparents."

"I doubt there'll be much to tell," I said.

"Like I believe that," she said.

Melissa followed me downstairs, leaving poor Boog stranded on the bed.

# Chapter Three

I didn't go straight home. Instead I walked back out behind Melissa's house and jogged toward Crow Valley. I wanted to see if I was right about my father's car. Needing to know if you are right or not can be a bad thing. But when I got out near the D'Angelo home, I could see that the car was gone. Instead a black Porsche was parked there, and I saw a man, Mr. D'Angelo, I guessed, walking down the drive toward the group of mailboxes by the road.

He had the shape that usually comes equipped with certain extras—a booming voice and obnoxious opinions. A tall, big-chested guy. Why those men are usually like that, I have no idea. It's not like the world would overlook them if they happened to be quiet and thought-ful. Maybe all that space just needs to be filled with something, even if it's hot air. Anyway, that's the way he looked. Big and self-important.

He went to his mailbox, pulled open the door with a hooked finger, and fished out a fat lump of mail. He gave it a casual look, a quick thumb-through, and a dismissal, which pretty well clinched the fact that he had a lot of money. I've seen my mother open mail. It is a search done while she holds her breath, that ends with a particularly good mood if there are only pizza coupons and flyers for roof cleaning. I could tell Mr. D'Angelo was someone not often surprised by things he couldn't handle.

He headed down the driveway toward the house, and I was about to go home when Mr. D'Angelo stopped suddenly. He turned his head quickly around as if he'd heard something. I hoped that something wasn't me. I continued walking casually past the house even though I was headed the wrong way, and tried to look interested in nature. But it wasn't me he'd fixed his eyes on; it was the hedge of trees and black-berry bushes that separated his property from Little Cranberry Farm.

I decided I must have been wrong before; his life mustn't be as simple as I imagined if he could be so startled by a rabbit, or whatever he'd heard just then. I never forgot that look; in fact I would think of it later over and over again. Those eyes both edgy and doubting. You could almost hear the argument going on inside his head as his eyes darted around those bushes.

I knew that argument. It was the one where there are only two sides, no middle—jump to conclusions or cover your eyes and keep both feet on the ground. I had that argument myself many times, later. Whenever I kick myself for being such an idiot, for not *seeing*, I try to remember what Big Mama told me.

"You acted out of instinct, is all," she had said. "You can't fight it, Jordan. When you're afraid, even a little bit, it's usually all or nothing."

That's one thing about Big Mama. She knows a lot about instinct.

Grandpa opened the oven door and let out a cloud of heat. "You sure you can handle this, baby?" he said to me.

"Just like taking a cool drink," I said.

"Don't encourage him," Grandma said.

"Grandpa's Hotter 'n Hell Hot Sauce," he said for the hundredth time.

"You're repeating yourself, Eugene," Grandma said.

My father opened the cupboard door and took out a stack of plates. He had been there when I arrived home, greeted me the same as always, as if nothing unusual had happened between us that morning. If it's true what they say, that anyone who does what he did is crazy, then maybe he was already beginning the process right then. Who knows if craziness is an instant thing, or if it takes time to grow, like splotchy green mold on a decent piece of bread.

All I know is, you wonder.

And I know too that if craziness *does* develop in a person over time, what takes longer is for the family members to notice. Or admit to noticing. That night, I was relieved to find him his old self, just Dad, instead of the different people I'd been so busy imagining him being. I was pleased with that relief. It was a false soothing, though, a drink of cold saltwater for the guy dying of thirst in the ocean. The car I'd seen in the D'Angelo driveway suddenly didn't seem like his anymore. Relief put me in a good mood. Sometimes you realize plain, boring, normal life is the best it gets.

Grandpa Eugene poked around the pan inside the oven with a long fork. It was too hot outside to have the oven door open for that long. When he came back up, his cheeks were rosy. His hair, usually sculpted into the style of a fifties greaser, was now a fuzzy frenzy that made him look shocked and alarmed. I've noticed that about people. Lots of times they stick to the hairstyle they had the last time they felt stylish, even if it was forty-five years ago.

"I like the sound of it, if it's any of your business. Hotter 'n Hell Hot Sauce. All those H's," Grandpa Eugene said.

"It's called alliteration," Grandma Margaret said. She used to be a high school English teacher and advisor to the Debate Club. Since she was retired and had no one else to teach, Grandpa Eugene usually got stuck being the student. He wasn't the teacher's pet in her eyes, either, but the slow kid who never did his homework. He took his role good-naturedly most of the time, probably because a good part of his day he spent away from her, at Eugene's Gas and Garage, which he'd owned for forty years and had just sold. He still got up and went to work down there every day anyway. He said he had a job to do, which wasn't scooting under cars and pumping gas anymore, but making sure Marty Abare kept his word about not making his station into one of those candy-ass places with a mini-mart. "You wanna buy deodorant and breakfast rolls, you go to the grocery store," he always said. "You want gas, you go to Eugene's."

"Alliteration, well, la-dee-da. Too bad they gotta stick a fancy name on everything. What about it, huh? We don't even have bums anymore. *Street people,* they call 'em. Sounds cleaned up, right there."

"The word *alliteration* is hardly new," Grandma Margaret said. "It's probably been around at least since the time of William Shakespeare."

"Pretty damn old, then, since you and he went to high school together." Grandpa laughed. He thought he was pretty funny.

"Eugene," Grandma said. Dad smiled. He took after his mother, but it was his father whom he seemed to enjoy more.

"Let's eat," Grandpa said, and clapped his hands together as if the idea had just come to him. He slid an oven mitt on each hand and removed the hot pan of ribs from the oven. A towel hung out his back pocket, taking the place of the grease rag that had been there for years. From the smell of dinner and the smoke pouring from the oven, I imagined we could all use a grease rag.

"This is a real treat," my father said. He opened the sliding-glass door and closed the screen to let in some air. "Someone cooking for me in my own house. You didn't have to do this, Dad."

"I don't have to do anything," Grandpa Eugene said.

"It gave him something to do. He's been planning this all day," Grandma said.

"Show you the poor man's red meat. We can't all afford steak," Grandpa said.

My father got that tight smile at the corners of his mouth where you don't know if he's really smiling or not. "Let me do that, Dad," my father said as Grandpa sawed at the row of ribs. Big food like ribs always makes me think of the Flintstones.

"I can cut meat. You think I haven't cut meat before?"

"He's just trying to help, Eugene," Grandma said. Dad raised his hands up in a *What are you going to do?* gesture behind Grandpa's back and rolled his eyes.

"I saw that," Grandpa said. "Here, baby." He freed a clump of ribs and eased them onto my plate.

"How much do you think I eat?" I said.

"Four million grams of fat never hurt anyone," my father said.

"You're too skinny," Grandpa Eugene said. "Anyway, saves you from asking for seconds. Now, this is a meal you'll be telling your grandchildren about." He eased a smaller slab onto Grandma's plate. "This could kill you, you old bird, so go slow."

"If your cooking hasn't killed me yet, I seriously doubt it will," she said.

I spent most of dinner getting up and fetching Grandpa more napkins, while Dad filled and refilled Grandma's water glass from the pitcher on the table and nervously eyed the line of sweat bravely forming on her forehead. Mostly we talked about how great Grandpa's cooking was, how he ought to bottle his sauce same as

Paul Newman, how he adds just a touch of dry mustard. It can be exhausting eating a meal cooked by a man. With a woman, it's, *Ho hum, pass the beans*. A guy, you have to act like he just built the Taj Mahal.

"What do you think of this new guy, Alonzo?" my father asked Grandpa after dinner.

"Overrated." They both studied the television, the Mariners playing some preseason game. Grandpa picked a tooth with the edge of his fingernail. "Look at him. Cocky bugger. Thinks his own shit doesn't stink."

"Eugene," Grandma said from the chair in which she'd sunk. She'd untucked her blouse, letting it hang loose over her pants, no doubt hiding the fact she'd undone the top button. Dinner had me feeling a little queasy too.

"Why is someone taking that guy's place?" I pointed to the television, at the player trotting in from first base. "He get hurt?" My theory was, sports would be okay to watch if they cut it down to the last ten minutes.

"Designated hitter," Grandpa said, as if that explained things.

"It means he doesn't run, he only hits," my father said.

I laughed. "You've got to be kidding."

"He's an outstanding hitter," my father said.

"If he hits so well, one would think he would be capable of running, too," Grandma said.

"Really," I agreed. "Sounds like whoever bought him got a raw deal."

"Snookered," Grandma said.

"'Oh excuse me, now that I've made my outstanding hit I must go sit down.' Puh-leez," I said.

"Prima donna," Grandma said, and shook her head in the way that meant, *There are some things I will never understand.*

"Another thing that's always bothered me," I persisted. "The way they call it the *World Series.* I mean, we're the only one that plays in it, right? I don't see Japan having a shot here, or Russia or Sri Lanka."

My father sighed and gave me a tired look.

"Arrogance," Grandma said from the chair.

"You call that pitching?" Grandpa said to the television. "They start with this hack and I'm not watching another game."

"It has suddenly become apparent what I should be praying for," Grandma said. "Take down the gentleman's name and jersey number for me, honey."

"Hey, Grandpa," I said. "Did Marty Abare set up a rack of deodorant yet?"

He ignored me. "Christ," he muttered to my father. "This guy's makin' a million bucks a year."

"Don't get him started," Grandma said to me. "He's on thin ice with Marty Abare as it is.

Marty is not amused by your grandfather's pranks, which, by the way, he is pulling again. Any more of it and your grandfather won't be allowed on the premises."

"Uh-oh," I said.

"You hear that, Dad? She's calling what you do at Eugene's *pranks*," my father said. Grandpa took off his glasses and wiped them clean with his handkerchief.

"Aw, get outta here. What the hell was that?" he said to the Mariners with disgust.

"Just consider it a small, quiet rebellion," my father said to Grandma.

"*Rebellion?*" Grandma said. "Foolishness, I'd say."

"Cut him some slack," my father said. "You only have to worry about him being ornery. At least he's not passed-out drunk every night."

"I could only hope for that kind of quiet," Grandma said.

I'd seen Grandpa Eugene perform his *pranks* at the gas station before. Just last year I'd spent a lot of time there after Grandpa hired Dean Forrester, who was this cute guy in my class. After Grandpa caught on that I wasn't really interested in how to change oil, he fired Dean Forrester, which I still feel badly about.

I got used to seeing Grandpa do his trick at Eugene's after a while, but the first time I saw him do it I was shocked. A man pulled up near the office and got out. He was all dressed up; the car was some expensive type. I could see a woman sitting inside, combing the edges of her hair with her fingers, all tense, you could tell.

"Can I help you?" Grandpa asked.

"Lost," the man confessed. He reached into the pocket of his raincoat and felt around, finally pulling out a wrinkled scrap of paper which he smoothed a bit and read from. "Three-five-three Raccoon Road?" He looked sheepish, as if he were somehow to blame for the name of his destination.

"Right," Grandpa said. He looked out to the street in front of Eugene's. "You see this road here?" he said. The man nodded.

"You come out here and take a left. Go straight until you see Spring Street, where you're gonna take a right. Now, keep going until you see Bobcat Road. With me so far? Another left and a right and just go through the stop and you're at Raccoon Road."

The man clutched his paper and nodded. "Thanks, I appreciate it," he said. He gave a half wave and got back in his car.

"Bobcat Road?" I said as we watched the car pull out. "Since when is there a Bobcat Road?"

"Since now," he said.

"They'll never find their way after that," I said.

"It's not my fault they're lost," he pointed

out, stubbornly shoving both hands in his pockets.

"But these people came to you for help!" I protested.

"They asked for help, I helped. The way I see it, everyone's going the wrong way anyway," he said. "So what's it matter?"

"Now they have no chance of getting it right," I said. "You can't do that. Did you see that woman? She looked ticked off already."

"Those're the only ones I do it to. The ticked-off ones." He jiggled the loose change in his pocket and thought for a moment. "They don't want to go where they're heading anyway. I'm doing them a favor. The way I figure, I'm giving them another shot."

"At what? A screaming match at each other when they're late?"

"No, to figure out where the hell they really wanna be."

According to Grandma, this logic didn't fly with Marty Abare. Any more of Grandpa's tricks and he wouldn't be welcome at the garage he began forty years ago. After a while, I didn't see what the big deal was. I've gotten directions from gas stations before, and I'd bet a million bucks they all do the same thing. Maybe not for Grandpa's reasons though. But the same way you sometimes say *Uh-huh, uh-huh* on the phone, pretending to take down a number you know you're never going to dial.

"And I don't trust him, not for a minute," Grandma said. She looked worried, probably because having Grandpa barred from Eugene's meant he'd be home with her. "Your grandfather, not Marty Abare, though I don't think much of him either. I don't like that man's eyes. I've had this uneasy feeling right in here." She tapped her chest. "Ever since Marty Abare told your grandpa enough was enough, I can't seem to be rid of it."

"Maybe it's just Grandpa's cooking," I said.

"No, more than that," she said.

"It's just June," I said.

"More than June, even," she said, shaking her head slowly.

Just then the phone rang. I'd forgotten all about Kale Kramer, and I admit my heart jumped around at the sound of it. But it was my father, not me, who had jolted at the ringing and who had leapt up with such force that he knocked into the end table, causing Grandma's tea to spill over her cup in a wave.

"Goodness gracious, Vince," Grandma said, but my father was already in the kitchen with the phone to his ear. When I went to get a napkin to mop up Grandma's tea, I saw him there, his back to the kitchen door, shoulders hunched around the phone like a drawn curtain. His voice was low and intense—I could hear the concentration in his tone, a hint of pleading. I was glad he was making up with Bonnie.

"He and Bonnie had a fight," I said to Grandma, and by the time I had soaked up the tea, my father had come back out of the kitchen, his eyes bright, keys jingling in his hand.

"I'm sorry to do this, but I've got to take care of something," he said.

"Invite her over for pie," Grandma said.

My father looked stunned. "It's Bill Raabe. Car trouble. I'll just be a few minutes," he said. Bill Raabe was a neighbor down the street and a good friend of Dad's. He and my father had grown up on Parrish together, left at the same time to go to college, and eventually ended up back at Parrish as neighbors. Bill Raabe and his wife, Betsy, owned Raabe Realty, whose green-and-white signs you could see all over the island. Dad and Bill were in the chamber of commerce together. They and a couple of men from Washington Bank got together for dinner twice a month.

"He's always been a terrible liar," Grandma said after my father left. "Isn't that right, Eugene?" This in a loud voice, more to rouse Grandpa than anything else, since he was now looking pretty comfy with his stockinged feet up on the couch, his glasses tipped to the end of his nose.

"Mmm-hmm," Grandpa said.

"One look at his eyes, and I'd know. 'Vincent John MacKenzie, are you telling your mother the truth?' I'd say. With that, he'd usually burst into a torrent of tears."

I smiled. "I guess he doesn't want me to know they've been fighting."

"Nothing to be ashamed of," she said. "Every relationship has its little bumps."

An hour later we gave in and had pie without him. Two hours later and after watching an entire stupid movie about some teenager who runs away from home and joins a street gang only to be saved by her avenging mother, Grandma looked at her watch for the hundredth time. "Well, I'm afraid we really can't wait any longer. I hate driving in the dark as it is. This really isn't like your father at all."

"Don't worry," I said. I wasn't worried; though he'd never left in the middle of a visit with his parents before, I figured my father and Bonnie had a lot to work out. He'd really been horrible to her that morning. What did worry me was that Grandma might want to keep waiting for him. Already, I'd been sitting there way too long with a heavy meal in my stomach, watching some dumb show and listening to Grandpa snoring. Even going to bed sounded fun.

"Wake up, Eugene." Grandma nudged him. His glasses were perched on his nose, still working hard and doing their job even though

Grandpa's eyes were shut tight. "Your snoring could wake the dead."

His mouth clamped shut, his eyes opened. "I'm not snoring, you old coot. And I'm not deaf, either."

Grandma looked him over. "No rhyme or reason to love, is there?" she said. Then, loudly, "Time to go home, Eugene."

"Where's Vince?" Grandpa said, sitting up.

"Never came back," Grandma said. "It's not like him to be so rude. He could have at least called."

"Something wrong with our company? You should have taught him better manners," Grandpa said.

"Speaking of manners," Grandma started.

I packed up the leftover Hotter 'n Hell Hot Sauce and unpacked it again at Grandpa's insistence. "Take some to your mother," he said. "I've got plenty more where that came from." I got Grandma's sweater, which she always remembered to bring, turned on the porch light, and walked with them to their car parked in the driveway.

"What's he still got this thing for?" Grandpa said, and knocked on the tarp-covered Triumph with his knuckles.

"He says that all it needs is a paint job," I said, defending my father even though, truthfully, he'd been saying that for years.

"Ha," Grandpa said.

I made sure they were safely off, and gave one look down the street for Dad's car. We were right; he wasn't at Bill Raabe's house, which was dark and quiet. The night was cool but clear, the sky heavily salted with stars. One thing about Parrish Island, you can really see the stars there, the way you can up in the mountains, even. With no sign of him, I went inside and went to bed. Kale Kramer never called, which was fine with me. I was sure that would make Melissa disappointed and ecstatic.

Later that night, when I was sleeping, the phone woke me. It took me a second to get my head together enough to stumble to my father's room where the upstairs phone was. When I picked it up and said a groggy hello, the person on the other end hung up.

I slammed down the phone. I noticed my father's bed was still made. He was like that. Tidy. Never letting the details slip.

I had just gotten back into bed when I heard the key in the lock downstairs. The glowing green numbers on my clock said 3:30 A.M..

"I'm not here," he'd mouthed earlier that day. I guess that even by then, those words were more true than either one of us realized.

# Chapter Four

Laylani's sister, Janine, helped out at True You on Saturdays, so I usually had the day off unless one of Janine's kids was sick. Mom liked me to come by on the weekends, and depending on my mood, I sometimes spent the night. So that next day after Dad had been out all night "fixing Bill Raabe's car," I propped a note on the coffeepot, stuck the bottle of Hotter 'n Hell Hot Sauce Grandpa wanted to give to Mom into my backpack, and cruised down the driveway on my bike.

To get to Mom's from our neighborhood, you've got to ride down Main Street, connect with the Horseshoe Highway until you see the old oil tank, then veer off onto Deception Loop. Right about then you start smelling the waters of the Strait of Juan de Fuca, a smell that's cold and wide and deep, and the houses begin to get rambly and far apart, and then suddenly there's Asher House, sitting in a sea of yellow grass. Dad's neighborhood is called Whistling Firs, which I haven't said yet, because it's one of those things that make you feel ashamed even though they're not your fault. First, most of the firs were cut down to build Whistling Firs, and second, the few that are left don't whistle. If you've lived around firs, you know that they do make a nice shushing sound when they are swaying around with their friends; but alone, with roots loosened, they are more likely to spit pinecones and even give up altogether, flinging themselves with angry desperation onto someone's roof.

I guess I don't understand why some neighborhoods have to be given grand names they don't deserve. Whistling Firs or Summerhill or Deux Chevaux Estates—it's like we have to be talked into believing we're someplace really great. Or that we're so dumb we might be fooled into thinking a neighborhood with basketball hoops on the garage is the English countryside or the south of France.

Whistling Firs was quiet that morning, no whistling, no noise at all. The Beenes' blinds were pulled tight to their sills. I rode down Main Street, the new air cold and wet and gray on my face. The day before, we'd been in shorts; that day I wore my fisherman sweater under a rain jacket. That was June weather. That was *Northwest* weather. It was like reaching under couch cushions. You never know quite what you'll find.

At the end of Main Street I could see a ferry boat docked at the ferry terminal and Joe and Jim Nevins in their orange vests sitting on a piling having a smoke, giving the nuns the weekend off to pray and do nun things. In a few weeks the long asphalt rows painted with white stripes and numbers would be jammed with cars full of tourists, even at that time of the morning, and there would be no time for a smoke again until Labor Day, when Parrish threw its Thank-God-They're-Gone celebration. To be fair, hotel owners like Jade Starr and Richie and Marty Gregors, as well as Cliff Barton of biplane fame, usually caused more trouble during the celebration weekend than any visitors in "I Love Whales" shirts did the entire summer.

Main Street itself was also quiet, except for a man in a spanking white suit unloading racks of bread from a truck at Johnny's Market. Officer Ricky Beaker, the Tiny Policeman, was already sitting in Boss Donuts's window table, looking like he wished something would happen. The change of weather made everyone sleepy; sudden gray can drop over you like a quilt.

What surprised me was seeing Bonnie Randall at the door of Randall and Stein Booksellers, her dogs waiting patiently beside her as she worked a key into the lock. I rode up the curve of the sidewalk and slid to a screechy stop in front of her, startling her so badly that she backed up against the door as if I were a gunman with a pair of pantyhose over my head or something. Bonnie was like that. She should have lived in Victorian times, because she was just the type you read about in those books who have vapors or consumption, whichever that is.

"Jordan!" she said.

"It's only me," I said. "I'm surprised you're up so early." I tried to put a Wink Wink, Nudge Nudge in my voice. She was easy to embarrass.

Bonnie didn't look as if she'd gotten much sleep. In fact, she looked like hell. Dark half moons cupped her eyes, and the buttons of her coat matched up with the wrong buttonholes. "I've got this discussion group. Books. A book." She pointed to the bulging bag at her feet.

"I just meant, after last night," I said.

"Last night? Oh. Oh no. This is awkward." She put her hands up to her face. I'd seen Max do that a hundred times. He thought it really made him disappear.

"Don't worry about it," I said. "I'm glad you two made up."

She peeked up from her hands and studied me a minute. Then she tilted her head, looked at me with sympathy. "Oh, Jordan," she said.

"What?" I said. She was making me a little nervous.

She clutched a handful of her sweater, near her stomach. Her eyes filled. "It wasn't me," she whispered. "Your father"—she cleared her throat—"I haven't seen your father in three weeks. He just left me a message one day and said it was over. 'Thanks for everything.' He won't even take my calls."

"You're kidding," I said. One of the dogs nuzzled her hand. "This makes me entirely pissed off," I said.

"Jordan, don't. It's okay."

"It's not okay. That is not okay," I said. "He can't treat you like that."

"I've got to go," she said. She concentrated on the keys again, gave the door a shove, making the bell that hung off the handle bang into the glass.

I wanted to say something, but what do you say? My eyes searched the window display—a row of books on Northwest hiking—and roamed the contents of the store through the glass. Theater posters on every inch of wall space, row after row of spines in every size and thickness. Two tables stacked with half-price books Bonnie would haul out to the sidewalk.

Millions of words, and I couldn't find one. Bonnie held the door for the dogs and went inside. The door closed behind her.

"Bonnie!" I called through the window. "I'm sorry."

I just stood there, straddling my bike, looking at her through the window. I didn't know if she heard me, didn't know if I should go in. She heaved her bag onto the counter. She looked down and appeared to concentrate on unfastening those mismatched buttons. Then she gave a nod. One small nod.

My throat got tight inside and my eyes hot. I'm not the crying type usually, but it felt strange to be so suddenly cut off from someone who had been so much a part of my life. I liked Bonnie. Bonnie made good brownies and remembered to water our plants. I would miss her. And then another thought nudged in: If Dad wasn't with Bonnie last night, then who *was* he with? I pushed hard down on my bike pedal, rode down the sidewalk and pumped hard down an empty Horseshoe Highway, past the oil tank which had sprouted new banners IT'S A GIRL! WELCOME HOME GABY!. My bike chain ticked with the speed of going downhill, and I curved onto Deception Loop.

I caught my breath then, let the ticking of the bike slow, and then pedaled calmly again. Deception Loop wasn't a place to go fast. There, stillness fills you like warm milk, whether you want it to or not. On certain parts of Deception Loop, the road is dark and tree-lined and drops right down to rocky beach. On others, like near Asher House, there are wide stretches of meadow or orchards that meander to the edge of the strait. But no matter where you are on that road, even when you are passing by the Rufaro School of Marimba next door to Mother's and hear the lively shaking of gourd rattles, you can't help but take the journey slow. Somehow you're supposed to match the rhythm of the huge, sighing whales you know are down deep in the cold water just next to you.

I bumped along the gravel driveway of Asher House, parked my bike next to Nathan's workshop, an old outbuilding left over from when the property was a farm. The building is made of dark wood, which you can see only when you're inside because Nathan had covered the outside with copper Jell-O molds set in cement. It was a shiny, cheerful party of fish and wreaths and hearts and those molds shaped like old ladies' church hats. Collected from every yard sale in the San Juan Islands for a year.

Nathan sells his sculptures out of the work-shop and also from brochures he has around town. The sculptures are mostly huge, twirling silver rings and ellipses set inside one another, which that morning spun in dizzy circles with bursts of wind, then slowed again. They hung from the tree branches, making the firs and hemlocks look like female giants in flashy drop earrings. Other sculptures displayed on the lawn turned madly on their own stands, like the one I called "the jester's hat," with its drooping silver triangles with copper balls on their tips. A length of clothesline was strung between two trees. Smaller twirling ornaments hung from this, as did the centerpiece of the yard, a brass-and-steel dragon (NOT FOR SALE, a sign said) whose wings pumped up and down.

This was not a place I brought casual friends to and said, *This is home.* Sure, Parrish has its share of oddities, even a nudist club with its own beach out by the Theosophical Society (which I liked to imagine that old prune Cora Lee peeking at with her binoculars). But this was an oddity I was supposed to claim. And to new school friends from the *other* section of town, who had moved here from mainland cities and whose parents walked around all the time with "Those Amusing Islanders" smiles. Who, if you listened to my mother, wanted to make Parrish into the place they'd just left.

My mother's yard looked like the yard of a mad scientist. Dad, who had been there many times, said it was the yard Leonardo da Vinci might have had if he'd been alive today on Parrish Island, listening to the Grateful Dead and eating bean-sprout sandwiches. Which pretty much summed up Nathan, if you also made Leonardo a nonpracticing Jewish guy with muscles, short hair, and little round glasses.

The smell of breakfast cooking had snuck outside, and it was so delectable and tempting that I decided to call the bowl of Lucky Charms I'd eaten earlier a prebreakfast snack. Nathan was a great cook, and you usually didn't have to praise him forever for it either—probably because he was used to being the slave. I climbed up the porch stairs and let myself in the back door. Nathan was in the kitchen as I had guessed, standing in front of the old gas stove in his Levi's, bare feet, and a raggedy T-shirt with the sleeves cut off. Nathan hardly ever wore shoes.

"Aren't you cold?" I said. I slung my backpack down on the counter.

"Doing this?" he said over his shoulder to me. "You can't be cold making bacon."

"Making bacon," Miss Poe, one of Mom's boarders, repeated, as if she were an advertising executive trying out a jingle. She already sat at her place at the kitchen table, which Nathan had fashioned from a huge slab of gnarled wood. "What a lovely sound," she said to the business section spread out before her. "Makin' bacon." She took a noisy slurp of herbal tea. *I ought to get her together with Grandpa,* I thought. Which reminded me.

"This is from Grandpa," I said. Nathan picked up the bottle, unscrewed the lid, took a sniff, then dunked in a finger and licked it. "Yowza," he said.

"Be a man, Nathan," I said.

He screwed the top back on, went back to poking the bacon with a fork. "You're right, you're right." He sighed dramatically. "After I'm through in the kitchen I'll down a mug of the stuff and burp the alphabet."

"I guess that means you'll be wanting the sports page, too," Miss Poe said. She fed bits of toast to our dog, Homer, under the table.

"Okay, all right, enough," I said.

"You started it," Miss Poe reminded.

Nathan stood back from the popping bacon grease, lifted the strips up with a fork, and laid them on a plate padded with paper towels. "Your mom's upstairs," Nathan said. "Tell her it's the last call for breakfast."

I found my mother in the second-floor bathroom, her braid tucked in the back of her shirt as she gathered up a pile of dripping towels from the floor. "Max thought I'd be mad that he didn't finish his apple," she explained. I saw the plunger propped against the toilet, the browning apple culprit in the bathroom sink, and Max sitting at the edge of the tub.

"Did you do this?" I asked him.

He nodded solemnly. "It don't go down."

He pointed to the toilet. He looked worried.

"No," I said. "Oranges, yes. Apples, no."

"Jordan," my mother said. "No oranges, Max." She put the last sopping towel on the pile, lifted the whole wet mess, and raced down the hall to the laundry chute. I followed her.

"Nathan says last call for breakfast."

"It's only us left." The towels stuck inside the curve of the chute, and my mother poked at them with a broomstick handle. They inched down as reluctantly as a wet bathing suit over chunky thighs until finally I heard them land on the washing machine with a splat. "Grant's working, and Hugh took a shower over at Janey's since there's no hot water. Why would a stopped toilet cause no hot water? Answer me that."

"Old plumbing?" I guessed.

"You could say the same for me, ha ha," she said. "The Romantic Couple already left for a kayak tour, thank God. You couldn't get me in a boat on a day like this."

That is what she called the people who came to stay for the weekend, the *Romantic Couple*, or when there was more than one set, the *Romantic Couples*. She had said this the way a vegetable gardener might say *canned green beans*—superior, sarcastic, and a with touch of sadness that there were people in the world who just didn't Get It. Years ago, when mom gave Russ Wagner her last penny to add on bathrooms to convert the farmhouse into a proper bed and breakfast, these were the people she imagined staying with her. But after a while she began to see them belonging to two camps: the real and home-grown, and the false and canned. I tell you, she could figure out what file to stick them in faster than any receptionist with a stack of pink phone messages.

The people who Got It were rewarded. They got to be Harv and Christine or Barry and June and got blueberry muffins made from berries from our own bushes. The others were simply Romantic Couples who got waffles with Reddi-Whip and pamphlets on island activities, and after a while there were fewer and fewer rooms left for them, because the rooms filled with other people Mom took a liking to. Permanent people. Like Nathan. Like Miss Poe with her Red Zinger tea, who got her kicks by letting Homer wear her good jewels around and who could most often be found sitting out in the meadow needle-pointing pillows that said stuff like, IF YOU DON'T HAVE ANYTHING GOOD TO SAY ABOUT ANYONE, SIT BY ME. Like Hugh Prince, who had been an air-traffic controller at Boeing Field for years until one night he gave the okay for a star to land. Now he has a low-stress job with the Parrish Island Water Department and is a regular at the marimba classes, though I think he just has the hots for Janey, the goddess who runs the school. Other folks just came at regular intervals, like Grant Manning, an eternal oceanography grad student who comes in May and stays through September to study at the university labs, or for extended periods, the way Big Mama did just before I moved out.

It started to get to me, when I lived there. I got tired of everyone always trying to teach me something and seeing people walking around in their bathrobes and hearing the toilet flushing in the middle of the night and the back door constantly slamming shut. And I know it sounds childish, but I wanted to have my mother to myself every now and then too. *There are other things to collect,* I'd say to her, *other than people. Stamps, say. Spoons from different countries you can hang in a wooden case.*

And she of course would say, *There are worse things, Jordan. We need good people around us. Like a plant needs good soil.*

*Plants don't have to see Grant Manning in his skivvies,* I would say.

*Plants don't stand outside his door and yell "Fire!" so he'll come running out,* she would say.

*Once,* I would say. *I did that once.* And then: *Okay, fine.* Which is the only thing you can say when you know you've lost an argument.

We started seriously veering away from each other, my mother and I, after I got my first period. It was when I first thought she might be crazy. Or at least so far away from where I was and needed her to be that she might as well not be in my life at all. It was not an easy time. I mean, not a year before it was still fun to poke the cups with your finger when your mother went bra shopping. Then suddenly, you've got all the guys at school snickering about hooter harnesses and over-the-shoulder boulder holders with the same nervous giggles people get when they go to funerals and serious stuff like that. And just when you think, *Okay, the breast business stinks but I can handle it*—boom. More than anything, you can use a little casualness, a little humor. Someone to laugh with about those advertisements for pads with wings.

Instead, my mother took me to the doctor, which was fine except that Dr. Mary's nurse was a guy named Larry, who looked like a construction worker. Larry wore tight jeans and had a red too-much-beer face and looked like he should have carried that squishy blood-pressure thing in a tool belt. When he asked what we were there for, I started blushing like crazy and I wore that blush the rest of the day, throughout Dr. Mary's talk about my *developing* (like I was, maybe, a roll of film), and all during the menstrual-cycle celebration I had to endure back home. Picture me with a wreath of baby's breath stuck on my head and in a circle around me, Miss Poe and

Mom and Janey from the marimba school and Mom's friend Bea Martinson, who had tried for years to be a lesbian, except she couldn't do the sex part. All of them holding glasses of sparkling cranberry juice in the air and making goofy toasts and Mom with a limp daisy stuck in her buttonhole and happy eyes like I'd just won the lottery or something. Miss Poe spiked her own juice and got rip-roaring drunk, and poor Hugh Prince wouldn't look me in the eyes for a week. I wondered why Mom didn't just rent a billboard, or better yet, paint JORDAN'S FIRST PERIOD on the island's old oil tank and tape on a few red balloons.

I thought she'd lost her mind. She was disappointed I wasn't more enthusiastic. Let me tell you, when my mother said, "Close your eyes, Jordan, I have a surprise," and took my elbow as we stepped from the car after the doctor's visit, I somehow wasn't expecting a period party complete with a cake that said, WELCOME, WOMAN.

Not quite a year later, Nathan became more than a boarder, something I only found out when Mom dropped the news that she was pregnant. The whole thing turned my stomach. I'd spent the last few months at school hearing about Ovary and Uterus, which if you ask me, sound like a couple of gossipy old spinster ladies who refuse to drive themselves around anymore. Now I was face-to-face with not only

them, but Fetus. Why they call babies something so unfriendly I will never know. *Fetus* is the
kind of word that comes to mind when you
think of aliens or cousins marrying, not when
you think of babies.

"We're having a commitment ceremony,"
my mother said.

"I thought only gay people had those," I
said. I'd had enough of her ceremonies.

That look again. And two weeks later, me
with another bunch of flowers stuck to my head,
standing out in the meadow, wind whipping our
dresses in a column around our legs as Reverend
Lee from Big Mama's church said hocus pocus
and waved his hands over our heads as if he were
a magician whose costume just happened to
have a white rectangle on the throat.

I thought they'd write their own vows, the
long mushy type you see on soap-opera wed-
dings, but they stuck to the traditional ones. At
"I, Nathan, take you, Claire," Nathan's jaw
started to quiver and my mom grasped his hand
and squeezed. At "sickness and health," his eyes
filled and his voice caught, and by the time he
got to "until death us do part," the most he
could do was wave his hand at Reverend Lee
and croak, "Go on, go on."

Afterward Cliff Barton buzzed by the reception in his biplane, and Hugh Prince did a
marimba solo he'd practiced for the occasion,

and Nathan fed Mom carrot cake they'd ordered from Nadine, who bakes for friends and sells the extras out of the back of her station wagon. Nathan got ahold of himself and walked around showing everyone his tomato plants, which in a few months would be as round and ripe as my mother would be. Tim Berg, D.D.S., who runs his practice out of a schooner docked on the sound out near Asher House, tried his hand at the gourd rattles.

The entire day I forced myself not to run away. My father had always been the weekend guy, the take-you-places-and-visit-the-grandparents guy. But I guess that day, for the first time, I started thinking about the possibility of living with him full-time. I imagined going home to his house after a day at a normal school. His house would be a quiet, regular home where the strangest thing that ever happened was the time the coffeepot started spitting water.

The day of my mother and Nathan's ceremony, Big Mama patted my shoulder a lot. She was living with us by then. If it wasn't for her, I might have done what I felt like doing, ripping the gourd from Tim Berg, D.D.S.'s, hand and screaming at them all to go away. But Big Mama was the kind of person you didn't want to disappoint. I'd started to count on her a lot in the months before, when everything caused an argument between Mom and me. Vicious arguments.

Fingernails in flesh arguments. Arguments that caused Miss Poe to make her point by walking around wearing a huge, puffy set of earphones connected to a Walkman.

Big Mama and my own mother had been friends for years and years, since my mother lived in Chicago. Big Mama came to live at Asher House after her husband, Clyde, decided he did indeed need a hole in the head. She and Clyde had come to Parrish a few months before, for Big Mama's job with the fisheries department. She had to finish out her two-year stint before she could go back to her home in Nine Mile Falls near Seattle, and she couldn't bear to go back to the small house she and Clyde had rented on the island. Big Mama's job had been a temporary one; Clyde Belle, or rather, parts of him, stayed on Parrish Island permanently.

Even though I knew Big Mama was suffering, she was there for me. She said things that made sense. Big Mama talked about God a lot, and salmon. She knew a lot about both things. She knew a lot about children too; she had four grown ones.

I liked to listen to her; her voice made me calm, like laying your head down on a pillow. I didn't know Laylani Waddell yet then, but let me tell you, Big Mama never went around like Laylani did, wearing Jesus shoes. Big Mama made God sound like the friendly next-door neighbor you actually wanted to see at the mail-box. Even if you happened to be in your robe with your morning hair.

In spite of Big Mama's help, my mother and I were a blow-up waiting to happen. And it finally did happen the night after my mother's ultra-sound test. She had wanted me to come with her and Nathan, and so I did. I even fetched her a hundred tiny paper cups filled with water until her eyeballs were practically swimming in their sockets.

When it was time for the test, she did a funny cross-legged walk to the table and had to be helped up; her naked belly stuck up tight and glistening as a slice of Swiss cheese. It was embarrassing. Then the nurse came in and squirted a splotch of goop on my mother and pressed this thing that looked like a microphone on her, rolling it around with this look of con-centration like Mom was a big crystal ball about to reveal our future, which I guess she was.

All during the test, my mother was making these little gasps because she had to go to the bathroom so badly. I guess they have to make your bladder float like a rubber boat, I don't know; I didn't exactly want to know the gory details. So anyway, Nathan is holding her hand, and here come the pictures on the screen, which look just like what Steve Pool shows on the weather forecast. Swarmy gray clouds, a cold front you just have to take his word for. Then they zoomed in on the heart, a gaping pulsing circle, and it's something you get the feeling you really shouldn't be seeing. It gave me the willies.

"No doubt about it," the nurse said. "It's a boy." She zoomed in on what she said was a penis, and everyone started to cry, although all I could think of was how the kid would hate that when he was sixteen, since it was all being put on videotape. My mother was gasping and crying and she looked up into my face, and I guess she didn't like what she saw, because she got this hurt look. Well, you know, sorry.

Finally the machine was switched off and my mother rolled off the table. "Bathroom," she breathed.

The nurse knocked on an adjacent door in that efficient way medical people have, like extra movements are simply too frivolous. They don't even talk with their hands, unless it's to describe the specific size of something—a needle, say. "Right here," the nurse said. She handed Nathan the videotape, gave her congratulations, and turned on her heel. Not an expression you use every day, but exactly what she did.

"Thank God," my mother said, waddling over to the door. She turned the knob, pulled. "Don't tell me. Oh no, no, no. Stuck. Nathan! Oh my God, it's stuck. Help me."

"Locked," Nathan said after trying the knob.

"Oh God, oh God, do something. Go get her. Hurry." Mother crossed her ankles, jiggled up and down. Nathan dashed out.

I was already getting a sinking feeling. Nathan's sneakers pounded away and back again, and he popped his head in. "No one," he said. "But there's a bathroom around the corner."

My mother moaned. She grasped the little gown around her, waddled to the door. "I can't make it. I can't make it."

Nathan looked desperate. His eyes darted around the room as if a blue sign with a white block woman in a triangular dress might just pop up to save the day. Instead he spotted a garbage can.

"Oh no," I said.

"Shut up, Jordan," my mother said.

She took the garbage can from Nathan. I turned my head. Think of the sound the Little Dutch Boy would have made if he took his finger out of the dike.

"I can't believe this," I said. I said it again, too, in the car, after Nathan had finally found the nurse and whispered to her, making these apologetic little gestures with his hands.

"Until you are in that exact place, you have no right to comment," my mother said to me.

So let's just say that night there was already some tension between us. The three of us, plus Miss Poe, were watching television, some sitcom, which didn't happen too often in our house. Mom was one of those people who thought animals mating and hyenas ripping zebras apart were the only appropriate things on television. I mean, you see less sex and violence on cop shows. Just another variety of animal.

Anyway, this commercial came on for Cover Girl, and I made the mistake of saying that I liked the names of lipsticks. Millionaire Red, Tropical Kiss. Mother let out a long, dramatic sigh.

"What?" I said.

"Nothing," she said.

"What?" I said.

"You probably think that singer you like is going to someday ride up in his mirrored suit and whisk you off too."

"I do not," I said.

Nathan pretended he suddenly had something urgent to do and got up. Miss Poe felt around the couch for the remote control so that she could turn the sound of the television up.

"Honestly, Jordan. You rely too heavily on romance for inspiration."

I just sat there, and okay, it's a cliché, but it was like she stabbed me. Shoved a pamphlet of island activities at me, the one half of a Romantic Couple. I knew her feelings about romance and other "flimsy" stuff as well as I knew the lines on her face and where the creaks on the hall floor were and to fasten the garbage-can lid down or the raccoons would get at it; they were what home was about just as much. Romance and shopping and fussing over your looks, she said, were life's advertisements. A shallow and meaningless diversion from the main program. The paths you got pulled down when you simply desired. Desired, without knowing exactly what.

So I liked the advertisements, so what? They were harmless. Fun even. Who didn't need a break sometimes from a heavy show? A chance to get up and make popcorn? What made her think she knew me so well, anyway?

"You peed in a garbage can," I said.

"So sue me," she said.

"Sue *me*," I said, "for finding it disgusting."

She lowered her voice again, pretended to laugh. "The queen of everything," she said. She turned to Miss Poe, who was suddenly very interested in a bald man on television shown side-by-side with his miraculous, bushy twin. "So this is how adolescence gets its reputation."

That did it. I shot upstairs, slammed my door. A few minutes later, I heard Big Mama come in from work, heard her and Mom talking in low voices. But by that time, I already had some clothes and my schoolwork and my own pillow stuffed into my backpack. I put on my jean jacket and tossed my hair from my collar; my hair was pretty short then. I could hear Big

Mama's voice. "She's just a young girl, Claire. They're breathtakingly wise one minute, a child the next. Don't you remember being that age?"

And my mother: "I don't like the direction she's going."

"She's a work in progress," Big Mama said.

I paused on the stairs. And then my mother said, "I don't know where I went wrong."

I was finished with her then. I wasn't some project she had messed up on.

"Maybe you'll get it right the next time," I spat at her when I passed and slammed out the back door. I could have gone out the front without her seeing me, but that would have been beside the point, wouldn't it? In a split second you can do something permanent, that's one thing I know. She opened the back door and called out after me.

I ran into the night, away from the rectangle of light she stood in, and past Nathan, who was frozen in place, barefoot in the darkness and holding a pile of ripe tomatoes in the tail of his shirt. That was the problem in that house for me right then. Too much ripeness. Too much realness.

I rode my bike in a fury to my father's house. I was probably lucky I didn't get killed on the Horseshoe Highway, riding like that in the dark. I pounded on the door. I was lucky he was home. I could hear the sounds of the television in the background when he opened the door. A poof of garlic smell from the dinner he had eaten escaped out the door for a night on the town.

He made me hot chocolate, with those teensy freeze-dried marshmallows already in the packet. I told him what happened. I told him the garbage-can story. He cringed at the right parts. He laughed a little. "It wasn't very funny, though, was it?" he said.

"No," I said.

"No," he said. He told me a story about the time he saw Grandpa Eugene pat a neighbor lady on the rear after he'd had too many beers at a block party. How he ran away to Bill Raabe's house for the night and slept on the floor with Bill Raabe's cat. It wasn't exactly the same thing, but I gave him credit for trying. I told him I didn't want to stay there only for the night. He thought about this.

"I don't know, Jordan. This isn't up to me," he said.

"Mom wouldn't care," I said.

"Of course she would care," he said. "And you. You'd have to change schools."

"I see," I said.

"What? What do you see?"

"I just see, is all." I felt like I might cry.

"You think I don't want you here?" He took my chin in his hand. "Look at me. Hey. We haven't lived in the same house since you were three years old. A baby. Do you even remember?"

"Not really," I said.

"Jordan, that you want to . . ." He shook his head as if it were something he couldn't quite believe. "That you want to come live with me . . . I cannot tell you how lucky that makes me feel."

He moved over for me, that's the best way to put it. And not with a reluctant, heaving sigh, but with a glad scooch and a pat on the cushion beside him. Moved his whole life over. At first it was strange, of course, changing schools, a lot of whispered conversations between him and Mom, and getting used to being there with him full time. He could come up with more rules than a recess teacher. Before, I was never uncomfortable with him, but I was always Dad-formal. Dads are usually the ones you talk to about what you learned at school, moms you tell what you saw that creepy Louise Schmidt do in the girls' bathroom.

But after a while, I could relax with him. We would do just regular stuff, like buy groceries and do homework, and other times, he would show me his Renaissance art books. Reading about that stuff was his hobby. I learned that a buttress was not some skimpy costume girl-acrobats wear, which is what it sounds like. A dream of his was to see the Baptistry in Florence, which is this small octagonal building they baptized babies in that I guess was important. In pictures it looks like some little jewelry box a rich lady might have, but there are some doors on it he said were so beautiful, the people called them the Gates of Paradise. I really liked that about him, the way his eyes lit up when he said that. *The Gates of Paradise.*

So I got to know him better, and I liked my new school, and I felt like I fit in there. I would go home to Asher House on weekends and listen to Big Mama talk about the salmon of six million years ago, giant beasts with fangs that weighed up to five hundred pounds. I liked to hear her tell how salmon went on voyages ten thousand miles long, just to reach home. Mom and I stayed careful of each other. When Max was finally born, I was a visitor, bringing flowers.

Max had a small scrunched face under a knit cap, a little hard nose. His fingers were so wrinkled, they looked like they really had been underwater all that time, like Big Mama's mysterious creatures. He smelled warm; salty and sweet at the same time, a smell that made you want to cry. I wanted to put my nose in his wrinkles and smell him forever. I guess this was where the Second Chance Guy was holding up his sign and waving it around, trying to get my attention. I decided this was none of his business.

"Just don't show me his belly button," I said and handed the baby back.

And that decided it, for Mom and me both. I would stay with Dad permanently. Maybe Mom and I were just too different.

"Nathan's got enough breakfast down there for twenty people," I said to my mother as she dried her wet hands on the hips of her jeans.

"No problem. I'm starved," she said.

"You have vageema," Max said to me.

At first, I couldn't understand what he was saying. You need a pocket translator for two-year-olds. It sounded like something we learned in history class. Battle of Iwo Vageema. Then he pointed.

"Oh, gee. Thanks for the news flash."

"Be nice," my mother said. She said that a lot.

"I liked it better in the old days when kids didn't know the real names of everything," I said.

"You're becoming a prude in your old age," she teased.

We went downstairs, passing Homer on his way up. He'd had his fill of Miss Poe's scraps, and now had one of Max's old pacifiers in his mouth. Mom shrugged.

"He's got this oral thing," she said.

It was just us in the kitchen, and we served ourselves up a big truck-driver breakfast and sat at the table. From the dining room, across the yellow meadow, you could see the wide expanse of the Strait of Juan de Fuca, and in the background, the jagged, snow-glazed Olympic Mountains. The high stem of Tim Berg, D.D.S.'s, schooner, *The Eclipse*, rocked rhythmically from the dock nearby. One thing about Asher House, you couldn't beat the view.

Mom followed my gaze. "I ever tell you why I always brought you to Dr. Gleason instead of Tim? You know how much I love Tim. But I hear that when you're feeling pain, he just turns his music up higher."

"Ouch."

"Yeah. That's why they send the tourists to him. You ever tell him, I'll be mad." She crunched a piece of bacon. Nathan makes it good and crunchy, not floppy and pale like some people. "So when are you going to let me in on what's bothering you?"

"Nothing's bothering me."

"Oh, right. Hey, I know you, even though you don't like to think so."

"Dad broke up with Bonnie."

"Really? I'm surprised."

"Me too."

Mom chewed thoughtfully. "I thought they were happy together."

"I know it. The weird thing is, I think he's got someone else."

"That's not so weird. Maybe he needs a change. Maybe he needs a little excitement in his life."

"We're talking Dad, here. Excitement? Come on."

"Okay, true." She laughed.

"I don't know, something just feels . . . not right." Homer had come downstairs again. He walked like an old man with a lot on his mind. He flopped down under the table and I rubbed his back with my foot.

"I'm sure it's fine, Jordan. Your father would never let anything bad happen."

"Only the predictable can be truly surprising," Nathan stated, waving around the hardback *Mr. Jones's Dream* as if in proof. "Theme of last week's book." Nathan had popped back into the kitchen, showered and redressed, his hair still wet. "Unlike me, of course. Predictably unpredictable." He kissed the top of my mother's head.

"That was fast," she said to him.

"Cold water, thanks to the resident apple flusher."

"Mom still buying you some dead guy's shirts?" I nodded toward his plaid number. Mom liked to shop at Second Hand Rose.

"Hey, I picked this." He took a pinch of his shirt proudly. And then, "Well, I'm off. Bye, Max!" he shouted. "Beer and Books club," he said to me. "Only for big macho guys who like lots of hot sauce."

"I didn't know you could read," I said.

"He reads, he creates, he sings," Nathan

said. He belted out a one-note demonstration.

"Maybe not sing," my mother said.

"Beer for breakfast?" I said.

"We usually meet at night, but Bud's repairing a leaky roof and has the place shut down. Randall and Stein is opening early for us."

"That's Bonnie's store," I said.

"You could get us the scoop," my mother said.

"Forget it," Nathan said.

# Chapter Five

I spent the day playing cowboys and two-dragons-without-their-mommy-in-the-forest with Max and helping Mom do laundry. I decided against spending the night. I wanted to get home. I had a few questions for Dad.

Around dinnertime I got on my bike and made the trip back around the Horseshoe Highway. The day had changed its mind and decided to be almost summer after all, so I wore my coat tied around my waist and looped my sweater around my handlebars. I cruised up the driveway, and noticed that the front door was open halfway. The car was parked at a funny angle, rolled almost to the curb, as if it had tried to make a getaway but decided it was no use. I set my bike down on the lawn. The garbage can was still at the curb from the day before, but the lid was off and balanced on its side as if it were waiting for someone to notice its fancy trick. The garbage men had come the day before, but the one thing you get drummed into your head if you live on Parrish is to keep the lids fastened on the garbage cans. If you don't, you wake up to find the raccoons have had the time of their lives with every orange peel and scrap of Kleenex. And let me tell you, neighbors do not like to wake up to any kind of lawn surprise.

So I was trying to fit the lid down tight when my mind caught up with me and told me I had seen something strange there at the bottom of the can. I took the lid back off and tried not to smell as I looked down. And then I forgot all about not smelling. What I saw there could make you forget crap like that real fast. It made me forget everything except the sick feeling that instantly twisted in my stomach and twined up, like a jute rope, to grasp my heart.

*What the hell is this?* I thought as I reached my arm down inside the can. *What the hell is this?* I lifted out the ripped-up pieces of the photograph. Right away, I knew who it was. I remember that a part of his face, a ragged tear against a cheekbone, one eye, stared up at me from what seemed like a long way down. Some of the pieces were soggy from wet coffee grounds. I didn't think about the feeling of them in my hands until later, that cold mushiness. I concentrated on keeping the sick feeling low and away from me, where it should be.

I tried to be careful with those pieces. I handled them gently. It seemed only right after the image on them had been so violently ripped apart. I knelt down, right where I was, by that garbage can. I laid the scraps out, fitted them together quickly. The sick feeling escaped from my hold, rose free on a wave of panic. I worked faster. I felt an urgency to see him whole again. Because seeing Mr. D'Angelo torn up in jagged pieces in our garbage can scared the shit out of me.

He was in a tuxedo. Mr. D'Angelo, lying there pieced together in our driveway. It was a younger him, a little narrower in the face, but him. Yes. He stood alone, with some flowers behind him, in a garden, maybe. He had a smug smile. His large chest strained against his jacket. A carnation was pinned to his lapel.

One thing was for sure. This photo, ripped up and discarded in anger, did not belong here at our house. This photo of a man who was not even one of us, dressed for an occasion we were not a part of. It frightened me. Frightened me in a way that I had never felt before. It was the sudden realization that terrible things might not just be for other people.

I gathered up those pieces. When I stood, my

knees were imprinted with the bumpy design of the rocks from the driveway's cement. My hand, the one that held those pieces of Mr. D'Angelo, trembled. If I had to put a name to my fear right then, I don't know if I could have. I just knew something was wrong. Very, very wrong.

I slammed the front door.

"Dad?" I called.

"Jordan! Just a second, okay?" I heard the junk drawer in the kitchen slam shut, then heard Dad run up the stairs.

I slid my backpack off. I yelled up the stairs. "Dad?"

"In here," he called from his room. "Just a minute. I'll be right down." I heard the slide of his dresser drawer. A moment later it slid shut again. My father appeared at the top of the stairs.

"What are you doing home?" he asked. He was slightly out of breath. He looked at the shreds of photograph I held in my hand and did not acknowledge them; I might have just brought in the newspaper or a flyer for lawn-care service that had been stuck to our front door.

"What is this?" I held the pieces out to him. They were shaking. I could see that. My hand was doing this ridiculous dance. My heart leapt around like crazy. That fear—it felt something like anger. Like rage.

"What is what?" he said stupidly. He came downstairs. He was getting ready to leave. His coat was on. He was tucking a scarf into his jacket with one hand. He held his keys in his palm.

"This. A picture. I know who this is."

"I was just leaving," my father said. He shook his head at himself. "I put on my seat belt, took off the parking brake, and didn't even have my keys. I'm dangerous," he laughed.

It didn't seem so funny. "Where did you get this?" I demanded. "This doesn't belong to you."

He moved toward the door. I followed. "I'm late," he said. "Date."

"Not with Bonnie. I saw her today too. I think you'd better tell me what's going on here. I think I ought to know what's happening here. I think maybe I have that *right*."

He looked at the photograph, still held out to him, still shaking. He sighed. "I met someone, Jordan. Okay? I met someone."

"I know you met someone. That's fine. Congratulations. That's terrific. I know who you met. I know who this is." I shook the pieces of the photo at him.

"Okay. She's married. Okay? That's true. There it is."

"So she's married, big fine fucking deal. I'm talking about *this*. This is not about married. This is not about some fling with someone *married*. I mean, it's creepy, all right? Her husband's picture? Shit, Dad. Where did you even get this?"

"Why do you need to use that kind of language? Would you watch your language?" I liked this. This was Dad talking like Dad again. I watched him. I couldn't understand why he was wearing a scarf when it was summer. He breathed in hard. He lifted his eyes to a corner of the ceiling. It looked like his eyes were filling with tears. It couldn't be, though. I'd never seen my father cry in all my life.

"I took it," he whispered. He blinked, kept his eyes focused on that corner of the ceiling. "It was in this album they have under the coffee table. I took it from this album." He didn't seem to be talking to me at all. For a moment I was confused. This was where he was supposed to say something comforting. This was where he was supposed to explain it all away as some petty fit of jealousy, like the one I had in the second grade when I poked a hole with my pencil stub through the school picture of my best friend, April Pettibone, when she decided she didn't want to be friends anymore. He was not supposed to make everything worse. I was not supposed to be picturing him sitting on some expensive floral sofa, lifting the corners of Wes D'Angelo's picture from their black triangular tabs and folding it the way photos should never be folded. I didn't want to imagine him tucking it into his jacket pocket.

His almost-tears made me want to be gentle. He suddenly seemed so fragile. My anger disappeared quick as breath on a window. But that fear was rolling and gathering layers sure as a slow, heavy snowball. It wasn't sure whether it should stop yet. It had no real place to settle.

"Jesus, you stole this from their house?" I said softly.

"Stole it, I don't know. Took it. Okay?" His eyes came back to me again. "Do you think I'm proud about that? It was a wedding album too. A wedding album." He laughed a little wildly. He raked his fingers through his hair. Shit, shit. I wasn't sure I knew this guy. I wasn't sure he should be here, in my and my father's house.

"God, Dad. Why would you do such a thing?"

"I don't know, I don't know I don't know," he said.

His eyes went back up to that corner of the ceiling. *Please God,* I prayed, *Don't let him start crying.* I wondered if I should call someone. I wondered who exactly I would call. "Jeez, Dad, come on."

"He mistreats her," he said to me again. "I hate that he mistreats her."

He looked at me. I wondered what he saw. I wondered if he saw me or just a body who happened to be there to hear his voice. I mean, this was not the kind of conversation Dad and I had.

"And this is your problem, how? What do you think you're going to do? Fight him? Disappear with her into the sunset?"

"I wouldn't fight him."

"Well, jeez, I guess we all ought to be grateful for that. What are you doing this for exactly? I mean, this is obviously going in bad directions already. No one is worth that kind of trouble."

"Oh, you're wrong," he said. "You're wrong about that." His hand was on that idiotic scarf. His eyes, those calm eyes that watched Mariners games on television and chose a tie from the rack in his closet and checked the rearview mirror twice before changing lanes, they had an intensity I had never seen before.

"I met her when she came into the office for an exam." He smiled. "And sure, I was attracted to her right away, but a man like me? With a woman like that?"

I wasn't sure I wanted to hear this. This was something he should be telling Bill Raabe, not me. I knew everyone liked to tell their little love story, but you know, thanks but no thanks.

"She came back later. She was sitting on the hood of her car when I came out. Wow. Just sitting there looking at me." He shook his head at the memory. He seemed lost in it. I wondered if he had forgotten I was there. "And then I went over to her and she just . . . she took my hand. Traveled it up underneath her . . ." He started to laugh.

I was sure I didn't want to hear now. I wondered if I should remind him I was his daughter. That I shouldn't be told these things.

"Shirt," he said. "Her shirt. And then she said, and it was something I will never forget, she said, 'I chose you.' Just that. 'I chose you.' Jesus, a man like me."

"Oh, Dad, come on. God, I'm sorry, but this is making me sick. This is a bunch of crap. And you hurt Bonnie. You treated Bonnie like shit. You're acting crazy. Stealing that from their house. Ripping it up like that. That's angry, Dad. An angry thing to do. Crazy." I twirled my finger around by my head in case he was in doubt about what I meant.

"Bonnie," he said. He was suddenly angry. He spit the words. "I've had a hundred Bonnies! I'm sick to death of Bonnies. My whole life has been Bonnies. I'm tired of being safe. I don't want to be safe anymore. Forget it. Just forget it," he said. "Forget this whole conversation." His face got red. That scarf he had on in the middle of summer couldn't have helped matters.

"I thought you were sleeping at your mom's tonight," he said. For a moment he was just Dad again. Normal Dad. Ha, ha. Just normal Dad.

"It's not that cold out," I said.

"What?" he said.

"It's not that cold out. For a scarf." I mean, it was ridiculous. He had this muffler wrapped around his neck and tucked into his coat like we were expecting a blizzard. "Look outside." I pointed out the living-room window. I realized I was still clutching the pieces of that awful photograph. I had made his damage worse; I had crumpled them in my hand. I let them drop to the floor.

"You don't need this," I said. I grabbed a pinch of the scarf.

"Don't." He shrugged off my hand.

"Come on, it's like seventy degrees." I took hold of the scarf again. Tried to pull.

"Knock it off, Jordan." He pulled back.

"What?"

"I said stop it."

"What are you hiding?" Shit. Shit, now what?

"Nothing."

"I want to see."

"Goddamn it, Jordan. I said stop."

I kept pulling. He grabbed my wrist. He took hold of my wrist and squeezed hard. He had never touched me before in anger. But now he was bending my wrist a little. My hand actually twisted around.

"Jesus, Dad. You're hurting me."

His eyes looked shocked. He dropped his own hand from mine. I was still pulling on that goddamned scarf. It dropped from his fist. It fell loose; an almost elegant slip from his collar.

"Oh my God," I said.

"Goddamn it, Jordan!" He put his hands to his neck.

"Oh my God!"

His hands could not cover the endless red marks that snaked around his neck, disappeared down into his shirt. My mind provided the image: her mouth bent to him, sucking hard. His neck arched for more.

"That is so sick!" I shrieked. "Sick!"

He eyed the closed door nervously. "Shut up, Jordan. Jesus."

"What the hell are you doing?" I cried.

"I'm late," he said. "Don't you understand? I'm *late*."

"This is *crazy*."

"I mean it, Jordan, I've had enough of this!" He yanked open the front door.

"What is she doing to you?"

"God." He sighed. "Never love anyone this much."

He put his head down, strode to his car, and got in. He gave the car too much gas, and it almost stalled. The engine ground as he turned the ignition again.

Pieces of Wes D'Angelo's wedding photo were scattered around my feet. The scarf just lay there on the floor, a red woolen puddle.

# Chapter Six

I followed him. I'm not even sure exactly why; my first feeling was of such disgust I would have been happy if I never saw him again for the rest of my life. And anger. The thundering kind of fury that sweeps you along and forces you forward, making you want to do something, anything—throw things, slam doors, get back on your bike and ride down to Crow Valley to see if your father was where you suspected he was. I was afraid for him too. It was as if I was watching him suddenly run out onto a freeway, this man who had always used the sidewalk.

But when I actually did see his car, parked a bit up the road from the D'Angelo house, I was so mad, so one hundred percent mad, there was no more room for fear. There is nothing that can piss you off half so much as being right.

"Get a fucking *brain*," I said.

The driveway was free of Mr. D'Angelo's black Porsche. My God. Could sex make a man so stupid? And hey, why was I alone there, left holding the bag of morals? Wasn't he the one who taught me all that stuff? Do Unto Others; Never Lie, Cheat, or Steal. What was all that, just some birdshit on a windshield? Erased with a flick of the wipers?

I didn't want to go home. I was too furious to be in one place. So instead I rode clear to the other side of the island, all the way to the Hotel Delgado, one of my favorite corners of Parrish. It really is like a corner; that's part of why it feels so good there. The big brag is that Teddy Roosevelt once stayed at the hotel, and it's a place you could picture him leaning over the porch rail or maybe standing at one of the shuttered windows, staring out through his round glasses over the cozy inlet of the Delgado Strait where the hotel sits. The hotel is over one hundred and fifty years old and wears a thick sweater of ivy whose loose threads trail down white trellises. Around the hotel runs a cobblestone street, with paths that lead to rose gardens full of flowers so ancient they are as big as grapefruits and smell as strong and powdery as an old lady's perfume.

Cobblestones are tough on a bike rider, so I

dismounted and walked my bike to a patch of grass where I laid my bike down. My chest burned from the ride. I loved that part of the island, but I rarely went there, and my thigh and calf muscles, already cinching up, reminded me why. I sat on one of the iron benches in front of the hotel and cursed myself. It's no big trick getting yourself somewhere. It's the going back that's hard.

I just sat for a while, trying to fit the new facts of my life into the old and watching the water. The harbor docks were nearly full; the owners of the yachts and schooners, which cruised the San Juans, stopped there to use the showers and to party. Already the commotion on the docks was starting. Guys walked down the docks with cases of beer under their arms, and occasionally I heard a "Hey, Marty!" or "Fuck, yeah!" and then laughter. I watched a seaplane land, like a heron in one of those animal shows my mother liked, and the driver got out and made his way across the docks.

I wondered where my father took her, Gayle D'Angelo, or whether they stayed there, at her house. I wanted to shake off the vision of him, his teary eyes lifted to the ceiling, his hands trying to hide the marks on his neck, but it was too ugly and so I couldn't. I thought about the time Gayle D'Angelo came into True You. I remembered the brochure, left behind on the counter.

The image of that brochure—the serious, concerned lettering "Find the True You," the chunky woman staring sadly out a window—would not leave me. It was as if my mind was sitting patiently, hands folded, with all the time in the world for me to catch up.

Which I did. "Oh God," I said.

She hadn't run into me by accident. That's what the image was trying to tell me. That realization started the fear churning again. If my life were a movie, you would have heard the creepy music start up seriously then. That's the feeling I had, like that eerie stuff was playing. Her visit had been planned. She had said it herself: "I'm only here for information." I wondered what it was she had been trying to find out. Hey, he had my picture in his wallet.

"I chose you," she had said to my father. The question was, for what? Maybe that's why she came in that day. To see how much power I'd have to keep him from doing what she wanted. Obviously she'd decided I didn't have much. I guess she was right.

She had planned that visit. And those are the only people you have to truly watch out for, the ones who plan and make it look like they haven't. Planning is the evil thing. You learn that when you're three and get scared by that witch in *Snow White and the Seven Dwarfs* as she makes that apple.

115

It was getting just dim enough that the lights on the boats started coming on. Bobbing dots of red reflecting into the water. From far off came the sound of someone beating on bongos. At night this place became something other than fat roses and shutters tapping softly like the toes of spirits. It became too much drinking and too much noise by people who didn't understand where they were and who would leave their mess in the morning. At night this was not Teddy Roosevelt's place. It wasn't even my place, though I probably wouldn't admit that to too many people.

I groaned at the thought of riding all the way back, especially now that I'd have to hurry to beat the darkness home. For a second I thought about calling Mom, but I didn't think I was ready for the questions she would have. My own questions took up all the question space I had in my mind. The words for what was happening seemed too heavy and too new to make real by speaking them aloud. Besides, it was my father who should have been worried about where I was, not Mom. He deserved to feel guilty for the rest of his life for whatever happened to me. I imagined walking down that pier, crouching through a boat's small door to join some drunken party, or getting hit by a car on Deception Loop on my way home, instantly dead. Tough shit if he had to identify my lifeless body. I imagined his sobs when he looked at my blue lips and my arms stiff at my sides. I was still mad enough at him that recklessness crooked its finger at me and beckoned, the same way Laylani says a box of chocolates does to a fat girl. Sure you know it's bad for you, but you can't stop thinking about the delicious possibilities.

Just then I felt cold hands close around my eyes from the back, and I jumped and let out a cry of surprise.

"Guess who."

The hands slipped down, and, with my heart thumping, I turned to see who was there.

"Jeez, you scared me," I said.

"So you came to find me, huh?" Kale Kramer said. "I was getting kind of pissed you never called me back."

It hadn't even crossed my mind that I might see Kale Kramer at these docks where he worked, but I wasn't about to tell him that.

"I didn't know you called," I said.

"Talked to some dude." He took a pack of cigarettes out of his jacket pocket, shook it until one slipped free. The cigarette hung out of his mouth while he struck a match. He cupped his hand around both and inhaled until the little flame disappeared. Then he took a long drag. He didn't offer me one, which was fine by me. Hey, I know what happened to the Marlboro man.

"I called and called and called until he finally picked up. Said he was on the other line, you'd call me back. Fucking call-waiting. So rude."

Kale Kramer never struck me as the type to be a Miss Manners fan, but okay, fine.

"That your dad, or some other guy trying to blow me off?" he said. He sat down on the edge of the bench next to me and looked at me sideways.

"Just my dad," I said.

"Good," he said. "Hey. Where's my hat? I thought you'd be wearing it."

The thought of me wearing that thing, well, I almost laughed out loud. But he was serious. Sometimes I can't believe the hilarious things that are happening all the time that no one else seems to notice. I mean, you'd think bunion pads cut to the shape of your toe and hunters in camouflage outfits would be enough right there to put us all in stitches for the rest of time. Could you see me, tromping about with that stupid flower hat on my head, la la la, like it was a diamond tiara or something? No, thank you. If this was what Melissa considered not thinking enough about other people, well, I guess I was guilty.

"I don't look good in hats," I said.

He turned and sat sideways on the bench, looked at me straight on. I could see that he'd just gotten a haircut. His face looked really big.

"Nah," he said.

"It's true," I said.

He put the hand with the cigarette on the back of the bench. A tendril of smoke curled up. With the other hand, he tucked a piece of my hair behind my ear. "I don't believe it. You'd look good in anything."

A little jolt of nerves raced through me. And I admit it, a thrill, too. "So what is this name, Kale?" I said. "I thought that was a leafy green vegetable."

Instead of pulling back like I thought he would, maybe getting offended enough that I wouldn't have to make some kind of choice, Kale only leaned in closer.

"Oh, a smart-ass," he said, and kissed me. Our lips did that kind of bumbling thing people do who meet on the sidewalk and can't figure out how to get around each other. Dodge left, smack, dodge right, smack, then finally a clean pass. He tasted like cigarettes: wrong and bad and different enough to be interesting. Over his shoulder, where my arm looped behind him, I could see the beginnings of a bruise on my wrist where my father had grabbed me. It was in the shape of a thumbprint. Kale and I kissed for a while, and I guess I sort of started to forget that I didn't like Kale Kramer.

Maybe I should say something right now about my vast experience with guys, ha, ha. I had had two boyfriends up to that point, the first being Mike Lewis, who worked at Jo Jo's Theater and read the movie times into the answering machine. You know, like, *Our feature presentation is* Video Cowboy *showing week- nights at five fifteen, seven thirty, and ten o'clock and on Saturdays a special matinee.* If you call over there, it is still his voice in the beginning of the message, where it gives the driving direc- tions to the theater. I heard he left town to go to college someplace, but his voice is still there at Jo Jo's.

Anyway, all we did was go to the movies a lot because it was free, and hold hands and kiss a little. When I first thought I liked him, I would call the theater during off hours just to hear his voice. I know someday this will embarrass me, because it is already starting to. The real him wasn't so great. Mike Lewis had a sister in a wheelchair, and I guess I felt sorry for him and thought he led this tragic life, which he didn't. Only his sister did. He was just a regular guy whose clothes always smelled like popcorn and who tried to say things in French to make him- self sound smart. For all I knew, every time he did it he could have been asking where the bath- room was.

After him, I really liked this guy Chuck Frasier. I know Chuck sounds like some squatty person with a crew cut who gets tutored in long division, but he wasn't like that. He was athletic, and his family had money, and he was in the gifted class with me. And he was cute enough that I did dumb things for love, like sending him notes signed "Love" underlined more than once and putting myself in embarrassing athletic situations, like playing racquetball with him because he wanted to. Most of the time I did less playing than screaming and ducking and covering my head, as Chuck showed his prowess by making the ball whiz past me so fast I thought it would slice off my ear. Picture me, Girl van Gogh. If you've never been in one of those cells with a racquetball madman and a ball that bounces like hell all over the place, I will tell you that what you feel like most is a stuck flipper in a pinball machine.

I guess you could say that Chuck and I had all of the hors d'oeuvres but never got to the main course. I didn't want to have sex with Chuck. I don't know why. I just didn't. Sometimes I really am a closet prude like my mother accuses me of being. That's just my little secret. I guess I got my father's carefulness, whether I like it or not. I broke up with Chuck after he threw a racket when I got a shot off him. I was glad when it occurred to me that I didn't ever have to go to Wayne's Sports Center again.

The kiss with Kale ended with the sound a straw makes at the bottom of a tall glass. Kale looked at me with these heavy lids that were supposed to be sexy, but looked like one of those pictures Grandma Margaret always takes where everyone has their eyes half closed. Or those books Dad had in his office, *Diseases of the Eye*, with the pictures in the back. There was some really gross stuff in there.

"Man," Kale Kramer said.

He started to lean in for more, and that's when I heard the bagpipe music. God, it was like a call from heaven or maybe a slap in the face. I jolted in surprise. I swear, the sound of that music just sort of took your heart out of your chest and lifted it up.

I looked around and saw Jackson sitting on a hill just behind Hotel Delgado. He had gotten a job there, I remembered Melissa saying. In the restaurant, as a waiter.

"Fucking fag in a skirt," Kale Kramer said. He took another drag on his cigarette, then blew the smoke out in a long stream.

But Jackson wasn't in a kilt; he never wore one. He was in jeans, same as Kale.

"Come on," Kale said. He took my hand and pulled, trying to get my attention again. "This guy I know's got this boat."

I wondered if Jackson was watching us. I wondered if he was playing there on purpose. I imagined I felt his eyes on us.

"I can't," I said.

"It's Saturday night," Kale protested.

"I'm expected back." I was suddenly cold. The bagpipe music stopped. I stood up, untwined my sweater from my handlebars. It seemed like a long time ago that I had put it there.

"I'm not saying we gotta do it or anything. It's just a party."

Gee, maybe he expected a thank-you note expressing my gratitude. "I know," I said. "It's just, I told my dad I'd be home."

"Okay." Kale Kramer held up his hand like a traffic cop. "Hey, fine."

"He's kind of protective." Sitting by the phone wondering where I was, yes, sir, that's just what Dad was doing. Well, he *used* to be protective. He used to insist I write the number of where I was going to be on a little pad by the phone. A flash of the truth, that horrible, ripped-up photograph, sped through my mind and I shuddered.

"Hey, it's okay," Kale said. "Don't worry. I got my ways." He took my head in the crook of his arm and kissed me again, hard. "Parents are tough," he said, after his mouth slipped from mine.

"Yeah," I said, even though we weren't having the same conversation.

"I'll call you later," Kale said. "*You* get the phone."

Kale strode off toward the docks. I was

relieved and sorry at the same time, mostly because I was left alone again. I kicked myself for not asking for a ride. I picked up my bike; the night was now getting serious about its task. I looked back up the hill and saw that Jackson was gone.

I got on my bike. I started to head toward home, resigned to the long ride back. And then I heard the bagpipe music again, a little farther off this time, over toward the woods.

It was the second time that night I had followed someone without knowing why, and it was even more stupid this time, as I was using up what little light was left to get around Deception Loop without being permanently tattooed by a Firestone Radial. Right then I felt like nothing so much as one of Big Mama's salmon, pulled forward by something no one quite understood and that no one had any real control over. But that music just took hold of something inside of me and *urged*. It called to me. Even though that sounds stupid as something that prune Cora Lee would say, I heard it. Calling me.

The music got louder as I moved closer, and then it got more distant again. I walked my bike toward the sound behind the hotel and to the entrance of the wooded trail just east of it. I knew where he was heading then; that place was one of the reasons I most loved this part of the island. But it was somewhere I had visited only in the daytime, and it made you nervous enough then. Now, with darkness falling and the firs tall and shadowy on either side of the trail, I was even more edgy and hyperaware. I thought about something else Big Mama said about her fish, how their feelings caused them to go places and do things that weren't always good for them—into the rough ocean and the mouths of mergansers and kingfishers, violently flinging themselves up rocks and inclines. It occurred to me that maybe what I was doing wasn't the wisest thing, walking down that dark trail. Big Mama said that most of the salmon don't make it back to fresh water.

I considered turning around, getting on my bike and riding the hell out of there. But then I had another thought, a crazy thought. Maybe, just maybe, it was the sound of bagpipes that calls to the salmon and guides them, under those deep, murky depths.

If you've ever been alone in a wood at night, remember that feeling. That's what my heart was doing, trying to be brave in the darkness, even though we aren't meant to be. My feet made soft thuds on the trail carpeted with pine needles, and my bike made a slow *tick, tick, tick,* as I pushed it forward by the handlebars. The woods looked deep, deep, and the trees whispered amongst themselves and shushed each other. And through all this floated the flutey cries of the bagpipe, muffled by the woods but sounding the way the moon would if it could call down to the earth.

I kept following after the sound, and I felt like a child in one of those magical movies, who follows a bird from branch to branch because it seems to be leading on purpose. The trail to the McKinnon family plot is long, and one of the reasons it has been mostly left alone, despite the wooden trail marker carved with the words HISTORIC SITE. Visitors, not knowing what is at the end, often turn around and go back, thinking the sign is wrong or that maybe it is the trail itself that is historic.

But I didn't go back. I knew what was set in the woods at the end of that trail—a large, round stone table surrounded by stone chairs, set on a platform, and reached by a curve of stone steps. Each chair had a McKinnon name etched on the back, and the owner of the name buried underneath. It was a damp, mystical place, a place that seemed as if it had been in the woods forever, built by knights and ancient kings and forgotten until you discovered it yourself. It made you feel that maybe some things *are* forever. Forever but just forgotten.

Down the steps, on each side of the platform were sets of wooden benches, built up like bleachers, and now soft and rotting. After the mourners had tromped down a wet and muddy trail, this was where they had assembled to do their job of watching the latest McKinnon sit down to his permanent dinner.

And that's where Jackson sat when I finally reached the burial site. On one of the bottom benches. You didn't dare climb higher, for fear of falling on your ass through rotting wood. His bagpipes were a pile of jangled bones beside him.

He just sat there, eating a papaya, slicing off hunks with a little knife and holding it to his mouth and sucking and chewing with total messy pleasure. He saw me there, looked up and met my eyes, then kept on with that papaya. I watched him eat; I'd never seen anyone eat like that before. Juice ran down his wrist and into his sleeve. His mouth was ringed with wetness. Watching him made me feel what I had felt kissing Kale. A stirring but a bit of disgust, too.

He cut off a hunk, held it out to me. I took it, held it to my mouth.

"Taste it," he said.

I took a bite, chewed. "No, *taste* it," he said again.

I closed my eyes, concentrated. It was sweet and sticky as a finger dipped in honey. And warm, probably from the ride in Jackson's pocket. I opened my eyes, and Jackson nodded.

Jackson wiped his mouth with his sleeve. "He hurt some cat," he said.

"That's just a rumor," I said.

Jackson said nothing. It was true, then. He'd been watching me with Kale. Jackson finished his fruit, folded up his knife and put it in his pocket. He wrapped the papaya skin in a napkin that he pulled from his jacket, tucked the ball this made back inside his pocket. It was the only thing that reminded me that he was a member of the Beene family: his care not to litter. He looked nothing like Melissa, or even Diane or Larry. His eyes stared up from a lowered head, not in a shy way, but direct; dark eyes that looked too long and let you and you alone in through the door to where he really stood. He had none of the Beenes' blondness. The Beenes were Santa Barbara and Fort Lauderdale. But Jackson, he was one of those places in my father's books: a small ragged church tucked somewhere in the Tuscan hills, decorated with paintings of a sad-faced Jesus. A place that smelled of wine and salami and the breath of old, passionate prayers.

"My father is having an affair," I told him. "With a married woman. He stole something from her house. This photo of her husband. He ripped it to shreds. I saw these marks." I ran my hand down my neck. "Bites."

He scratched his head, stared off at the McKinnon table. Then he looked back at me. "It won't do you any good. Chasing your own tail," he said.

"What do you mean?"

"I mean, you're doing this." He twirled his finger around in a circle. I thought of myself, making that same motion to my father when I told him he was crazy. Jackson grinned and I laughed. Jackson picked up a pebble and threw it. It sailed past the spot where Gaylord McKinnon's head should have been, and fell with a *ping* on his ghost lap. "I mean, he's the guy driving the boat. Man, the wind is blowing. I can see that by looking at your face. Blo-wing! But he's steering, and you can't do a thing about that."

"So what am I, the passenger?"

"Not even."

"What?"

"Some guy in another boat."

I thought about this. "No one should get to drive their own boat unless they know what they're doing."

"Probably," he said.

"It's a bad plan," I said.

"Yeah, well." Jackson threw another pebble. It hit the small of Gaylord's back. If I were him, I'd be getting pissed by now, but his chair just sat there all stony and calm.

"Come on," Jackson said.

"Where are we going?"

"Home," he said. He lifted up the bagpipes again. "Too dark to ride."

"I'm not afraid," I said. I was, but I wanted

him to know how brave I could be.

Jackson only laughed. "You can be not-afraid in my truck."

I picked up my bike. We walked back toward the path. Jackson put one hand on the bagpipes as he walked, as if he were a father carrying a baby in a front-pack, only this baby was a pouchy alien with four thin arms that clattered to the beat of our steps.

It was so dark now that you could see only the barest lacy outline of tree limbs, spread out like the wings on Nathan's dragon. It wasn't scary out there anymore; shivery, but not scary. It's funny how just having another person nearby can make you feel fearless. I mean, it's not like you ever see dogs walking next to other dogs for support when they are in some nervous situation. But people? It's like inside every one of us is that girl who takes her friend with her on a trip to the bathroom. I never liked those kinds of girls.

Jackson, with his thin frame and scraggly hair, well, he was not the type you imagine saving you against bad creepy stuff. But I felt calm with him there, walking on the path, my bike *tick, tick, tick*ing again and the sky so black and filled with stars it looked like nothing so much as a huge mug of rich dark coffee just given a good shake of sugar crystals.

We didn't say anything for a long time. And

then, because I'm an idiot sometimes, I started to feel that the silence needed something. An idiot, because silence can be more rich than words.

"It was really great, you know, when I heard you playing in the woods," I said.

"Yeah?" he said.

"Yeah. I couldn't see you, but I heard the music. It was really strange but great. Definitely."

He nodded a little. More silence. "Just this music, floating in front of me," I said. My voice sounded high, a little silly. "I thought, maybe that was what it was like when you got lost hiking, hearing the bagpipes."

Stupid. Stupid, stupid. I knew it the second the words slipped out. Melissa had told me it was something he never talked about. His step lost its rhythm; I thought he might stop walking altogether, but he didn't. The abruptness of a slammed door sat suddenly between us. I could feel my face get hot. We kept walking in silence. All the noises of the forest seemed too loud. It was the kind of silence where every second lasts a thousand, the kind of silence that makes you want to run away and stick a pillow over your head, pretending it was yesterday.

Finally he spoke. "Be real with me," he said. "That's the thing I like best about you."

We reached his truck, in the Hotel Delgado lot. Jackson didn't seem mad anymore. He lifted my bike and set it in the back of the pickup. His license-plate holder said, CATCH AND RELEASE WILD TROUT. I pointed to it.

"You fish?"

"Naw. Slim Wilkins?" He looked at me to ask if I knew the man and I shook my head. "He's the guy I bought the truck from. Actually his wife, Slim being dead. He's the fisherman."

Jackson unlocked the car door, and I stepped up into the cab. Jackson climbed up into the driver's seat, shut the door with a loud metallic slam. "All this stuff is his." Jackson flicked his finger at a round compass ball on the dashboard and a fuzzy creature with google eyes hanging from the rearview mirror. "Look," he said, with obvious pleasure. He opened up the glove compartment. "Maps." Maps and fast-food paper napkins and little foil pouches with those stinky wet cloths for wiping your hands.

"This Slim was a good friend of yours?" I asked.

"Oh, no." Jackson did a half-laugh. "Never even met him. I just like having the stuff around. There's this book he wrote in, the dates he changed the oil and got tune-ups. I like that." Jackson turned the key and started the engine. "All written down, right there. Slim's a good guy. Nice to drive around with."

Okay, this was weird. But more weird was that I kind of knew what he meant. I could almost picture Slim, riding around with one tan hairy arm out of the window, shirtsleeves rolled up. I could see a bunch of rakes and tools sliding around the back of the truck, and a couple of thick branches he'd just pruned off some tree that was starting to take advantage. Happy at his day's work, and singing out loud the wrong words to some country-and-western songs he'd turned up high on the radio. I too liked this idea. It was funny, but I guess I saw myself in the unusual package that was Jackson Beene.

I watched Jackson work the clutch and accelerator. His window was rolled down just an inch, enough that I could hear the rush of the wheels on pavement outside, and enough to make the top of Jackson's hair blow around as if it were trying to coax him into an adventure he was reluctant about.

He looked over at me. We were curving around Deception Loop. I could hear my bike scrape against the truck bed with the turn.

"You ever just feel happy?" he asked.

I nodded. Despite everything, I did right then.

"That worry," he said. "About your dad? Worry is like watching your feet while you're dancing."

That Jackson talked strangely, but I liked it. He gave you the pieces of the puzzle; you were supposed to fit them together. Only you had no top of the box to look at. You might be making a flower garden or a lighthouse or the Cathedral of Notre Dame.

"This isn't a good dance, though," I said.

"Still a dance," he said. "Here you are."

Jackson turned onto Whispering Firs and stopped in front of my house. He kept the engine running, but hopped out and slid my bike from the back. I looked at my empty driveway.

"He's not home," I said.

Jackson looked too. "Nope," he said.

"Thanks for the ride," I said.

"Sure," he said.

We looked at each other, and for a split second I thought we were supposed to kiss. Instead Jackson turned back to his truck. I picked up my bike and headed up the drive. I heard the noisy clang of Jackson's truck door as it slammed closed and then a moment later, "Hey."

I turned around. Jackson leaned out the window of his truck.

"That Kramer guy's eyes. Vicious. A baboon's eyes," he said.

"I've never looked that close at a baboon," I called back to him.

Jackson rolled up his window, put the truck into gear. He made a loop back to his house.

I might be stupid sometimes, but I knew jealousy when I saw it.

# Chapter Seven

"I just heard the most wonderful lyric on the radio," Laylani Waddell said as she waltzed into True You and shook free of her coat. "'Tall from side to side,' it said. 'Tall from *side to side*.' Isn't that apt? That's something we can use with the team members, as an option. I don't want the girls thinking of themselves as *fat*."

Laylani was in a good mood. She and Buddy had probably just had sex. You could always tell.

"Girls, some days I know just how Jesus must have felt, helping to heal the afflicted, making the lame whole," Laylani said.

This was not my area of expertise, but I did know for a fact that Jesus never told his disciples to get on their stationary bikes and ride, ride, ride.

Melissa didn't even look at me. She sat at the desk and stared at the phone all stony faced, as if it were her job to watch and see if it might ring. Usually by now we'd be shooting each other glances that said, *Next she'll want to start the Church of the Thin Thighs*. Which, if you ask me, would probably get a pretty good following. According to my mother, half the problems in Today's World are because, somewhere down the line, vanity got turned into a virtue.

Melissa was making it clear she was pissed at me, and I got the message loud and clear. At school she'd skipped Ms. Cassaday's class and sat by Chantay West at lunch. When Laylani disappeared into her office and shut the door, Melissa got up and stomped around True You as if she had boots full of snow.

The square button to Laylani's phone line lit up. You could hear waves of Laylani's voice, cooing to Buddy in a disgusting manner. "Okay, Melissa," I said. "What's wrong?"

"Like you don't know," she said. She slammed a file cabinet drawer shut, making the little sign on top, YOU CAN BECAUSE YOU THINK YOU CAN, shudder.

"Tell me," I said.

She whirled around at me. A real whirl—her hair fanned out like a twirling skirt. "I saw you," she said.

"So?"

"With my brother?"

I wasn't really surprised. My horoscope that day said, *What was hidden will be uncovered.*

"So? He gave me a ride home."

She crossed her arms, looked at me with eyebrows raised.

It was the look Mrs. Beene gave Boog whenever he forgot to scratch on the door to be let out.

"It was a ride home, Melissa, jeez. It didn't mean anything," I said. It wasn't true. It did mean something. I just wasn't sure what.

Melissa kept on with the Bad Doggie look.

"I got stuck out at the Hotel Delgado, and it was getting dark," I said.

"You were out at the hotel?" she said. Her voice gave an inch.

I nodded.

"Seeing Kale?"

I *had* seen him. I nodded.

"Why didn't you say so?"

"I mean, the way you were slamming things around here. And you ate lunch with Chantay West, for God's sake."

"She had this meat-loaf sandwich," Melissa said. "It was like this thick." She held out her thumb and forefinger a good two inches apart. "With these veiny red lines of catsup. I thought the fumes would make me heave."

"Ugh," I said.

"Tell me about it." She sat in the chair behind the reception desk. "I've got phones," she said.

She seemed to know she deserved something from me, which was fine. I'd do the measuring that day. "Okay," I said.

"I'll do phones tomorrow, too."

"Okay," I said.

She spun the desk chair back and forth with the tip of her shoe. "I know it's a free country and all, Jordan, but if you somehow liked my freaky brother I'd never forgive you," she said.

"Don't worry," I said.

It occurred to me that I'd been lying a lot lately. Then the phone rang. "True You," Melissa sang. She checked out her nails while she listened, a color we'd bought together. Peach Shimmer. "Just a minute," she said. She clicked down one of the phone buttons, then another and another. "Oh, shit," she said. "Shit." Four lines were blinking. She punched a button. "Hello?" She hung up, hard. Her eyes opened up wide, she started laughing. "Oh my God, oh my God," she said.

"What?"

"I punched the wrong one," she whispered gleefully. "I could have *sworn* that was Buddy telling Laylani how much he wanted her."

Melissa's eyes glimmered like the blinking phone lines, and she spun in that stupid chair, trying to squelch her laughter as she answered the other calls. I laughed too, though I knew Melissa was wrong. It was Buddy, or the man had said something else or there was some other explanation; I didn't know. What I did know was that I was laughing and it wasn't funny. I was laughing, but the idea made me as sick as the thought of Chantay West's meat-loaf sandwich.

After Laylani's second lecture on "Doing Good Deeds For Yourself," I told Melissa we could go to Boss Donuts, my treat. But when we got outside, Kale Kramer was there in his car waiting for me, rolling the radio dial with his finger, causing Melissa to instantly finish up her forgiving. Kale took us to Boss Donuts and laughed with us at all our Laylani stories and drove us home. I actually had a good time. Melissa called me later.

"Everything is going just perfectly," she said.

It was the wrong thing to say; a careless thing to say. Big Mama may know some things I don't know. But sometimes I still think life is a big Soak 'Em game and God has the ball. The trick is, blend in with the crowd, keep your mouth shut, and stay toward the back.

It's when you wave your arms and call attention to yourself that, *bam!* He's sure to get you out.

For a few days, I wondered if my father had called it quits with Gayle D'Angelo. I thought maybe he had stepped to the edge of something ugly and scared himself back. I was grateful for whatever it was.

My father was calm, and lighter somehow, as if the recent rain had washed some of the June danger out of the air. We never spoke of the night I found the photograph and pulled off his scarf. Instead we just stepped around each other for a while until he was himself again. I was so relieved he was himself again. He slept soundly, hummed along with his lame CDs as he made dinner, read *The Vision Of Landscape In Renaissance Italy* with his socked feet propped on the couch. He told his usual corny jokes and talked with a pen in his mouth as he balanced his checkbook.

"You know what happened today?" my father said one night as he stir-fried vegetables for dinner. He shook his head with disbelief and laughed. "This woman comes in because every time she gets her picture taken, her eyes look red."

"You've got to be kidding," I said.

"She thought something was wrong with her."

The pan hissed, and the snug smell of frying onions wafted up. I watched his hands, one grasping the pan's handle, one efficiently working a wooden spoon. Capable hands.

"Oh, man," I said. "What'd you say to her?"

"I told her she could sell her extra stupidity by the side of the road."

"You did not."

"I told her to look just to the left of the flash next time and then spent a half hour looking at pictures of her and her husband posing in front of palm trees and bad sunsets from her trip to Hawaii."

"What a guy," I said.

"There should be a law against that bathing suit he was wearing. It was like a slingshot."

"Oh, Dad," I said.

"Lost in the hills," he said.

"Oh, gross," I said.

Getting a fix on fathers, just regular fathers in regular situations, can be tricky. It can be like looking at Big Mama's salmon under water. You can see those fish swimming, you know they are there, but they're hazy and indistinct under the ripples of the stream. And my father right then, well, he wasn't in a normal situation. He too was making his way across a stream—rapids—really, by stepping from one small shaky stone to the next.

Just as suddenly, things were once more not so normal. My father started looking like hell. Wrinkled and sleepless. Dark crescent moons under his eyes. I heard his voice drifting down the hall in the middle of the night, sounding sometimes charming, sometimes aloof, sometimes pleading. He was distracted, left home without his coat or breakfast or the mail he was going to take to the post office. He didn't listen when you talked to him; conversation seemed only to agitate him and make him lose his patience. He left the house at odd hours, came home joyful. He jumped when I came into the room, as if he was always about to be caught. It was like living with a CIA agent—a bad, nervous one not cut out for the job. He was on some ride, or maybe just Jackson's ship, and from where I stood, it didn't look like much fun. It looked like it made you seasick. If that's what love was like, it sucked, if you ask me.

The last week of school, my father called me from his office. Understand, the only time my father had ever called from his office before was when Peppy Johnson at the radio station got carried away and reported that a fire was raging on our street. This was after Mr. Lucassi's sheepdog, Shelley, knocked over a stick of Mrs. Lucassi's lighted incense and burned a hole in her area rug.

"You've got an activity after school on Friday?" he asked.

"An activity? What, you mean the end-of-school picnic?"

He was almost whispering. I could hear Janet, his technician, talking to a patient in the background, an old man with a fragile voice.

"That's it. What about it?"

"I want to go," he said. "I thought I'd like to go."

He was trying to be off-handed, cheerful. You could hear the strain of it. My hands got sweaty. The phone was heavy to hold. I knew why he wanted to go. I knew, that more than anything, I did not want them to be there together, where I would have to see and pretend that I didn't.

"You do? Why? You've never gone. It's, like, five o'clock. You'd miss an hour of patients. *I* don't even like to go."

"Aren't parents supposed to come?"

"Well, yeah, but it's usually just like the PTA people. It's not like we'll be having quality time or anything. The parents just sort of hang out together on their own. Last year I just hung out with Melissa."

"That's fine. Where is it?"

"Where it always is."

"Come on, Jordan."

"You won't even see me," I said.

"I *understand*."

I sighed. "Point Perpetua."

"All right," he breathed. "Okay. It's all set then."

He hung up. I slammed down the phone. I felt sick again. That sickness you feel when you remember that the people you love can be the biggest strangers.

Since I'd met Gayle D'Angelo, I had begun to see the name everywhere: *Many thanks to*

*Gayle and Wes D'Angelo for their help in supporting this year's Parrish High* Bugler; *Baseball thanks all the parent-volunteers this year, Bernie and Sharon Myers, Wes and Gayle D'Angelo, Art and Donna Hawkins* . . . And over the intercom, "PTA vice-presidents of hospitality Paige Woodruff and Gayle D'Angelo invite all honor roll students to a luncheon in your honor . . ." They were the kind of people who liked to show themselves. I would have bet Mr. D'Angelo would be at that picnic, making sure he got the points for being the involved dad. By now, I knew he'd be there. What I wondered was if my father knew too.

When it started to rain Friday morning, I was glad. The announcement blared over the intercom that if the weather kept up, we'd have the picnic in the gym. I figured Dad would drive out to the park and find a soggy sign pinned to a tree. I hoped the Second Chance Guy would be there too, in his yellow hat and rain slicker and dorky boots, standing under his umbrella. Big Mama says second thoughts are God talking a little louder into a stubborn ear, something most people are too impatient to listen for. I don't know about that. I just think the Second Chance Guy is easy to ignore; you call him a dweeb who doesn't like to have any fun, and poof, he's gone.

By afternoon the sun had come out again. Mother Nature was screwing with the heads of the weathermen, who had changed th[e] [fore]cast midday to predict a late-afternoon st[orm.] You've got to feel sorry for any weatherman i[n] the Northwest. I think they all ought to give it up and just simply say, *Well, gang, today we're going to have weather.*

Kale Kramer offered to drive me to the picnic. It was one of those school things you hate but don't want to miss, and now, with my father going, I felt I had no choice but to go. So I said yes. I had begun to think I had been wrong about Jackson Beene and the jealousy I thought I saw that night at the McKinnon family plot. The few times I had run into him since then made me feel stupid for even imagining it; he'd looked at me as if I were about as interesting as a change in the temperature. I felt bad about bringing up his hiking accident. It was a habit I had, saying stupid things at just the wrong time. If there is an extremely tall woman behind me at the grocery store, that's when I will surely say something like, *Wow, who in the world is supposed to be able to reach the stuff on these shelves?* At True You it was the worst. *Big, fat raindrops,* I'd say. *A tight squeeze. Humongous cantaloupes.* Sometimes I think the little person in charge of the Humorous Affairs Division of my brain gets a great big kick out of this.

It seemed best to forget about the goofy feelings I thought I had for Jackson Beene. Anyway, Kale Kramer was the kind of guy you

...o like, and there he was, pursu-
... as a bee does a rhododendron
... admit, I kind of liked the special
...t because I was with him. People
...mething they hadn't before. I start-
...saw it too. Like the fat girls at True
...en they lose a little weight, start raising their hands during discussion time. I don't
think it's confidence so much; confidence is
probably something you give yourself. This was
more about permission. Someone else allowing
you in a door, and you're suddenly sure that's the
place you belonged all along. Even if you haven't
taken a real good look around; even if you
haven't figured out yet it's not so hot a place to be.

So on the last day of school, I said yes when
Kale Kramer offered to drive me out to Point
Perpetua for the picnic. Melissa piled in the back
with Andrew Leland and Jason Dale and Jason's
girlfriend, Wendy Williams, who sat on Jason's
lap and made slurping noises with him all the
way there. At the park, a few barbecues had
already been set up in a row, and poofs of smoke
rose from them. The odor of burning charcoal
mixed with the salty air drifting upward from
the strait gave everything the wet, smoldering
smell of camping.

I didn't see Dad or the D'Angelos. A few
other parents, though, had gathered at one of
the picnic tables, and Mr. Wykowski the art

teacher, in his Cleveland Rock 'n' Roll Hall of Fame T-shirt, manned one of the stalled Webers. A few students were trying without much luck to get a badminton net to stick into the rocky ground, and Custodian Bill stalked around the park wearing a concentrated look and waving a metal detector around the patches of grass. A group of Franciscan nuns finished up their picnic and looked anxious to get out of there. They waited in a gaggle as one of the sisters threw away their picnic trash in one of the swinging-lidded cans. Whenever I saw them in a bunch, it cracked me up. I always imagined that if you ran straight toward them they would flap and fly off cawing into the air, like a group of crows.

"Fuck, this is always so lame," Kale said as he looked around the park.

"Why do you come every year then?" Wendy Williams said.

"Free food," Kale said. Andrew Leland laughed.

"Right," Melissa said.

"Good company." Kale put an arm around my waist and pulled me to him.

"Don't you have a blanket in the car, Kale?" Wendy Williams said.

He tossed her his keys. "I'm not your servant boy."

Mr. Newburg, the football coach and driver's ed teacher, spotted Kale and waved him over. I stood with Kale and smiled politely as he and Mr. Newburg joked around and hit each other on the arm. The park began to fill up; the nuns were gone, but there were a lot more students now, and a few more parents and teachers. Custodian Bill was seriously going at the metal detector now, letting the thing stop and sniff under the table where the nuns had been. He reminded me of those clowns with the stupid joke-leashes, that make them look like they're walking an invisible dog. I saw Ms. Cassaday drinking a can of Coke and talking to Heck Kwa, who teaches math. The joke is, if you say his name real fast, it sounds exactly like what the kids in his class say every day after listening to him teach.

Someone turned on a radio, and Kale and Mr. Newburg stopped punching each other in their manly fashion, and we walked back over to Wendy Williams's blanket and sat for a while. Kale took off his shirt, which made Melissa blush. It wasn't that warm, but I guess if I had a chest like that, I would probably take any opportunity to show it off too. He rolled up his shirt and put it behind his head, showing off an intimate fluff of armpit hair. He pulled me down by him, his chest warm and sweaty against my cheek. I could smell his deodorant, one of those that's supposed to smell like the woods. I felt embarrassed down there, where everyone, even Ms. Cassaday, could see.

"Too bad I didn't bring any suntan lotion," Kale said. "You could rub it on me." He swirled a wide hand over his own chest.

I sat up. "Too bad," I said.

"Hey, where you going?" he said.

I got to my feet. "I'll be right back."

Kale sat up on his elbows. "What is it with girls, they've got to piss every five minutes."

"Truly," Jason Dale said, earning him an elbow from Wendy.

"Just because guys can hold it for three days," Wendy said.

So, you know, the conversation was going downhill fast. I felt relieved to make my escape. I wanted to poke around, see if Dad had shown up. I had only gone a few paces when Melissa caught up to me.

"Thanks for leaving me alone again," she said.

"You were hardly alone," I said.

"Jordan. You know what I mean." She looked back over her shoulder to Kale. "I don't see how you could be in such a hurry to leave him."

"I had to go to the bathroom." No arguing with that.

"You know, he's really average height for a short person," she said.

Sometimes I just didn't understand why I liked that girl.

We stopped at the park bathroom now that

I had said that was my plan, and I hurried the hell in and out of there. If God really wanted to punish you, he'd make you stay in a park bathroom for all eternity. I mean, fire is nothing. I waited outside for Melissa. I stood there, breathing through my mouth and listening to the fuzzy drone of Melissa's voice talking to the girl in the next stall, who she thought was me. Just stood there, kind of laughing to myself about Melissa spilling her guts to some chick wearing Birkenstocks.

And that's when I smelled it. Her perfume. Gayle D'Angelo's perfume. I swear, I smelled it before I saw her. It was not a smell I could forget, ever. Later I would smell that perfume on some woman in a department store, and I would feel so sick, I actually gagged. Covered my nose and mouth with my hand and stood there shaking outside until some woman with a loaded shopping bag asked if I was all right.

Gayle D'Angelo stood in a sprinkle of other PTA women, tucking one corner of a red-checkered paper tablecloth over the edge of a picnic table, as Wendy's mother, Please-Call-Me-Cathy Williams, smoothed the wrinkles from the surface with her hand. I heard a booming laugh and saw Wes D'Angelo and the baseball coach, Mr. Chester, hauling either end of another table, then setting it down to meet the covered one. I thought about Wes D'Angelo in his wedding tuxedo, torn to pieces, and felt a pang of guilt that I knew what he had looked like on that day. Today he looked relaxed, joking with Mr. Chester and trying not to bang his shins on the table as they carried it. Markus D'Angelo stood near the badminton net, which lay in a heap on the ground, given up on. He was talking with a couple of guys from the baseball team; he cracked open the top of the drink can he held, took a long swallow. He looked like his mother, but he seemed shy and nice. One of those nice guys who does well in school and doesn't step on anyone's toes and becomes a doctor, or something. Whose Adam's apple bobs when he drinks. Adam's apples can make a person look so easily hurt.

His brother, Remington, walked up from the car with a cooler in his arms. He was husky, like his father, with big round shoulders that bulked from his tank top and carried his load as easily as a handful of spare change. He set the cooler on the table's bench, opened the lid, and rummaged around inside. I watched him; the curve of his shoulder blades. I wondered if he knew, they knew, what I did. I wondered if any of them had seen a white page in the wedding album and puzzled over why it was empty. I wondered if I might catch their eyes darting around and trying to find mine. Trying to spot my father. But Remington only found what he wanted in the cooler, popped it into his mouth, and chewed. He went over and said something to his dad, who clapped him on the back and made a remark that caused Mr. Chester to laugh and nod. Remington looked embarrassed but pleased. Wes D'Angelo's big hand stayed on Remington's back for a moment, squeezed his shoulder, and dropped.

And then, as if Gayle D'Angelo's perfume rode on a last drift of dangerous June air and called him forward, my father, at that moment, strode across the park from the parking lot. I remember reading later, in one of the books Ms. Cassaday would give me, about those sirens in mythology. The ones who sat on the rocks and with their singing lured sailors to their deaths. When I read that, I thought of my father then, walking across the park. His hands were in the pockets of his khaki pants, and his face wore this hopeful, uncertain look. Young, that's what he seemed from that distance; not something you would ever say about him up close, with his eyes with the crinkles at the edges, eyes that looked like they'd seen some things, and his face so much a man's face, a father's face. He saw me too. He gave a wave, then poked his finger in the air to indicate where he was headed, a goofy dance-move gesture. It made me worry for him, that gesture. Like when you see a kid walking to school with really short pants and you just say to yourself, *Uh-oh.*

"Gee, thanks," Melissa said, stomping out of the bathroom and drying her hands in the armpits of her shirt. She was right not to use that endless loop of towel in there. "God, I am so embarrassed. Why didn't you say you were coming out here? I just described how Andrew Leland kept putting his leg right up against mine in the car to a perfect stranger."

"How was I supposed to know you were talking to me?" I said. "I was out here." I wondered if I might soon be struck by lightning. Someday I would use my last allowed fib.

"Well he did," she said. "The entire ride over."

Four people in the back seat, where else could he put his leg, out the window? But of course I didn't say that to her. "Let's get something to drink," I said.

I walked over to the row of coolers on the ground, right next to where Markus D'Angelo stood. I bent over, took a cold can from the slushy, melting ice. I could see Markus D'Angelo's leg, the tawny hair on it, could see that the lace of his shoe was coming loose. "I bet that was a surprise," he said to one of his friends—Gary Redding, I think his name was—who laughed. "Hell, yes!"

We stood in a line, Markus and I and Wes

D'Angelo, points along one line, with me between them. My father was off to the side now, talking to Mr. Wykowski, who was arranging slick pink hot dogs in rows on his grill. Someone had turned up the music so that you could feel the beat in your feet, pulsing under the ground. Mr. Wykowski was pretending to listen to my father, but I could see his foot tapping under the barbecue to the music.

Which was fine, because my father, too, was only pretending to talk. I could see it in his face. His smile was frozen in Mr. Wykowski's direction; his eyes darted away and came back only out of politeness. I knew what would happen next. I knew it would happen and it did; his eyes drifted and I followed them to where they stopped and connected with Gayle D'Angelo's.

I held the cool, sweaty soda can to my forehead. Shit, shit. It was hot outside, suddenly very hot, and my feet and legs felt dirty and sticky from walking around the dusty park in bare legs and sandals. I wanted to cut that glance, break it with my hands or slice it with a pair of wicked-sharp scissors. I looked at Markus, who was still laughing and talking, looked at Remington, who had picked up one of the badminton rackets and was swinging it like a baseball bat as some girl pitched him birdies. I looked at Wes D'Angelo. Mr. Chester stood in front of him, animatedly telling him a story. But Wes D'Angelo's eyes were not on Mr. Chester, baseball coach and proud leader of an honorable season of ten game wins. No, his eyes looked just past Mr. Chester's shoulder. His eyes were on his wife.

Gayle D'Angelo gave my father a half smile. It could have been a stranger's smile or a lover's smile. She drew her fingers across the base of her throat; a secret gesture, or only surprise at attention she didn't expect. She dropped my father's gaze, chatted again with Mrs. Williams.

He was stupid, stupid, my father. Wes D'Angelo looked back at Mr. Chester, laughed loudly at something he said. It was a laugh that meant my father was no threat. He was wrong about that. But right then he was making it clear. Gayle D'Angelo was his wife. His toy. And that's what she was: a toy. My father never did see that.

"God, it's hot over here by these barbecues," Melissa said. She took a pinch of her T-shirt and waved it in and out. "Let's go back. They're probably wondering where we went."

I heard Gayle D'Angelo's voice. "Oh, a little bit of work. But it was my pleasure. Really." She seemed to practice sincerity the way other people practiced the piano. That was easy to see when her attention was not on you. I wondered what Wes D'Angelo's horoscope had been that day. I wondered if it too had said, *What was hidden will be uncovered.*

# Chapter Eight

"Are you all right, Jordan?"

Melissa had her hand on my arm. It felt cool, the one she had around her own soda can. I remembered why I liked her. I wished we were alone in her room, sitting on her bed, and listening to Jimmie Dix on her CD player. Just us doing little stuff.

"I'm okay."

"You look funny." She glanced over and spotted my father. He'd given up Mr. Wykowski and was now standing and looking around awkwardly like the dance was over and he'd just lost his partner. "Your dad's here? Jeez, I told my mother I would kill her if she came."

"My dad drives his own ship," I said.

"Oh, please. Where'd you get that crap?"

We started back to Kale's blanket. Past the cement bathrooms, I could see Wendy Williams sitting with her yearbook open on her crossed legs, probably reading aloud to Jason all the things other guys wrote in there. I wished I was home. The funny thing was, at that moment I wasn't quite sure where that was.

"Boo."

Kale leapt out at us from behind a tree. Melissa gave a little scream and grabbed my arm.

"Shit, Kale," I said. "Don't do that."

"Scare you?" He laughed. "Hey, thanks for getting me one." He pointed to my Coke.

"One per customer."

"They didn't say that," Melissa volunteered.

Kale ignored her. "That is so lame. Wait here." He pointed at us, trotted off, and came back a second later with four Dr Peppers lined up inside the waist of his shorts. "Man, that was cold," he said.

He looked so silly, rubbing his red stomach after stealing something he didn't even need to, that for a second I forgot my dad, who was stealing something else on the other side of the park. I tried not to crack up. Melissa was shooting me a nasty look. "What is it with guys and Dr Pepper?" I said. "Name one girl who likes it."

"I do," Melissa lied. She hated it too.

"What the fuck does it matter?" Kale said.

"Here." He handed the extra cans to Melissa. "Why don't you take these to everyone else?"

"Okay." I watched her go. I felt so sad for that back, clothed in a flower shirt that tried too hard to be cheery. She was worth a hundred Kales.

Kale put his own can in his pocket, making an unseemly bulge. He backed me up against a tree and put his arms on either side of my head. I looked smack into his eyes. A half-inch more and I'd have a clear view of the top of his head. "Are you avoiding me?" he asked.

"Why would I do that?"

"That's what I didn't get." He pressed his hips up against mine. I could feel the coldness of the soda can through his pants. "I see your dad's here, checking up on us."

"My dad drives his own ship," I said again.

"Fuck, you're weird sometimes." Kale kissed me, and I let him. I didn't care who saw. Maybe my father would see Kale stick his tongue in my mouth and be shocked at my alarming behavior. I thought about the look that passed between my father and Gayle D'Angelo. I thought about the fact that where we were kissing was two steps away from the spot where Big Mama's husband, Clyde, made her a widow. I knew if I peeked, I could see the actual rock that still had his blood on it, right over Kale's shoulder, next to the lighthouse.

Kale pulled away. He put his forehead against mine and sighed with frustration. His hair smelled like someone else's cooking. "Man, what is the matter? Where are you at?"

"I'm sorry," I said.

"Where's my cigarettes?" He had something in every pocket, that Kale. He could have been a magician.

"You're going to smoke in front of all these teachers?"

"Hey, I don't see a sign. They won't do anything to me anyway." He shook the wrinkled pack of cigarettes, then gave up and pinched one out with his fingers. "You got something on your mind, I wish you could tell me."

He lit the cigarette with his lighter, and blew smoke out his nostrils in two fierce streams. If his nose were a rocket, that burst of exhaust would have shot it clear into space.

"I would," I said.

"You can tell me things," he said. He put his chin down to his chest, gave me a look that tried hard to be full of feeling. "That's what a boyfriend is for. So you chicks can spill your guts and we can comfort you, right?" He punched my arm playfully. Smoke from his cigarette zigzagged and made the outside air smell wrong.

"Right," I said.

"So spill."

"It's just . . . Not here, okay, Kale?"

"Oh, sure, you want your privacy. I understand that. You want to be alone. Hey, I'll make sure we get our *privacy*." He leaned in, licked my ear. I shivered.

"That's more like it," he said, happy again. "Don't think I'm gonna forget, 'cause I won't. You know, your problem is my problem."

"Okay," I said. "Thanks."

I guess the cigarette served its purpose. He threw it to the ground and stepped on it. I thought of our dog Homer. I wondered if Kale had an "oral thing" too.

Kale took my hand. "Let's get something to eat." We took a couple of paper plates off the stack, and some napkins held down by a rock even though no breeze was blowing. We stood in line for hot dogs in squishy buns and decorated them with a couple of squirts of catsup. The dishes that emerged from Remington's cooler had been lined up on the picnic table and joined by others, all of these perfect, pretend foods with little folded cards to identify them. MEXICALI ROLL-UPS in calligraphy. I'm not kidding. The kind of thing my mother would have hated. These were the people, Mom said, that donated an espresso maker to a needy family at Christmastime. She read it in the *Parrish Island Journal*. I'd told her that even the poor deserve a good cup of coffee, which didn't go over very well.

"Jordan." Ms. Cassaday stopped me at the

end of the food line. "Can I talk to you for a minute?"

"Sure," I said. Kale was back at the drink cooler, putting more Dr Pepper in his pants.

I carried my plate and followed Ms. Cassaday. My father sat at one of the tables, with his own plate in front of him. Gayle D'Angelo sat across from Dad, a can of diet soda in front of her. Women like Gayle D'Angelo didn't eat.

Ms. Cassaday leaned against a tree, folded her floppy arms, and gave me a good long look.

"Okay, this is none of my business, but what the hell. You're a good student and I like you. You've got a brain in there, you know." She tapped the side of her own head.

I smiled. "Thanks," I said. Ms. Cassaday stared off, right where my father sat. For a second, I thought she was going to confess to knowing about his affair.

"It's about Kale Kramer," she said.

"Oh," I said.

"I've seen you two around together. Just now. At school . . . I think you ought to be careful, Jordan. He seems cool and smart-ass and funny and all, but he's not exactly what he appears. Smart enough to be dangerous, but not smart enough to care what that means. I'd say that to his face. And this is probably stepping way out of line, but if you haven't at least heard the rumors about Kale, you're probably the only one."

"I've heard them," I said.

"Well, I saw that cat. I saw what he did. He twisted its neck."

She let this sink in. "Its *neck*. He lured it to him first. With a piece of chicken." There was something particularly ugly about that detail, this chicken. "Jordan, if someone is capable of doing that to an animal . . ."

"I know what you're saying."

"It was in my neighbors' yard. Last summer. They tried to press charges even, but no one would take them seriously. You know, it was a cat, he's an *athlete*. Kale's parents paid some fine. Anyway, I thought you should know. I wouldn't have told you unless I thought you were someone who would care about this."

I looked at Kale strolling back to the blanket, his pockets bulging with "stolen" soda. From here, he didn't look dangerous. Just the kind of guy who harbored dreams of being a football player a little too long, when he wasn't that good to begin with. Maybe you couldn't tell with danger. Maybe it didn't walk around with a sign hung around its neck with a strand of yarn. My plate warmed the bottom of my hand. Mrs. D'Angelo's Brie Rounds and Miniature Spinach Quiche looked cold and make-believe. Less nourishment than decoration; faux jewels. I didn't even want that food anymore.

"I don't mean to upset you or anything. I just thought you ought to have all the facts."

I looked up at Ms. Cassaday. Her eyes were warm and concerned. She had been indulging in the Mexicali Roll-ups. She had a piece of olive between her teeth. "Thanks," I said.

"Well, I hope you have a good summer. A careful summer, right?" She gave my shoulder a little shake.

"Right." I smiled.

"I'd better go watch over Mr. Wykowski. If I don't remind him every two seconds to turn those hot dogs . . ."

"Okay. Thanks," I said.

The whole way back to the blanket, I felt like shame was creeping behind me, its hands arched just over my neck. Ms. Cassaday was someone like Big Mama, someone who understands bullshit; someone who sees things as they are. A person you couldn't stand to disappoint.

"That lesbo trying to get you on a date?" Kale said. The middle of the blanket was piled now with a small mountain of Dr Peppers. Jason Dale was hunched over Wendy Williams's yearbook, one arm covering his writing like some paranoid kid who's sure he knows all the answers on a test. Melissa knelt behind Wendy, French braiding her hair. If Melissa wasn't careful, pretty soon she'd be bent over the lot of them, waving a fan made of peacock feathers and feeding them grapes. When I looked again, I saw that Kale was pouting.

"She was just wishing me a good summer," I said.

"Lesbians. That's something I will never understand," Wendy Williams said.

"God," Melissa agreed. "Truly icky."

"Icky," Andrew Leland said. "I think I actually heard her say 'icky.'"

Melissa blushed horribly. I thought about socking him.

"Ow, that's too tight," Wendy Williams complained.

"Do it yourself, then. She's not your servant girl," Kale said.

I liked him right then, despite what Ms. Cassaday had said. That cat wasn't very real to me. She might have been right; but at that moment I was sitting on Kale's blanket, and the guilt I had about that fact was quickly turning into Who Gives a Shit, which wasn't truthful but felt better. That cat incident had been a year ago.

We sat around and ate, and everyone but me went back for Gayle D'Angelo's Dark Chocolate Brownies. We hiked down to the beach and threw rocks in the water. When we got back, it was getting dark and Custodian Bill had set up a movie projector, pointing it at the wall of the lighthouse as a screen. Custodian Bill had pinned a name tag that read LISA on his green unisuit. Those guys in Custodial Management were real jokesters.

The students who were left had laid out blankets in uneven rows in front of the lighthouse, ready to watch the movie. Someone had lit a fire, and the air became thick and smoky and filled with sharp pops and crackles, sounding like Miss Poe when she chews gum. Most of the teachers had left, but Heck Kwa and his wife sat in a pair of woven lawn chairs in the front row of movie-watchers, waiting for the show to start. Mr. Wykowski was still there too, sitting way back near the projector, ducking behind his hand and into a sweet, weedy-smelling cloud. Mr. Wykowski must have a thrill-seeking nature, because in the parking lot was the Tiny Policeman, clear as day. He sat alone in his patrol car, the dome light on and illuminating his tiny head. Just waiting for someone to do something wrong. You had to feel sorry for a guy like that.

The two picnic tables, now cleared of food, held only a sprinkle of parents. The talk and laughter there was loud. You were an idiot if you thought there was only coffee in the couple of thermoses and white Styrofoam cups that had appeared. My father sat with the holdouts, not wanting to give up Gayle D'Angelo's company unless he had to. He gave me a big wave when I came up from the beach. His face was happy with alcohol and company.

Gayle D'Angelo now sat next to him, Wes across the table. Mr. Chester had gone home to Mrs. Chester. Wendy Williams's dad, tie loose around his collar, had apparently come straight from work to join Mrs. Williams who now wore his suit jacket against the cold. Another couple in twin Mariner jackets also sat at the table, along with Paige Woodruff and Mr. Woodruff, whose son Michael was on one of the blankets, whispering things to his girlfriend, Kristine, that were causing her to frown and elbow him.

On my father's other side was Jake Levin's mother. Jake Levin was this nice guy on the baseball team who I sat next to in Contemporary Science. He was real quiet, probably because he had a slight lisp, which nobody cared about but him. His mother was this kooky woman, with hair down to her butt. In another six months, she would be diagnosed with ovarian cancer, and neither Paige Woodruff's fund-raising efforts nor the stuff that prune Cora Lee from the Theosophical Society gave her would make a difference. Jake ended up moving to Hawaii to be with his father, who was supposedly some hotshot surfer guy.

But right then Mrs. Levin was still alive and shooting my father these creepy, flirty looks. Custodian Bill finally got the film looped in the machine properly, and after everyone yelled "Focus!" at him, a grainy image began flickering against the lighthouse wall. It was getting cold, and Kale had put his shirt back on; helpfully leaving it unbuttoned so that we could still peek at his chest, a landscape of tight rolling dunes that looked like those pictures you see of the Arizona desert.

"*Pink Panther*. I love this," Wendy Williams said. "Look at those groovy outfits." In the movie, a group of mod museum-goers were gathered around a dome with a diamond in it. Everything looked slightly curved from the lighthouse wall, as if we were watching the film through a peephole. The sound for the movie was small in the huge park, the voices of little people trapped in tin cans.

"Jordan and I are going," Kale said. This was news to me, but okay. Maybe if I left, Dad would too. Kale slipped his hand in my back pocket.

"I want to watch the movie," Wendy said.

"Find your own way home then," Kale snapped. Wendy Williams seemed to rub him the wrong way.

"Fine, asshole," she said.

"I need to tell my dad I'm leaving," I said.

"He'll probably follow us in his car," Kale said.

A roar of laughter came from the picnic tables. "Shut up! We can't hear!" someone yelled at them. My dad's face glowed red from the light of the fire. It was way, way past time he went home. He belonged there, laughing and drinking spiked coffee with the D'Angelos and Williamses and Woodruffs, as much as I belonged there with Kale. And he, too, felt good being accepted by them. I knew that. Somewhere inside, I did.

"Miss Texas," Mrs. Williams said.

"You are *kidding*," Gayle D'Angelo squealed loudly. "Missouri. I won the talent comp."

"Don't get her started, I'm warning you," Wes D'Angelo said. Everybody laughed. "You think I'm kidding."

"Pageant girls," Mr. Williams said. "Expect you to throw roses every time they walk down the hall to put towels in the linen closet."

"No shit," Wes D'Angelo said.

"Oh, quit," Cathy Williams said. "You don't know how lucky you are."

"I thought you weren't supposed to admit things like that anymore," Mrs. Levin said. "Like being a cheerleader. I thought it was something embarrassing."

No one paid any attention to her. "I can still fit into my gown," Cathy Williams said.

"Somebody shoot that woman," the lady in the Mariners jacket said. She looked rough. The kind of face you get when you spend a lot of time at Smoky Joe's Tavern.

"I *can*," Cathy Williams said.

"Sometimes my song just runs through my head at night," Gayle D'Angelo said. "Like I'm right up on stage."

"Gayle," Wes warned.

I walked up behind my father. "Dad?" I said.

He ignored me. His eyes were focused on Gayle D'Angelo. "Sing it," he said.

"Oh, I couldn't," she said. She laughed a little, stuck her hands in the pockets of her lamb's-wool jacket.

"Dad." I tapped him on the shoulder.

"Come on. Sing it."

"Gayle," Wes said again.

"It's 'America,'" she said.

"Dad, I'm going. I'm going with Kale."

He looked back at me and nodded. "Don't we all want to hear it?" he said. "Yay, come on!" He started to clap. He was making a fool of himself. Wes D'Angelo looked as if he was struggling not to stand and wrap his hands around my father's neck.

"Oh sure, come on. We're patriotic," the woman in the Mariner jacket said. Her hands were folded around her Styrofoam cup like she was afraid someone might snatch it from her. Her partner nodded and smiled a glazed smile. He had passed into the land of booze zombies.

"Well," Gayle said. "All right." She stood up.

"*Jesus,*" Wes D'Angelo said.

"Dad," I said.

"Just a *minute*," he said. "The beautiful and talented Miss Gayle D'Angelo," he announced into his fist. He set it back down, flat on the picnic table. The only people there who could possibly miss the fact that she and my father were sleeping together or about to were the ones too drunk to notice. My father reminded me of Nathan's old cat, Sophie, thinking she was this great, expert squirrel hunter when all the while she had this noisy little bell on her collar.

"Miss Martins, I was then," Gayle said.

And then Gayle D'Angelo began to sing. Oh, God, she began to sing this horrible, sappy, warbling. She started out low and slow, with her eyes closed. Built to this peak of emotion that led her to grasp a handful of her lamb's-wool jacket and raise her face to the sky. My insides clutched up in embarrassment. So much that my stomach began to hurt. I stared at my sandals and concentrated. Leather and sandals, cows and leather. Sandals woven by a woman in a hut in some poor country so that she could feed her children. I concentrated on that woman weaving.

And then, when the worst seemed over, there was a second verse. Who knew that song had a second verse? I can still feel the awful cringe, creeping up along my body when I think of it *Above thy frui-ted plain!* That worst kind of humiliation, the kind you feel for someone else who doesn't have enough sense to feel it themselves.

She stopped. Thank God, it was finally over. I looked up from my feet, which I had been staring at so hard. Several of the movie-watchers had looked over their shoulders to watch, too stunned to be rude. Wes D'Angelo was gone from the table. With his fist, he was stuffing a pair of Styrofoam cups into the now over flowing garbage can. Paige Woodruff was drawing a design on the table with her finger as if she had decided to devote her life to it. Mrs. Williams's smile looked like it wanted to slink off and hurl itself into the fire but was being held there against its own will.

"Did she say she won with that?" the broad in the Mariners jacket said. "Maybe she had a baton or something."

"That was great," my father said.

The bizarre thing was, he seemed to mean it. His eyes were glossy as he looked at her. Could he have drunk that much?

"You think?" She beamed.

"God, yes," he said.

"Warms the cock of my heart," Mr. Mariners jacket slurred.

"Whew, I forget how much that takes out of you," Gayle D'Angelo said. She fanned herself with her hand.

"Took something outta me too," Mrs. Mariner Jacket said.

"Well," Mrs. Levin said. She rose to leave. Her Rapunzel hair swung around her shoulders all pissed off–like as she untangled her legs from the picnic table. She had given up on my father.

"You ought to sing at a baseball game or something," my father said.

"Over my dead body," the broad in the Mariners jacket said.

Wes D'Angelo walked back to the group. He slapped both palms down hard on the table. He was the type to do that kind of thing—slap his palms, clap his hands together once to make his intentions known, hit someone on the back too heartily. His eyes were flat. He had lost all his patience somewhere back at the garbage can. "That's it, Gayle. Time to go."

My father rose, as if he were the one that was supposed to obey the command. Gayle tapped her fingernails on the table. "Well, I may not be ready yet," she said. My father's praise had given her sudden rights.

"You're making a fool of yourself," Wes D'Angelo said to her.

"Wait a minute here," my father said.

The table got quiet. *Please God,* I prayed, *Let my father sit down and shut up.* Mrs. Levin froze where she was, looked at the toes of her shoes as if we were relying solely on her stillness to keep things calm.

"You've had too much to drink, and you're

making a fool of yourself," Wes D'Angelo said to his wife.

"Hey, now," my father said. "I think you," he had tapped Wes D'Angelo's chest with one finger. "Ought to apologi—"

Wes D'Angelo yanked away from him. "Get your hands off me."

"Oh, gosh," Cathy Williams said.

Mrs. Mariners Jacket's eyes were big, like this was television ice hockey and things were just getting interesting.

"Now, come on, guys," Mr. Williams said.

But a peacemaker turned out to be unnecessary, at least then, at that moment. Wes D'Angelo had turned away in anger, strode in the direction of his car, raising both hands in the air as if to say, *I'm not looking for a fight.*

What I saw next sickened me. Made me realize, too, that all the rules were beginning to change for my father. I guess inside I knew this already; I saw what happened next only because I looked for it. My father sat back down beside Gayle. Under the table he grasped her hand. She let go. She rubbed her hand up his leg, laid it on the V of his khaki pants and squeezed. Mrs. Levin saw it too. I saw her eyes, rising from beneath the table. She turned and left in a hurry, her keys already tight in her fist.

I grabbed Kale by the arm of his jacket. "Let's go," I said. I didn't care about Ms.

Cassaday right then, about any of the things she had told me. I didn't care about anything but getting the hell out of there.

We walked past the patch of movie-watchers, who had returned their attention to the screen. I could see Heck Kwa and his wife in their lawn chairs, watching the movie, their shoulders moving up and down with laughter.

Big Mama says that male salmon grow hooks on their jaws to protect their eggs against predators. It seemed to me then that God had left us all only half-equipped. We could have come with all the options, if He'd wanted. Instead we were all on this big survival campout, but some animals got only a knife, some a tent, or a can of insect spray. The game was, no one got it all.

My father could have used one of those, those hooks. When I went off with Kale, he didn't even turn around.

"It's cool. This hard-to-get stuff," Kale said. "I could use a change like the next guy."

Kale and I sat in the dark on the hood of his car, in Parrish Island Historic Park. Parrish Island Historic Park is basically this huge stretch of straw grass that ends at the widest sandy beach on the island. The place is so full of rabbit holes that walking around in the dark will earn you a sprained ankle for sure. What's historic about the place is that it was the site of a near war between the British and the Americans, who still hadn't figured out who owned the place. The war almost began when a British pig rooted around in an American settler's potato patch. For that wrong move the pig was shot, which made both sides mad enough to bring in the armies. I'm not kidding. You can see why the park rangers there have a chip on their shoulders.

Kale's car looked like it had a mean streak. I'm not good with car names, but it was one of those oldish cars shaped like a shark, the kind that make a lot of noise when you step on the gas. The year before, it was dull gray with primer. I remember it in the school parking lot. Now it was painted a slick black.

We'd dropped Melissa home and brought Wendy and the gang back to Jason's house, and then Kale had brought me to the park and tried to convince me to have sex. I couldn't do it; down deep I thought I had better love Kale, and down deep I knew I was having trouble even liking him. So instead, Kale had a smoke, then laid a soft, red plaid blanket on the hood of his car. Climbing up, I tried to be careful of the paint. It was so shiny, even in the dark.

Kale leaned back on his elbows, checked out the black starry sky. I circled my arms around my knees, set my chin there. Kale tilted his head at me. "So," he said.

"So," I said.

"No, you're supposed to spill your guts, remember? You promised."

"Oh," I said. I didn't remember promising.

"Hey, it's okay," he said. He rubbed my bare ankle with his hand. "You know, I'm here."

I thought for a while. "Well, it's my father," I said.

"That, I could've guessed," Kale said. "He's just gonna have to get used to the fact you're a big girl now. It's not right, following you around and everything. I'd tell him, 'Hey, I'm grown up. You got to give me some room. I make a mistake, I make a mistake. You can't protect me every second.'"

"It's not that," I said.

"It's not?"

"Most people think he's just this regular optometrist."

"And he isn't?" Kale said.

"Uh-uh."

"So what is he, some secret agent?"

That would have been good. "No. When he was in his twenties? He was a marine." The thought of my father as a marine cracked me up. It'd probably take him being chased by a herd of pissed-off elephants to get him over a rope wall and into a sand pit, like you see those guys do in the movies.

"No shit," Kale said.

"Yeah. Hard to believe, huh?"

"Fucking unbelievable." Kale's eyes gleamed in the dark, shiny as the paint on his car. I heard a boat out on the strait. The putting of an engine. That gasoline-on-water smell floated over.

"Well," I said. "They were doing this reconnaissance training once, and things got out of hand. He got into a fight with one of his superiors." I paused. "A *bad fight*."

"A bad fight?"

"Let's just leave it at that," I said.

"Shit, he killed him?"

I put my hands around my own neck and made strangling sounds. Kale's eyes danced happily. His foot jiggled back and forth at the end of the car hood. "He ran," I said. "He's been hiding here since. The secret's about to kill him."

"I thought your family was from here."

"You'd think this is the first place they'd have looked, wouldn't you? If you knew what I do about the armed forces, you wouldn't sleep so good at night."

Kale seemed to like this. "Anyway," I said. "His conscience has been bothering him. He's been talking about giving himself up. I mean, can you imagine? He's an *optometrist*." I paused, looked at Kale, who was thinking this over. "And on top of that he's been in this dangerous situation with this married woman."

Kale chuckled. "Go, Pops," he said.

I stopped then.

"So anyway," I said. I rubbed my arms from the cold. I wanted to go home.

"Just a sec," Kale said.

He inched himself off the car, then opened the front door and leaned inside to get his keys out of the ignition. He smiled at me from the back of his car. His teeth were really white in the dark. He popped the trunk and disappeared from view. I though he was getting me another blanket, or a jacket, maybe. That's actually what I thought. Oh God, a jacket.

He slammed the trunk down. Smiled again. He held up something. I didn't think it was real. A rifle. What he held up was a rifle. He put it to his eye.

"God, Kale," I said. I started getting real, real nervous then. I regretted the story about the marines. I regretted the lie about violence.

He slung the rifle over his shoulder, casual as if it were a beach bag stuffed with cartoon-stenciled towels. "Watch this," he said.

"No Kale," I said. "That's not loaded, right?"

Kale sat back inside the car, one leg still out the driver's side door. *Shit*, I thought. *Shit, shit, Jordan. You've got yourself in some mess now.*

My heart started pounding. I had no idea what he might do. None. I thought he might start the car and drive off, with me still on the top. I scrambled off the hood. I thought about running. I pictured one of those old westerns, a bullet in my back, arching forward with the impact.

"No, stay there," Kale called. "You'll see better."

See. I did not want to see anything. Nothing that involved a rifle. I knew that gun had bullets in it, all lined up one against the other, end to end. That's how I pictured them anyway.

I did not climb back on top of the hood. Instead I just stood where I was, backed up against the front fender of Kale's car. The engine thundered to life. The sound made me jump. I wanted out of there. Badly. This was the wrong, wrong place for me.

Kale gunned the engine, just for show, making it roar like an angry giant. Then it quieted to a low rumble.

Kale stuck his head out the driver's door. "Okay, watch!" he called.

He flicked on his headlights, two bolts of light so sudden and bright it was like looking directly into the eye of the Point Perpetua lighthouse. My arm went instinctively up to my eyes. I blinked. That light was horrible. Painful bolts. But not bright enough that I didn't see them, at the same time as I heard the sound, the tremendous *crack, crack* of Kale's gun.

The rabbits. Dozens of rabbits. Rabbits

emerging from their holes, some frozen blind, some stupidly nibbling at the ground as if it had merely suddenly become morning.

"Jesus, Kale!" I yelled. "Jesus! Stop it!"

Pieces flying. Actual pieces of animal flying, and the thud of something hitting the ground. Oh, Jesus. A rabbit skittered under the car. Kale raised the gun to his eye. I screamed. I must have moved; I remember clapping my hands over my ears at the sound, turning my head away.

"Stop it!" I cried. "Stop it, stop it, stop it!"

"Got him," Kale said.

He drove me home. He was full of a bouncy energy. He kept apologizing. He thought I would think it was cool, he said.

It was going on midnight by the time we reached my house. The moment we drove up the street, the Beenes' electric garage door rumbled up and showed its bright cheery contents—bikes and Mr. Beene's car and the lawn mower and fertilizer and equipment from various sports Mrs. Beene bought Mr. Beene that he never used. Jackson stepped out of the garage, hauling the garden hose and a sloshing bucket of water, which he set down next to his truck.

I got out of Kale's car. Kale yanked the parking brake and got out too. He leaned his back against the driver's door. "Aren't you gonna kiss me good-bye?" he said.

I kissed him, I'm ashamed to say, but I did it. Mostly because I wanted him to go away. Mostly because I never wanted to see him again. His lips were cold and dry. He tossed his keys in the air and caught them in his fist. He looked at my father's Triumph, sitting under the tarp.

"I want that car," he said. "That's a fantastically great car."

"It's my dad's," I said.

Down the street, Jackson had turned on the hose. I could hear the sound of the hard spray hitting the metal side of his truck. I could feel his eyes on me.

"Fuck, that guy's a spook," Kale said.

After a few minutes of stupid talk, Kale got back in his car and left. In the streetlight, I could see that my feet were speckled with blood. Blood from the rabbit that had tried to escape under the car. It was my fault, those rabbits.

I walked to the curb, where a stream of soapy water from Jackson's hose had trickled across the slope of street and was gaining speed in the gutter. I stepped into it, let it wash over my feet.

I looked up the street toward Jackson, but he had his back to me. I heard the Beenes' upstairs window slide open, and Diane Beene's voice jump out loudly into the darkness.

"What in the world are you doing, Jackson?" And then, more muffled, "He's washing his truck, Larry. Twelve fifteen at night and he's washing his truck."

"Do mine while you're at it!" Mr. Beene shouted.

# Chapter Nine

Grandpa Eugene had Elvis hair. Except for the times he'd just come from underneath someone's car or out of the laurel hedge with his pruning shears, his hair was sculpted like the King's, the sides swept back like wings, a swoop of meringue on top. Dyed black as the habits of the Franciscan nuns who work the ferry terminal. His hair just got stuck there in the fifties and never came out.

I leaned against the office door of Eugene's Gas and Garage, and I looked at that hair and the stubble on his cheeks that felt as prickly as stickers on a rosebush when he'd rub it against your face on purpose. Even though things turned out the way they did, right at that moment I felt like I was doing the right thing. I was sure I was. Because Grandpa Eugene could fix things. He wore that capable feeling, the way a lot of old guys do, as if they slap it on their face every morning along with the Aqua Velva. Like they had already seen plenty of broken dishwashers and insurance policies and car mufflers, and none had gotten the better of them yet. When Grandpa Eugene was in his unisuit (like Custodian Bill's, except gray) and was gripping a wrench, you knew both you and the wrench were in good hands. Whenever Grandpa Eugene was fixing a stalled car or leaky pipes, or cleaning gutters choked with leaves, I got that reassured feeling, just seeing him work the problem.

Grandpa Eugene leaned back in his chair, which complained with a long squeak. He scratched at a wide roll of packing tape with one finger. "How much time you figure we spend trying to find the end of the tape roll? Three, six months out of our life?"

"Here, give it to me," I said.

He tossed me the roll of tape, and I caught it. "That ass-wipe Marty Abare got a bunch of ordering catalogs for candy and snacks and crap. You want Ritz Crackeeos or what the hell, you go to the supermarket. You don't go to Eugene's. I'm packing them up and sending them back, thank you very much." He leaned back up with another long squeak and thumped the brown box on his desk. Marty Abare's desk.

"Good for you," I said, although I wasn't sure it was. I found the end of the tape roll, transferred the sticky end from my finger to his.

"So what's this problem," he said.

The phone rang. "Hell's bells," he said. "Eugene's," he barked into the phone, crooking it between shoulder and ear as he taped the box of offensive material. "What?" He listened for a moment. Leaned back in the squeaky chair. Through the office side door I could see Will Cutty sweeping up spent fireworks fuses that were scattered on the lot from the night before. My personal theory was that once Will's face cleared up he'd be good enough looking to increase business at Eugene's a good 75 percent.

"You gotta be kidding." Grandpa shook his head in disbelief. "None of your goddamn business." He hung up the phone with a slam. "You'd think they was selling vacuums," he said. He shook his head again. "You know what that was?" He didn't wait for an answer. "A goddamn religious telemarketer. I'm not kidding. You ever heard of that? Wanted to know where I 'worshipped.' Drumming up business for the Church of the la-dee-da. You think they was selling vacuums," he said again.

"For chrissakes," Grandpa said. "I went to the Seven-Eleven the other day and got blessed from the kid handing me the Big Gulp. I said,

'You hear me sneeze? I want that, I'll ask a priest. At least he's got credentials.'"

"You should see the woman I work for," I said.

"I don't want to see, I see enough. So what's the problem?" He tilted his chin down, looked at me from the top half of his glasses.

I can see him now, too late. The Second Chance Guy, poking his head around the corner during that pause. Wearing a big brimmed hat and standing in a cloud of smoke like a detective in an old movie. Peeking from underneath that hat, urging me to think it through. That I didn't listen is just one of those things I will have to live with.

"Dad," I said.

I knew things were getting bigger than me, that's why I did it. She had been at our house. I had gotten up that morning to find her downstairs in the kitchen. In our kitchen. She had poured herself a glass of orange juice. She had been wearing a pair of sweats, the kind that could make real sweats roll their eyes—dark purple with a monogram in a small diamond at the neck. She balanced herself with one hand on the counter; the other gripped her running shoe behind her back in a stretch.

"Good morning," she said. Her hair was up in a ponytail. She looked like an advertisement for a runner, not a real one. She looked beautiful. The word tastes bad in my mouth when I say it, but it was true. She looked beautiful.

"What are you doing here?" I said. I was tired. The night before, Melissa and I had gone to watch the fireworks lit from the small hump of Jubilee Island. If you listen to that prune Cora Lee at the Theosophical Society, Jubilee is the most "energized" spot in the San Juans. We'd been out late. I was in my old robe, my old ragged buddy. Both of us disapproved of Gayle D'Angelo. Both of us were embarrassed at our own disheveled condition.

"I think we met once," she said. "Gayle D'Angelo?" She dropped her shoe and put out her hand. I took it. The nails were as perfect as the first time, the skin as cool. "Your father"— she gestured to the downstairs bathroom—"told me I ought to drop by some morning," she said. "Such a perfect day for a run. I think summer has *officially* started."

My father emerged from the bathroom. He was in his own bathrobe, a responsible green plaid, his hair all weary yet rebellious, as if it had gone and had a party behind its parents' back. If he wasn't in the shower by now, he'd be late for work. His car had been there when I got home the night before. I didn't know why he looked so exhausted.

"Oh!" he said. As if I were the one he was surprised to see in our kitchen.

"You have company," I said.

"Look at you," Gayle D'Angelo said to him. "Frazzle boy." She licked her finger, smoothed his eyebrow. I wondered if she wiped his chin after he drank.

"This is my friend Gayle," my father said.

"Friends are strangers you haven't met yet," she said.

"I think it goes the other way around," I said.

"I *know*," she said. She waved her hand at me, a light, frilly gesture. A baby-doll pajama gesture. Something Bonnie Randall never would have done. Honestly, she was proving to be the kind of person you want to push down an escalator.

"Sure you can't stay for breakfast?"

"Oh, no. This is more than I should be having anyway." She clinked the edge of the juice glass with her nails.

"Right, you're a stick," my father said.

She smiled. She was one of those thin women who loved to be told they should eat more. One of those people that think they deserve congratulations for tight upper arms. You take care of your own body, hey, wow. You and the guy that finds a cure for cancer ought to get a medal.

"You see the fireworks last night?" she asked me.

"Yes," I said.

"Oh, I did too." She smiled and caught my father's eye. "They were *great*. As usual."

My father twined the end of his belt around his wrist. He was actually blushing.

"Well, time is a-wastin'," she said. "Better be on my way."

"Thanks for coming by," my father said to her.

Stupid thing was, I believed it. That she had just dropped by that morning as she had jogged past. Wes D'Angelo, I even thought, wouldn't be too much of a threat for those few minutes, even if he was only a half-mile away. I believed it all through their whispered conversation by the front door, I believed it after my father went upstairs and got showered for work. I believed it, until he left. When I saw his bedroom door shut tight. When I went in and saw on his bedroom mirror a message written in lipstick. YOU SAVED ME.

I rode my bike through town, past the nuns at the ferry docks, past Johnny's Market and Randall and Stein Booksellers. The town was sleepy and hungover from its late night. Colored wrappers littered the ground, and the air still carried the smell of lit matches. That gash of lipstick, in a color that might have been called Cherry Blush or Passion Pink or Desert Red, sickened me. The way it sat there, so bold. A mark, claiming ownership, announcing the fact that she had been there overnight as I slept unaware in the other room a heavy and naive sleep. A red mark, like the one left on a cheek after a slap. And my father had not wanted to wash it off.

I rode to True You to pick up my paycheck, came out of the cheery rose-colored room and back into summer on Parrish Island, where the blues are so blue and the sun, in a good mood from months of vacation, graces everything with bright halos. The air was grassy and warm. I tried to talk myself out of the fear I had about my father and Gayle D'Angelo. They were both adults, weren't they? That kind of thing happened all the time, after all. Every affair didn't end up on the evening news. And it wasn't that I was so innocent or so morally pure to be shocked. For all I knew, Gayle D'Angelo could be in an unhappy marriage; she and my father might have found true happiness together. Or maybe it was only temporary, a passing fling. Maybe I was experiencing some kind of psycho jealous Freudian thing. Any of those possibilities I could live with.

Well, that lasted until I rode just past the doughnut shop. Because down deep I knew my feelings about Gayle D'Angelo and my father had nothing to do with morality. Not about morality or jealousy. Those feelings were fear, pure and simple, fear that I didn't want to look at and that I couldn't shake off. Those feelings were about Wes D'Angelo ripped to shreds in that goddamned photograph. About this desperation I saw in my father that wasn't there before. Somewhere inside I knew that his wanting was the dangerous kind, wanting for wanting's sake, the kind that destroys people. My mother had warned me about that kind of wanting. Nothing, *nothing* about this was temporary. Though I didn't have the word for it then, what I felt was instinct. *Instinct* isn't about words, anyway, according to Big Mama. "Instinct," she said, "is God's vibration. That certain something that only one sockeye in a hundred will feel strongly enough to get him back home."

I don't know if what Big Mama says is true, but I do know now that it's what made me ride back downtown instead of anywhere else. Back past Johnny's Market and down a block, where my grandfather's gas station had been for forty-one years. Where you bought gas and not cartons of milk, for Christ's sake.

"You can't go accusing lightly," Grandpa Eugene said to me. He pointed his eyebrows down in a V to let me know what his disapproval would look like, in case I needed to be reminded.

"I'm not."

He tapped the end of a pencil on his desk. Marty Abare's desk. The pencil was printed with

EUGENE'S GAS AND GARAGE in dark green. We had some at home, in the pencil cup by the phone.

"Mister Don Juan," he said. "Is that it? Thinks he's Mister Don Juan?"

"I don't know," I said. Grandpa had the air-conditioning blasting. I got little goose bumps up and down my arms. Or maybe it was just a little thrill at his anger. Or the energy-shiver you get when someone sees something the same way you do, finally.

The bells on Grandpa's office door banged against the glass. I stepped away from the door and a man popped his head inside; a sincere guy in glasses, his shirtsleeves rolled up and his tie giving him a struggle in the heat.

"Excuse me," he said.

"You get gas?" Grandpa barked.

"Yeah." The man waved his thumb over his shoulder in the direction of the pumps.

"Gotta be careful of those hot dogs." Grandpa chuckled. In spite of his joke, I could see the tightness in his face. The anger. Grandpa didn't like funny business. That's what he called it, too, the bad, serious stuff. Funny business. I knew the subject of my father was closed. Taken care of sure as an overheating radiator.

The man smiled and handed over a credit card. Grandpa found his old imprint machine under a stack of invoices, stuck the card in, and yanked the handle over the top. "Get rid of this thing," he said to the man as he handed back his card. "You have a problem with real money?"

"Plastic's a curse all right," the man agreed. He put the card back in his wallet, took a slip of paper from it. "One more thing. I gotta find . . ." He looked at the paper. "You know the Parrish Medical Building?" He handed Grandpa the paper.

Grandpa read the address, looked at the man from the top half of his glasses. He eased himself up from the chair, opened the office door, and we stepped into a blast of warm air. "This street here?" he said. "Go back the way you came. Out to Front Street. Not more than a mile, mile and a half, you'll see Alder. Turn right, you'll see a big gray building."

"Thanks." The man took the slip back from Grandpa and got into his car. Marty Abare pulled up in his BMW and parked over by the air and water pumps. He got out, wiped a swag of dust from one shoe.

"What, no Bobcat Road?" I said to Grandpa. "You finally listening to Marty Abare?"

"What, are you kidding? Eugene MacKenzie doesn't take orders." He jabbed his chest with his fingers in case I'd forgotten who he meant. "Especially not from a guy like that. Look at him, ass out to here. Walks like a goddamn duck."

"He does," I agreed. We watched Marty Abare walk toward us.

"That customer didn't need Bobcat Road."

"Oh, really," I said.

"What are you, Miss Smarty Pants? I known you since you was a baby. I say the guy wasn't lost, the guy wasn't lost. Look." He hooked his thumb at Marty Abare. "Now he's gonna talk to you. You gonna stink like his frou-frou water all day."

Marty Abare reached us, stuck his hand out to shake mine and then Grandpa's. "What you shaking my hand for, I saw you an hour ago," Grandpa said.

Marty Abare ignored him. "School's out? You enjoying the summer?" he asked. His tiny crocodile eyes were attempting to calculate my bra size.

"Very much," I said.

"Eugene," he said in a louder voice. "If I remember right, all customer questions regarding directions were to be referred to Will."

"Will's busy," Grandpa said.

"Will can be interrupted," he said. "You know, we talked about this little joke of yours. Any more of it"—he laughed, looked at me—"your ass is grass, and I'm the lawn mower." He chuckled. Trying to pour syrup over the blade of a knife. Grandpa's face looked suddenly sewn shut. His mouth had these tight lines, like the trussing on a turkey.

"You ever need a summer job, you come to

me," Marty Abare said over his shoulder as he walked away from us toward the office. Inside, I saw him toss his keys onto the desk.

"He's got a comb in his back pocket, for Christ's sake," Grandpa said. "Look at that."

"A regular peacock," I said.

"You got that half right. You hear what he said to me? 'Your ass is grass, and I'm the lawn mower,'" Grandpa mimicked in a high voice. "'Your ass is grass, and I'm the lawn mower,'" he sang. He stuck his butt out like Marty Abare's and said it a few more times, prancing around.

I started to laugh, and as mad as I could tell he was, he started to laugh too. "'Your ass is grass,'" he said high and girlie. "'And I'm,'" he pretended to comb his hair. "'The lawn mower.'"

I was laughing hard now. "God Grandpa, stop." Will Cutty had just slid the contents of another full dustpan into the garbage can, but now he looked up and smiled grandpa's way.

Grandpa liked this. He stuck his old rear out and strutted back and forth some more.

"'Your ass is grass,'" Grandpa sang.

"Oh, jeez, he's looking at you."

Grandpa waved to Marty Abare staring at him from the window.

"Oh, jeez," I said again.

"Hello, you ass-wipe," Grandpa sang.

"Oh jeez, stop," I said, laughing. "Grandpa."

Nervous laughing. I didn't want Marty Abare to see us busting a gut at his expense.

"Man, oh, man," Grandpa was chuckling good now. He took off his glasses that Dad had gotten for him and wiped his eyes with the back of his hand. "Sometimes I think I'm the only one who sees clear around here," he said. He put his glasses back on. His eyes looked kind of big through the lenses. Big and a little smeary with age.

"You want a frozen burrito? I got a couple we can pop in the microwave. Don't tell your grandma. She thinks they're gonna give me a heart attack." He grasped at his chest and made a pretend dying sound. "Hell, I been eating 'em all my life. I'm gonna start eating some celery stick?"

"What, use the microwave in there?" I asked, nodding to the office. Marty Abare was on the phone. He rocked back and forth in the chair, pretending not to notice us when we were obviously the only thing he was paying attention to.

"I don't care about that ass-wipe. See that there?" Grandpa said. He pointed to the sign that bore his name. EUGENE'S GAS AND GARAGE, dark green on white, in letters as bold as Grandpa himself. "Look at that."

"I see it," I said.

"He can't hurt me," Grandpa said.

Grandpa had been right. I did stink like Marty Abare's aftershave, even after a good wind-whipping from the bike ride back. It was giving me a headache. Loud perfume is basically the same as someone else's blaring boom box, if you ask me. Once I was home again I tried to wash it off, and when I came out of the bathroom I saw the message light on the answering machine blinking. Melissa. "Oh God, oh God, oh God. Come over right away. The most awful thing has happened."

The first thing I noticed when Mrs. Beene opened the door was that she'd redecorated the living room again, and sitting on the fireplace mantel was this big brass urn. It was a serious looking thing, right in the center. I'd never seen it before.

"Oh," I said. I stood in front of the urn. "Jeez, Diane, I'm sorry. Is that, uh, Grandpa Lawrence?" I pointed to the urn. Melissa's Grandpa used to own a drapery business. He was a quiet little guy who, every time I'd ever seen him, was eating dried apricots out of a bag. Real nice; he always offered me one.

"What?" Mrs. Beene said.

I pointed to the urn again. "Did he, um, pass away?"

"My vase? Oh my God, is that what you think? That it's one of those . . . For *ashes?*" Diane Beene grabbed the urn off the mantel by its handles, held it at arm's length and looked at it with a tilted head. "Tell me honestly, you thought it was one of *those?*"

Honestly, yeah, it looked like something some dead guy's ashes were in, but that seemed kind of indelicately put.

"I don't know," I said.

"It does, doesn't it? Tell me."

"It's just . . ." I said. "Melissa called all upset."

"She's perfectly fine," Mrs. Beene said. "She just had a slight problem. I told her not to use that facial-hair bleach when she had a tan. Oh, now I don't know," she said to the urn. "This is terrible. I'm going to have to give this some thought. I'd hate for people to think I'd . . . Larry's mother still has her second husband in the closet behind her *shoes.*"

Upstairs, I stepped over Boog where some-one had left him in the hall. Melissa sat glumly with her arms looped around her knees. I tried not to laugh when I saw her, but I probably laughed a little. She looked like she was sporting a first-rate milk mustache on her upper lip. She could have been in one of those ads for the Dairy Farmers of Washington.

"It's not that bad," I said.

"Lie."

"Let's see." She moved her arm down so I could get a good look. The hairs on her lip shone all sparkly silver-blond like they were dressed for the disco. "You won't even see it with some makeup," I said.

"I tried," she said. I could see that she had. Squat brown bottles were scattered on her dresser. Also, a round plastic lid holding a pyramid of white powder and a flat paddle scoop. Stuff anyone unfamiliar with Jolene Hair Cream might easily mistake for drug paraphernalia. "I considered doing the rest of my face," she said.

"Oh, jeez, don't do that," I said.

"You don't think I should?"

"It'd probably give you some horrible disease in ten years."

We played around with Melissa's lip for a while. I could hear Jackson in his room next door, in a Texas mood, on the telephone: "If my name isn't Archimedes Pesto . . . impeachment is what they deserve for ignoring the spotted owl . . ."

"Kale call today yet?" Melissa asked.

"I haven't been home. I'm sure he will. The more I ignore him, the harder he tries. You'd think he'd take the hint, all the times I've hung up on him."

"I'm starting to feel sorry for him," she said.

"You've got to be kidding."

I'd told Melissa about the rabbits. I left out the part about my made-up story. I still couldn't bring myself to tell her about that, or about my father and Gayle D'Angelo. It made me feel as if it were *me* doing awful things. If I had my wish, I'd stuff all of it in a closet and shut the door, fast.

"Maybe what happened at the park was just sexual frustration," Melissa said. She seemed to like the idea of this. It was the way she said the words, swishing them deliciously in her mouth.

"Great. His animal nature makes him want to kill nature's animals."

There was nothing funny about that night, though. The horror of it still grabbed me and twisted sometimes. At night sick pictures flashed in front of my closed eyes. I shuddered when I put the sprinkler on the front lawn and the cold drops of water splattered my bare legs, and when a passing car's headlights made a quick slash of light in the dark living room window. I would have to be desperate or crazy to see Kale again.

From Melissa's bed where I sat, I heard the skipping thuds of Jackson going downstairs, and a few moments later, the *bamp bamp bamp* of a basketball being dribbled in the driveway. The sound was loud through Melissa's open window. Melissa shoved aside her Venetian blind and stuck her face to the screen. "You don't even play basketball, you freak," she said, and let the blind bang back in place again.

"I bet if you sit in the sun the rest of the day

your lip will burn and be tan in time for work tomorrow," I said. I don't know if this was good advice. "I'll go out with you."

"You probably just want to watch my psycho brother play imaginary basketball without a hoop," she said.

She may have been right.

"I meant the backyard," I said.

I picked up Boog on the way out and placed him in the kitchen in front of the refrigerator, where it was cooler and only a small slide over to his water dish. I swear he smiled at me with his black lips. Diane leaned against the kitchen counter, sipping a glass of iced tea and looking at the new vase, which now sat by the back door.

"What's that doing here, Mom? It looked fine."

"Jordan thought it looked like one of those urns. For cremated people."

"Jordan, jeez. It looked fine, Mom. Great. Don't listen to her." She shot me a nasty look. "God," she said when we got outside. "What did you say that for? Do you know what you're going to put me through for the next two weeks?"

"Well, it did," I said. "It looked just like one."

"I know it did," Melissa said. "But jeez."

Melissa pulled out a couple of lawn chairs for us and handed me one to unfold. "It should have been engraved," I said. "'Grandpa Lawrence Beene. I never met an apricot I didn't like.'"

"You're sick," she said.

"You love me," I said.

Melissa rolled her eyes. She plunked herself down on the lawn chair and pointed her milk mustache toward the sun.

It first hit me that I had done something terribly wrong when I saw Grandpa and Grandma's car in our driveway the next night. That car, sitting there all solid and functional and, I don't know why, but *unexpected* and suddenly, *bam!* The "Oh Shit." I had betrayed my father. Hell, I *told on* my father. And I knew this would matter. A lot. The car in the driveway would matter. Because my father cared what Grandpa Eugene thought of him. He cared in a way I thought (I *hoped*) you somehow got over when you got old enough.

I knew because of the steak. Not just the steak, but that was one thing. When Grandpa came over, that, not hot sauce on ribs, was what we usually had. Broiled or barbecued to red, fleshy steaky perfection. Dad and I rarely ate it when the two of us were alone; not that good for you, and neither of us liked it that much. But Dad served it whenever Grandpa came. Because steak meant Dad made enough money to buy steak.

Seeing that car, I felt the panicky shame all tattlers feel. The wish to be back in the group again instead of standing by the teacher's side, both higher and lower than everyone else. When I went inside it was with that guilty silence that makes you want to walk on your tocs. My father was still jovial though surprised by their presence, caught steakless. My grandmother wore a dress that was as nervous and spotted as her old hands. My grandfather asked me to leave the room.

If I jumped out my bedroom window, I would be dead on top of the garbage cans; if I put my head under my pillow, I wouldn't be able to listen. I settled for going to the top of the stairs and plugging and unplugging my ears, letting chance decide what I would hear. "Well, you know I'm a grown man." My father laughed that laugh that isn't the least bit funny. And next, "Fifty years, your mother and I been married," and "That's not the way you were raised," and my grandmother's voice, "We're only concerned for you, Vince."

And then, "Not my business? Is it gonna be my business when he comes after you with a gun?"

And my father "This isn't the movies. This isn't some make-believe drama you saw on television."

Until I could hear with ears plugged or not,

my grandpa's voice raised to a thunder. "Goddamn it, you old bird, don't tell me not to get upset! I'm upset!"

"I'm not a kid, Dad!"

"You oughtta at least think about your daughter! She's the one that's upset, you know that? Or you too busy in the bedroom to notice?"

"Eugene!"

"I can handle my own daughter."

The front door slammed, and my bedroom window rattled. From my room where I'd taken refuge I could hear my grandmother by the front door, speaking softly now. My ears were so on-edge, I think I could have heard her thoughts.

It hurts to remember. It hurts, hurts, hurts. "He's just upset," she said to my father. "Marty Abare let him go today."

The front door closed. Outside I could hear my grandmother's voice, surprisingly strong. "I'm driving," she said.

"You're not driving anywhere, you old coot," my grandfather said.

"Move over or I'll stand here all night," my grandmother said. "You are not driving in your condition. Look, your hands are shaking. I'm afraid when you get so worked up."

"Worked up, hell," he said. But he must have moved over, because a few seconds later Grandma gave the car too much gas as she backed out of the driveway.

My father waited until they were gone, and then he thumped up the stairs. I was crying by then. Sniveling into my pillow like the coward I was. He stood in my doorway. That's all he did. Stared at me, with this look that couldn't decide between contempt and bewilderment. I hated myself. I wanted to vomit, and he just stood there and stared, his hand on the door-jamb. His tie still on from work that day, a guilty reminder of everything he did for me. Then he turned away from me. I heard his keys scrape against the tile counter as he gathered them up, heard the rattle of the doorknob. Another slam. His car rumbled angrily to life. I cried hard then. Heaving cries, as I grasped my pillow to my chest. At that moment, I felt that he was lost to me.

I told myself a bunch of self-pitying lies. Then I got myself together. I wiped my face. Away from my father's staring, I remembered why I had told Grandpa in the first place. I decided there was no way in hell I wanted to be home when my father got back. He, after all, was the one that was doing wrong, and maybe he'd better remember that.

I stuffed a few things in my backpack, got my bike out of the garage. I would spend the night at my Mom's.

The funny thing was, I wasn't even surprised to see Jackson's truck at the end of the block, just sitting there waiting for me with the engine idling. He didn't say anything when he saw me. He just got out, lifted my bike, and put it in the back of the truck. He got back in and didn't say a word. Not even a sigh that said I required a great deal of patience.

# Chapter Ten

*My mother had wanted to* name me Daisy Blossom. Daisy Blossom MacKenzie. I'm not kidding. Thankfully the only outrageous thing my father had ever managed to do was marry my mother, and even that had been more than he could handle. He put his foot down about the name. Not only was it ridiculous, he'd say as he told the story, but a poor choice; daisies stink worse than the inside of his shoes. So I have my father to be grateful to for sparing me the misery of going through life with a name that sounds like it belongs to a stripper with tit-twirling tassels.

I regretted almost immediately going to my mother's that night. First of all, I could tell she was trying something new with me, and nothing ticked me off more than her thinking I required techniques. It was probably something she read about in some book called *Daughters on the Cusp of Womanhood*. She tiptoed around me in wide arcs, giving me space, I guess, holding herself back from asking what was wrong. Keeping her mouth shut was not something my mother did without looking like she was at a gym, trying to bench-press her weight. Every one of her actions screamed what she wasn't saying, which did not encourage me to become open and communicative. Screaming, any way you do it, never does. Actually, it only made me curious to see just how long she might go before the words came out in some messy explosion. I became so comfy and involved watching her bustle around pretending to be casual, as her face got tighter and tighter as the skin of a balloon, that I almost forgot what it even was that I was keeping from her.

And then there was the problem of my mother in the summertime. In a loose sundress lax on the job, sometimes letting a part of her that shouldn't pop into view, she was so much my mother that it bugged the hell out of me. You were certain to see grassy patches under her arms, not mowed since winter, and freckles that speckled her back in various patterns, looking like those paintings Mr. Wykowski showed us in class that are made by a thousand dots of color.

I don't know. Now I think that maybe you judge a mother in a way you don't judge a father. Maybe just daughters do. In my mind I was simply my father's child, no question—restrained, polished. And shaven.

So by the next morning I wanted out of there, but I wasn't ready to face my father yet. My plan was to stay around until it was time to go to True You, avoiding Mom. Miss Poe had gone out to pick raspberries, Hugh Prince was relaxing his strained nerves through the rhythms of the marimba gourds next door, and Grant Manning was at the university lab trying to get orcas to sing into his microphone. So my only option was to go out to Nathan's shed and watch him work. Usually he was too preoccupied to talk much and I could just sit on a stool or his old rocker and watch the sparks of his blowtorch and the silvery drips of his soldering iron.

Mom had Max strapped into a high chair he'd outgrown, trying to still his wiggles long enough to give him a haircut. "It was a surprise to see you last night," she said. So casual it was killing her.

"I know how you like unexpected visits," I said, and banged out the screen door. I trotted down the porch stairs and almost ran smack into Homer slinking around the corner, sucking away on Max's pacifier. He dropped it like a drunk caught with a bottle of booze, then came over for a pat.

I scratched his tan head. "You're neurotic," I said to him. He smiled up at me like this was the best news he'd heard all day.

Homer trotted amiably behind me to the workshop. The Jell-O molds cemented to the outside of Nathan's shed actually get hot to the touch in the summer, and standing next to them, you felt them radiate a surprising warmth. A sign on the building had a picture of Max tacked to it, and the message, IF YOU HAVE ANY QUESTIONS ABOUT MY DAD'S ART, JUST COME TO THE HOUSE AND KNOCK. Visitors to Parrish often pulled to the side of the road and ventured over to gawk at the yard.

I pushed in the heavy wooden door to a shady coolness and the sound of Bob Dylan whining as pitifully as Homer when no one will throw his knotted sock. Nathan, in tank top, shorts, and sandals, bent over what looked to be two copper pinwheel blades on a silver stand. The huge round globes of his safety goggles were down over his eyes.

"You look funny," I said.

He wiggled his arms out in front of him. "Scuba diver," he said.

"More like fly eyes," I said.

"Run! Protect your children and women!

210

The Human Fly will eat you all!" He flapped his arms like a chicken.

"You're so weird," I said.

"I'm melting pennies on it," he said. He rubbed his hand along the flat blade of the sculpture. At his feet, I saw the wrinkled Front Street Market bag packed full of copper. "Everyone's contributed to this one. Even the guys at Beer and Books empty their pockets when they see me coming. I like the idea of it, pennies, all the places and pockets they've been. Old ladies' coin purses, sweaty little hands of kids. Cash-register drawer of some diner, who knows where. Life layers. I'm hoping they'll show through the work when I'm done," he said.

"Oh," I said. You know, whatever. I sat in the rocker he had in the corner of the shed, drew my knees up. Homer nosed around in the basket of toys Nathan kept there for Max, looking for something to put his slobbery lips around. "Homer, quit," I said.

Homer overcame his compulsion for a moment and dropped down on the floor in front of me. I just sat there for a while, watching Nathan and listening to the *har-har-har-har* of Homer's heavy breathing. It sounded like he was remembering a joke that truly cracked him up. I couldn't have been there more than ten minutes when Mom popped her head through the door.

"Jordan?" My first thought was that she had finally caved in; my brain had started negotiations on how much of the truth I wanted to tell her. Then her face got all funny.

"God, Jordan," she struggled. Her voice wobbled with tears. When the rest of her came into view, I saw that she held Max under one arm, his bangs cut only halfway across like some baby punk rocker. He hung under her arm in a haphazard fashion but looked too stunned at the sudden change in plan to care. Nathan switched off the blowtorch, and the workshop got too quiet. He lifted his goggles to his head.

"What?" I said. I was getting worried now. *My father,* I thought. *Oh Jesus, it happened. Something has happened to my father.*

My mother met Nathan's eyes. She wiped her own teary face against Max's small shoulder. "The phone," she said. She pointed back toward the house. "God, Jordan. I'm so sorry. It's your grandpa. Your grandpa. Eugene."

"What? He's in the hospital?" I said. "He's in the hospital?"

"He's dead. He's dead, Jordan. He . . ."

"He can't be," I said. "I just saw him last night."

She didn't say anything. Her shoulders just started moving up and down in a swallowed sob.

"I just saw him," I said again.

"After," she said. "Later. Last night. Oh, honey," she said.

"But I just saw him," I said. I mean this was ridiculous. He was perfectly fine last night.

"Honey," she said.

*Oh shit,* I thought. *Shit. Whatever had happened to him had been my fault. My fault.*

She came to me, put her free arm around me, and pulled me to her. I was confused more than anything else. My chin rested over her shoulder. Her body racked against my still one, and soon Nathan came and put his arms around all of us. I didn't cry then. I mean, someone can't just be here one minute and dead the next. I concentrated on the back end of Max, which from my viewpoint I could see sticking out from my mother's arm. I saw his little shoes, both laces undone. It can take a person a long time to die in your mind.

"I loved Eugene," my mother said in a small voice. She released me. "We need to get her to her grandma's," she said to Nathan. We walked hurriedly across the yard. I wasn't sure what the rush was now. If he was dead. We crossed paths with Hugh Prince and Marimba Janey, who had just strolled across the grass hand-in-hand, happy smiles on their faces. My mother thrust Max into Hugh Prince's arms, and rushed into the house after Nathan. Poor Hugh looked like a spectator who had wandered down to the field to get a hot dog and had just been handed the football during a crucial play. His face was a mirror of what I felt right then, that someone had just handed me something unfamiliar, unwanted. Something I had no idea what to do with.

My grandmother's house was full of people when I got there. When it comes to death, people move fast. I guess they think they'd better move quickly to show good manners and compassion so Mr. Death will figure they're nice people and pass them by. A lot of little old people grasped my hands with their thin, loose skinned ones, and some folks I recognized from the gas station patted my shoulder, and I just basically walked around and said the things you do, except that it all seemed like we were only pretending. My aunt Sonia, my father's sister; her husband, Bob; and the two kids would be coming into town the next morning. I had to call Laylani and tell her why I wasn't at work.

"Oh, Jordan," she had said. "You just know your grandfather is in a better place." Well, no, actually I didn't know that. But that's what people say when someone dies. All the old people and friends from the garage said it too. He's in a better place. Like he packed his bags and went to Hawaii. Like he and his Elvis hair had themselves resting against some lounge chair, working on a tan. I wondered where he really was. I wondered if he was cold there. It still seemed then that he was going to walk in and ask what the hell all those people were doing in his living room. I just kept expecting him. He would be very pissed off at these people who came over without calling first. He would be very pissed we were pretending he was dead.

Grandma had thrown an afghan over Grandpa's chair, the one with the footstool that popped out, with the seat all soft and worn. The one where he died. People avoided looking at it, as if it knew something they didn't know and didn't care to.

My grandmother was doing what they called "holding up well." Maybe that's another reason all the people come fast, in a swarm. To catch you before you fall into that pool of raw grief. To make sure your eyes don't stay too long on the jar of Hotter 'n Hell Hot Sauce when you open the refrigerator door. Instead your eyes are forced to move, looking for the 7-Up Mrs. Carpenter asked for because she was feeling a little faint.

The only problem, though, is that those people don't stay forever. They don't follow you into the night, pile into bed with you. That's when you really need them, too. You could use Mrs. Carpenter lying across the foot of the bed with her hair curlers in, and old Franklin, the neighbor man, in striped pajamas with his plate of midnight snacks balanced on his stomach, and Will Cutty shyly elbowing for more room in his plaid boxers and white T-shirt, punching his pillow to make it more comfortable. That's when you need them; that's when the person missing becomes hugely gone and Dead seems the biggest thing of all.

It was decided that I would stay with Grandma that night until Aunt Sonia and her family came the next day. I didn't like the idea, but my father and Grandma and I were doing this guilty square dance and Grandma, Lost My Partner What'll I Do?, got me. I didn't want to stay there. That house felt strange to me with Grandpa's pill bottles sitting half empty on the kitchen windowsill, his black grandpa socks tossed by his side of the bed, the TV channel knob still marked to the place he had watched the night before. In the bathroom drawer was the tube of toothpaste he expected to finish. It seemed like he had not done a sad thing, but a mean one—selfishly going off to the better place and not packing up his things. Leaving his black socks for Grandma to pick up one more time.

Grandma gave me one of her nightgowns. Actually it was more like a floral housecoat. If Melissa could have seen me, she'd have laughed like crazy. All I needed was a hair net with rollers underneath. But nothing was truly very humorous right then. Because there in the darkening house with Grandma asleep in the other room and the sound of the kitchen clock ticking, ticking, the idea of Grandpa being gone was catching up to me. There is nothing quite so empty sounding as a clock ticking in a house that is not your own. I was trying hard not to cry. I felt scared. I got a sheet and blanket from the linen closet and made myself a bed on the couch. The linens smelled the way everything in their house smelled, like vegetables cooked until they were pale.

I lay down very still. Set my cheek on one of the couch's rough, needlepoint pillows. I could hear Grandma rustling about in the other room. I tried to sleep, but it was hard. It felt like Grandpa was everywhere. He was more present while gone than when he sat right on that same couch next to me watching baseball. I wondered if he was still hovering about, he felt so close; floating all around like those tiny specks of dust you can see only when the light is right. I kept hearing his voice when I shut my eyes, like he was giving me a big dose of himself before he left for good. A few moments later, I heard Grandma call out.

"Honey?"

Her voice gave me a start. I was feeling responsible for her, and I guess down deep I was a little nervous something might happen to her on my shift. That dying business makes you edgy.

"What, Grandma?"

"Would you mind coming here?"

She was propped up against both pillows. She looked small in her bed. Her hair frizzed out all white and wiry from her head. "Do you need something?" I asked.

"No," she said quietly. "Yes."

"Are you all right?"

"I'm just . . ." she said. "I'm very alone." Her voice was small. "I keep trying to tell myself he only went to take out the garbage. So I can sleep."

"But that's not working, huh?" I said.

"Garbage day is Friday," she said. She started weeping softly.

"Do you want me to come in for a while?" I asked.

I saw her white head bob in the darkness. I went back to the couch, got my blanket, and lay down on the bed beside her. "You're gonna have to share a pillow, though," I said. She slipped a pillow from behind her head and handed it to me. I propped it under my head. I thought about Grandpa's body, lying there in my place. I just kept wondering where he was.

"I don't know if I can sleep without his snoring," she said. "I hated that snoring."

"I'll snore for you," I said. I gave a couple of loud snorts.

"Oh, honey." She laughed. She patted her lap, and I inched closer to her, laid my head down on her thin legs. "Sometimes it would make me bolt upright in the night. *The train is here, and I haven't even packed!*"

She raked her hand through my hair, the way she used to when I was small. I tried not to, but I couldn't help it. I started to cry too. Darkness does this. It finds all the places you are hiding in. It finds all the things you are holding onto tightly and makes you let go.

"I knew something was going to happen," Grandma said. "I felt it coming. Since Marty Abare bought the station, I felt it." Her soft, knobby fingers brushed against my temple. "He was just sitting there. Sitting there right in his chair, plain as day. Eating a bowl of ice cream. Scraping the spoon against the bottom of the bowl in that irritating fashion he has. 'Eugene, must you?' I would say. I tried to get him to come to bed. You know how upset he was. Oh, he was angry. But Eugene never did anything he didn't want to."

"No," I said.

"He just looked at me," she said. "'What the hell did they put in this soup?' he said. Those very words. Soup! Then down went his head. Drop. Right to his chest. It was the oddest thing.

Sixty years, I've known him, and his head just went down like that and he was gone," she said in wonder. "In a way I wish he'd have lingered. Just . . . waited a moment. But Grandpa wasn't the type to do anything halfway, now, was he? All or nothing. Still . . ." She breathed a shaky breath. "I would have liked to say good-bye."

I cried at that for a while. "It was me," I said into the blanket. "It was my fault." It was good to get those words out, that blackness. "I didn't think it would make him so upset."

"Oh no, Jordan, no."

"Marty Abare . . . and what I told him. I'm so, so sorry Grandma," I cried into the blanket. "I didn't mean to hurt him."

"No, no," she said. "Jordan, no. It wasn't your fault. No, sweetheart. Nothing did him in."

I was glad she said it, but I didn't believe her. That I would never believe. She started to cry softly then too. I just lay there real still until she stopped. For a while, she was so still, I thought she was asleep. But she'd only been sitting there, thinking.

Finally she spoke. "They zipped him into this plastic bag," she said. "Like those pieces of luggage you put your good suits in? A garment bag. With the little opening for hangers on top."

"I know what you mean," I said.

"The two boys that came, they asked if I wanted to leave the room, but I said no. I was interested. Eugene hadn't let me watch when my mother died. He made me go into the kitchen and turn on the radio! And my father, well, he'd been in the hospital, and they do all the shushing off when no one is around. Seeing it, well, for a moment, I did panic. My heart pounded. I worried he wouldn't be able to breathe in there."

"That's probably why they didn't want you to look."

She thought some more. "It was burgundy," she said finally. "That bag. A nice shade of burgundy. I've always thought a little color can make things more bearable."

"Me too," I said.

"And then there he went," she said. "Right in his pajamas. Now I suppose they'll be required to give them back so I don't sue."

I didn't say anything. I pictured someone saluting and clipping their heels together, handing back the pajamas folded into a triangle.

"I don't want them back," she said.

"I wouldn't," I said.

"I asked the boys for a receipt. Before they carried him off. You should have seen the look! They were laughing at me, with their eyes, I could tell. The one even caught the glance of the medic, who only shrugged, like he'd seen worse. They didn't think I noticed, but I most certainly did. I was a teacher for twenty-five years, don't forget. Not much slips past me. But that was perfectly fine, they could laugh to their heart's content. Go right ahead. I held firm. I made them write one on the back of an envelope."

I smiled in the darkness.

"Eugene would have been proud. Eugene told me to always get a receipt."

Somebody tell me why we look at dead people in their caskets, on purpose. My father says that it helps make it more real, death. Well, it sure does drive the point home, doesn't it? If you need the point driven home by then. But, hey, we don't have to watch ourselves get surgery to face the fact of being sick, do we? Or stand barefoot in the snow to understand winter is coming? I seriously doubt you turn thirty-five and suddenly start accepting this logic. If you ask me, people are just afraid to say what a stupid idea this is. No one wants to look like a chicken.

And the thing is, it's not like it's only a quick peek either. No, they put goddamn benches in those places so you have to sit and look at that chalky profile until you are convinced you see the chest going up and down. Until you see those folded hands rise up in a little wave. Until the last thing on your mind is how much you loved that fake person in there. Instead you start wondering if it's true what they say about those funeral guys putting toothpicks in the eyes so they don't pop open and surprise someone. And you start wondering about those funeral guys themselves. Walking around in their dark suits with faces like those palace guards in London. You just want to walk right up to them and sing "Beans, Beans the Magical Fruit" just to see if they're really human.

One thing I knew, that fake guy up there had nothing to do with Grandpa Eugene, and he'd have been the first to tell people he wasn't about to do no goddamn tap dance, so what the hell were they looking at? Most of the people there had done this kind of thing before and seemed to disagree with me. They sat on the benches, whispering back and forth as if waiting for the matinee to start. My father wandered around up front, rattling the change in his pocket. I wished he'd stop it, because although I was sure it was only nerves, it made him look in a hurry to leave. Some people got up and stood there beside Grandpa Eugene or patted his hand, which gave me the creeps. That body up there is what Grandpa Eugene would look like if they made a copy of him for a wax museum. It was not him, the man who wiggled his old ass around.

"He looks really good," the woman behind me whispered. She said she was related to me somehow, but I was having a hard time keeping it all straight. I had never seen her before in my life. For all I knew she could have been there for the ham sandwiches later.

"Oh, he does, he does," her companion whispered back. "He looks wonderful." This I did not understand. Sure he looked like he'd just had a clean shave and his hair was in a perfect Elvis confection, but he did not look great. He looked dead. Dead people look amazingly dead.

"My Humbolt," Miss Poe piped in. She had come along with Mom, Nathan, and the gang, and had latched herself to the two suspect relatives. "What a mess they made of him. He looked terrible. Not even a bit like himself. He looked like Winston Churchill."

"I'm sure you were the only one who thought so," the suspect relative said. Kindly, I thought.

"Well, look who's here," she said.

"Who?" Miss Poe said. I was worried about Miss Poe getting too cozy with those two. I wondered where Mom had gone, but I didn't want to get up and walk around to find out. I was worried that I might accidentally see something else I didn't want to see in that place.

"Nancy. Sonia's cousin's wife," the suspect relative said. I looked toward the doorway where a couple was entering. "She just had her breasts enlarged, not that you can tell by looking at them. That kind of surgery at her age. Might as well flush your money right down the toilet if you ask me." Not so kind after all. The suspect relative had a mean streak.

"I say if it makes you feel better about yourself, go for it," the companion said. That *All right! Power salute!* in her voice.

"You obviously haven't read any of those articles," the suspect relative said testily.

"Well, either way, they certainly are a nice pair of whoppers now," Miss Poe said.

I hoped Grandpa was still hovering around. He would have liked that. If anyone could have used a laugh right then, it was Grandpa.

Mom appeared. I scooted to make room for her. She sat down next to me and took my hand. She was nicely covered today, in a loose green dress. Black was for dead presidents, maybe, she'd said. But not for Eugene.

"How are you managing?" She squeezed my hand.

"This is weird," I said.

"I know," she said. "For me too, and I've done this before." She watched the front of the room for a moment. "Jordan, your dad . . ."

"What?" I said.

"Is he all right? He doesn't look well. He looks like hell, actually."

"His father just died. How do you expect him to look?"

"Not just that. I haven't seen him in a while."

She followed his movements with her eyes. "He's so thin. I thought maybe he'd been . . . sick or something."

Not there. Not then. "He looks the same to me."

"Okay, okay," she said. "I care about him is all. And you. You know that." Her voice cracked. I tried not to look at Grandpa.

"I know."

The church service was held at St. Anne's, a few blocks from Eugene's Gas and Garage. I had to walk with Grandma and Dad and the rest of the family behind the casket as it went down the church aisle. It made my throat close up, seeing Mom and Nathan and Hugh in their seats, looking over their shoulders at me, and even Bonnie Randall, sitting in the back, and Laylani and Buddy, which was nice. And that ass-wipe Marty Abare with his crocodile eyes and his wife, Charlotte, which would give Grandpa something to complain about. Now that Grandpa was covered up and less distracting, the ritual seemed more real and I fought back tears. Grandpa's casket looked very alone up there. Making the trip ahead of us.

I sat next to my father. On my other side was Sonia's daughter, my older cousin Alison, who was dull and white and plain as an envelope. The priest was talking about Grandpa's earthly vessel, which I liked the sound of. It sounded like a particularly beautiful ship. I heard someone whisper behind me.

"I didn't know Eugene was a good Catholic, having the service here and all," the suspect relative said meanly. She was becoming a pain in the ass.

We got up and down a lot, and let me tell you those Catholic things are very confusing and stressful, especially when you are in the front and you don't know what you are doing and everyone can see you get up when you aren't supposed to. You've got to shift around a lot to make it look like you've done it on purpose, pretend you were only adjusting for comfort. Once our whole row eased up and down by mistake until we all sat down to the sound of nervous giggles.

"I think we just did the Wave," I whispered to Alison, which made her scowl at me. Alison was always the good cousin.

At the end, the priest, a large red-faced man, swung this little ball of whirling red incense over Grandpa's casket. The smoke made my eyes burn, and my father cleared his throat once and then again. I wasn't sure if it was emotion or the strong smell of the stuff. My father looked like he had aged overnight, or maybe it was just my own fear that he had, now that Grandpa had moved aside and let my father move closer to the front of the Your-Turn-to-be-Dead line.

The limousines got lost on the way to the cemetery. The driver got twisted up in the heavy summer tourist traffic getting off the ferry and ended up turning by the oil tank, that day sporting the banner HAPPY BIRTHDAY CHUCK! The driver must have been new. Grandma, too nice to say a word, poked my leg and I nodded.

"Wasn't that a wrong turn?" my father said.

"It's all right," Grandma said.

"It's not all right, if it's wrong," my father said tersely.

The driver ended up going down a dead end, the sign changed with black tape by some comedian to read, DEAD WENDY. The driver started to sweat. Actual drops were rolling down the sides of his face. You should have seen all the cars trying to turn around. Headlights on and these sashes reading FUNERAL flapping from the windshields.

"There are only two main roads on the whole goddamn island," my father said.

"Vince," my grandmother said. "Just get back on Deception Loop, dear," she said to the driver.

So we ended up making a complete circle around the entire island, the driver apologizing the whole way, and my father getting more and more hacked off.

"Gosh, I can't tell you how sorry I am," the driver said again when we finally arrived.

"You obviously can, because you've done it a hundred times," my father said.

"It's all right," my grandma said. "It turned out just fine. You know why? Eugene would have loved the ride."

I got out, then ducked my head back in the car. "Next time just make a left on Bobcat Road," I said.

Then it hit me. Finally.

He was gone.

My father got stormy after that. Dark and stormy. One afternoon I stood in the kitchen, cracking ice cubes out of a tray when I heard my father and Gayle burst in the front door. The door slammed shut. Gayle D'Angelo was laughing.

"Vince," she teased.

"My God, Gayle," he said. He sounded scared.

"Vince, relax," she said.

"How can I relax? He knew we were there! He knew what we were *doing* there."

"You're not at a motel for a round of bridge." She laughed. "He's just playing games. He's trying to *frighten* you."

"Well, it worked, okay?"

I decided I wanted them to know I was there. I clinked the ice into my glass noisily. Flicked a cube with my finger so it skittered across the counter and shattered on the floor.

"Damn," I said loudly.

If they heard me, I couldn't tell.

"Taking your car and leaving his in the parking spot. Goddamn, Gayle. That's not a game. He's telling us something."

"I told you how he is," she said. "I told you the way he treats me."

"I can't stand that. You deserve so much more."

I opened and shut the refrigerator door with noisy smacks. My father was supposed to be at work. I tried to ignore the sounds of their kissing by staring at the catsup bottle and the fat container of mustard and the cartons of milk. What I wondered was, what was happening to the old ladies who needed their cataracts checked, the ones who came to my father's office clutching their purses in their laps in case there were thieves lurking about? What was happening to the seven-year-olds getting their first pair of glasses?

"If I could leave him I would," Gayle D'Angelo said. "You know that. You know what he'd do if I left."

My father was over the edge then, make no mistake about it. The Second Chance Guy had packed his plaid suitcase and was going through the tunnel toward the airplane door, folded newspaper under one arm and chewing gum in his pocket for the takeoff. The Second Chance Guy had given up on my father.

I started hearing messages on our answering machine: "Vince, it's Mother. Where were you yesterday? I needed your help with those papers of your father's. I'm worried about you. . . ." And, "Vince? Bill. Where the hell have you been? I got to tell you, Betsy and I are getting concerned."

My grandma said if Grandpa Eugene hadn't died right then, she didn't think any of it would have happened. He would never have done it if his father was alive. She says sometimes a man goes over the edge when he loses his father.

But maybe that's just the kind of thing you come up with when you ask yourself why. One of those pale reasons. My father was a man who never hurt anything in his life, and you ask yourself this question over and over.

Why?

Maybe Grandma is right. Maybe the strings that hold us in place are more fragile than we can ever understand.

# Chapter Eleven

Every day for the next few weeks, I made a point to ride my bike past Eugene's Gas and Garage after work at True You. Two weeks was all it took before the trucks started to come. First the old pumps were dug up, replaced with ones you could slide a credit card through. Next the sign came down. The new one was stuck on a tall pole. ABARE'S in bold red letters, set on a rectangle that spun an endless, slow circle. Finally Grandpa's old office was covered in plastic, a sign—YES WE'RE OPEN! REMODELING TO BETTER SERVE YOU!—stuck to the outside. It made me think of the plastic Grandpa himself was wrapped in before he was carted off. About Grandma's moment of panic in thinking he couldn't breathe.

"Don't tell me about it," Grandma said, actually clapping her palms against her ears. "Not another word, I can't bear to hear it."

But I went every day, until the mini-mart was almost finished. It's amazing how fast those things pop up. That's how I saw Kale Kramer coming out of Abare's with a Dr Pepper in one hand that day. I just stood there, straddling my bike, my work clothes stuffed into my backpack in exchange for the tank top and shorts I had on for the ride home. I should have turned and pedaled away, but I didn't. The heat of the sun made my tank top suddenly feel stuck to my back. Kale walked up to me as if he expected me to be there all along, which he probably did.

"Change your mind?" he said.

"About what?" I said.

"About what." He shook his head. He was shirtless; tan with the orange glow of an apricot.

"I said I was sorry." He passed me the soda can, took hold of my handlebars, and stared at me over them. "A mistake, okay? I call and call. You don't ever call me back. You're making me miserable."

He gave me his sleepy eyes, leaned in, and kissed me. His mouth was cold from the drink. "Jesus, you kiss good," he said. "If you didn't kiss so good . . . " I could have said the same thing about him. In fact, it was his finest quality.

"You know, I don't know, Kale," I said. There was a lot of noise from Grandpa's plastic-covered office, the high pitched whine of a saw.

"You want me," he said.

"No," I said.

"You do."

I was sick of the whole idea of wanting. She'd been coming over a lot lately, Gayle D'Angelo. Wanting was in my face every time I turned around. Gayle D'Angelo was there, sitting at the kitchen table at breakfast time, wearing a Chinese robe. I heard her voice in the night and would look out to see her car parked plainly in the driveway. She would arrive at our house, dressed up to go out. Arriving in the car her husband bought her, with the license plate reading GAYLE D She bought me presents—little bottles of perfume, a teddy bear holding a stuffed heart. Everything about my father was too much, like he was being followed around by this crazy shadow of excess. His laugh was too bright, his shows of affection were too heartfelt, his snappishness too harsh. He started drinking wine at night, too much. I started sleeping badly; the light, ready sleep of an animal. Like salmon, who just float with an eerie stillness, with their eyes wide open.

I put my hand on Kale's shoulder, just ran my fingers on that shoulder all warm and solid.

Beauty can do funny things to you. Like those stupid photographers who tumble over cliffs because they leaned too far over for a better shot of the waterfall.

"Shit, you do want me," Kale said.

More kissing. My tongue warmed up that cool mouth. His tongue gave me some rational excuses for the rabbits. Sometimes, why think about rabbits?

I handed him back his soda can. "Keep it," he said. He wore a really big shit-eating grin. "Just think of me when you put your mouth on it."

"Maybe I'll think of you when I throw it in the garbage," I said.

"Right," he said. "I'll call you later."

"Fine," I said.

"That same car," I said to my father. "I've seen it maybe three days now. With that guy sitting in it."

We got into my father's car. The Ford, not the Triumph, which still sat under its plastic cover in the driveway. We were heading to the Front Street Market to do the grocery shopping.

"Don't worry about it," my father said. He started the engine and backed out of the driveway. The seat of the car was hot against my legs, and the air inside was baked and suffocating from the sun insisting its way through the windows. I reached for the sliding knob of the air conditioner.

"Broken," my father said.

"You're kidding," I said. I rolled down my window and stuck my head out. "That guy is following us," I said. "I swear, he started his car right when we did." I popped my head back inside.

"I said not to worry about it."

"You know him? Jeez, Dad, roll your window down. It's a hundred degrees in here. Why don't you get this fixed?" I slid the air-conditioner knob back and forth. My father rolled his window down. His combed hair started blowing around goofily, like a kid sticking his tongue out and waving his fingers in his ears.

"You're the one who's always going on about the upkeep of a car and the responsibility that goes with the privilege and all that," I said. "You know this guy? Look, he turned right when we did. I think he really *is* following us. This is getting creepy."

"I see him," my father said.

"Well, who is he? This is weird. I mean, it's like the movies, or something. He's *following* us."

"It's Gayle's husband," my father said. He looked over his shoulder to change lanes. "They're separated."

"That's not her husband," I said. "He doesn't

look anything like that. That's not their car."

"Her husband hired him," he said. "Okay?" He stared at me for too long, making me wish he'd keep his eyes on the road. "It's nothing to worry about. They're separated," he said again.

"This guy's following you around? You mean an investigator? Jesus, Dad. Isn't this a little scary? If they're separated and everything's so fine, why's he following you? Aren't they supposed to hide or something? Those guys who follow people? This is scaring me."

"Don't worry about it," he said. But when we reached the store and the other car parked too, the fear I'd been carrying for weeks settled into a knowing dread. Something bad, bad, was going to happen to my father. These kind of things did not happen to regular people. Regular people did not have creepy-looking guys following them around in their cars. This was the kind of thing you saw on TV right before someone ended up dead. This was not what happens to a normal girl who goes to school and to her father who helps lazy eyes be responsible members of the human body.

I was scared. In the store, my father spent a long, long time walking up and down the cool aisles. His face looked thin in the bright lights. Distracted with worry. I wanted to stay there too. In that light where nothing ever goes very wrong, with those boxes of comforting things like toilet paper and lasagna noodles and Prest-O-Logs and vegetables that are too shiny.

When we finally left, my father's eyes shot to the place the car had been.

"He's just trying to send a message," my father said to himself.

I wondered about that message. In my mind I saw Wes D'Angelo in that tuxedo with the carnation in the lapel. My father looked at the parking space that now held a Volvo station wagon with a baby seat and a dog in the back. The window was rolled down, but it was hot. I felt sorry for that dog.

Kale said, "I want you to call me next. I want you to call me when you're ready." We stood in front of my house. It was nearly one in the morning, and the air was finally breathable and the cement under my feet cool as clay again.

Melissa had changed her mind about Kale. She didn't think he was right for me after all. Honestly, she told me, he frightened her a little bit. I was acting differently lately, and she didn't want me doing anything that would get me into trouble. I ignored her. Kale and I had gone to a movie, then made out in his car, which was now parked in front of my house. He stuck his hand up the front of my shirt.

"They like me," he said.

"At least someone does," I said. I whacked Kale's hand away. My father's car was gone from the driveway. If you asked me, he should have been supervising me better. I looked down the street to see if Jackson Beene might suddenly start washing his car again, but he didn't. Their house was still and dark.

"This is where you pretend you don't care," Kale said, kissing my neck. "I'm catching on to you."

"You're too short for me," I said.

"Fuck you," he said, but then he started laughing. "You almost got me with that one. Next time you're calling me."

I had begun seeing things in our house that didn't belong to my father or me; I started looking for those things. Items Gayle had asked him to hide for safekeeping. Boxes of jewelry, those small velvety ones that close with a snap. A man's Rolex watch. Papers, that looked important, with their names on them in capital letters. Wesley James D'Angelo and Gayle Earline. She must have hated that middle name.

They said it was Wes D'Angelo's gun. Gayle had asked my father to keep it. "We don't want to get ourselves shot," she told him. I never saw that gun. But I imagine it sometimes, in my mind. Clearly enough that I forget I *hadn't* seen it, there in his drawer, rolled into a pair of black work socks. When I see it in my mind, I am unrolling that ball. That gun is black and hard. Permanent looking, the way very hard things are. I imagine my father feeling its hardness in his hand. Weighing it.

Kale got in his car. "Okay?" he said. "I'm done chasing. You call me when you're ready."

"When hell's the temperature of a penguin's balls," I said.

I went inside the house and got into bed. A few moments later I heard my father come home too. I lay awake for what seemed like hours. Lately it seemed that my body was waiting all the time.

About five or six in the morning, I heard Jackson practicing his bagpipes, slow and repetitive as a lullaby. They sounded foreign and far away but somehow familiar as grass. I heard someone yelling at him to shut the hell up. But by that time I was close enough to sleep to drop into it with relief and gratitude.

*Lunar cycle high,* my horoscope read. *Make room for travel, romance. Clandestine arrangement adds spice! Study Sagittarius message.* But my lunar cycle was anything but high the next day, and neither was my father's; he was a Capricorn too. I was slow and sleepy from the late night, so even less equipped for the condition of my father, this haggard man I saw in the kitchen. The funny thing was, he was pouring the remains of yesterday's coffee in this potted plant he had on the kitchen table. I couldn't tell you the name of that plant if you offered me money, but I did know it was usually as neglected as the Beenes' poor dog, Boog; we gave it a bit of water only when it started looking dry as a potato chip. It was a gift from Bonnie Randall, and she was the one who used to water it. Neither Dad nor I had been very good caretakers, but now it looked positively zingy with new shoots and a round knob that might even have been the start of a flower. Apparently he'd been giving it the old coffee for a few weeks now, and it appreciated the caffeine with its whole heart. It just goes to show how things sometimes can thrive even with faulty, perverse attention.

Or not. My father put the coffeepot back in its stand and turned around. I almost gasped, he looked so exhausted. Like a man walking around carrying his beating heart in his two cupped hands. Sure, maybe something can appear to thrive with faulty attention, but it seemed my father's roots had turned black. Plants need water, not coffee—just water, pure and simple. And air and sun. Good things.

"What happened, Dad?"

He sank into his chair at the kitchen table, put his head in his hands. His robe was too loose around him and I could see his chest start to cave in, actually fold inward with a sob.

"I'm such an idiot," he said, his voice cracking.

The sight of my father crying made my own throat cinch up tight with tears. That's what a father's tears can do. Make you feel like the ground underneath you is soft and fragile.

"What?" I whispered.

"She's going back. To him. Oh, God," He took a big breath. He wiped his eyes with the sleeve of his robe. "I'm sorry. . . ."

"No, Dad, no. It's okay." Tears gathered in my own eyes.

"I just . . . I don't know."

"Maybe it's for the best," I said. "Her going back." I put my hands on his shoulders. "This is killing you, Dad. This is *destroying* you. If you could only see yourself."

"It's money and fear," he said. "Money and fear, money and fear. That's what is keeping her there. Goddamn it. *Goddamn it!*" He exhaled shakily, which started his tears again. "She says she has a physical *revulsion* to him. I don't understand. No, I do. I know why she went back."

"Dad, come on," I said. "She never really left." It was horrible to see him like that, slumped over, his face shiny with tears, his eyes red and old-looking, and that stupid plant reeking coffee fumes. But it was good, too. To finally have it out, to say all the things that had so badly needed saying that they had become acid in the mouth.

"No," he said.

"It's true, Dad, and you know it. She's playing with you! She's just *one woman*, Dad. There are lots and lots of women."

"No," he said. "Not like that. *Not like that.* I don't understand it myself." He put his palms over his eyes. "God, I feel like such a fool. She makes me so crazy. She makes me feel like . . . I don't know. Like I'm *breathing*. But this back and forth, back and forth . . ." He shook his head angrily.

I honestly thought he'd had enough. Relief started seeping in. Relief is simple-minded. The big dumb guy of emotions, wearing clodhoppers and a loud bow tie, willing to believe anything you tell him.

"Jesus, look at yourself, Dad. This isn't love. God, I hope not. There are others, you know? You'll find someone else to be crazy about."

"I've got to get myself together," he said.

"You do," I said.

"I can't go on like this."

*We made it,* I thought. It had been disturbing and awful, but it was over. I was filled with the energy a narrow miss brings. I was surprised at how worried I had actually been—something you don't realize until you aren't any longer.

Big Mama assures me that real love is deep

and true and careful. And finding it is like a long, long walk on the beach. Where a lot of other things get put in your pocket—rocks ugly when dry, jagged parts of shells, all called treasures— before you find that whole, white sand dollar. That whole sand dollar that you trust has the five bony seagulls inside, but you'll never break it open to find out for sure.

Which is a nice and comforting thought. That whole, white sand dollar. I need comforting sometimes.

But I don't forget the other things she says about love. The other things she says sometimes go in the pocket. Those shiny and dazzling things that can make you want them with a desperation that can destroy you. Sometimes love gets all confused with wanting, Big Mama says. Then love is the slate where we draw our own needs, the ground where we show our darkness.

My father's resolution to get himself together lasted two days. Until the flowers came. I saw them on the porch when I came home from True You. Placed in the shade and stapled under a tent of waxed paper, but still looking a bit soft and wilted from what was now August heat. I opened the tiny card, of course, plucked it from the pronged fork sticking out from the vase of roses. Signed, IF ONLY. G.

"Dad, don't be an idiot. I see his car there all the time," I said to my father as he carefully undid the staples from the waxed-paper tent. But I could see by his face that he was gone again.

"I think this falls into the category of my business," he said.

"Dad, no," I said. "Please."

"I know what I'm doing," he said.

He actually leaned in to sniff those god-damned flowers.

I would give you another kind of weather for that night if I could, the kind of summer night on Parrish where the light on the strait twinkles so brightly it hurts your eyes, then dims to a magical twilight; where the cool, when it finally comes, brushes across your sunburned shoulders and makes them tingle. I would give you the kind of night where the new drove of tourists just off the ferry have happily scattered—to drink Red Hook ales under the outdoor umbrellas of Scully's, to shed their shoes on the round-rocked beaches, to mount their bikes for a calm evening ride past the oyster beds where Ms. Cassaday and her friend Elaine Blackstone worked summers. The kind of night where Cliff Barton happily buzzed around in his biplane, pissing off Jade Starr, who always brought her sister in to sing at the hotel's outside café; and where Max walked around outside with only a diaper on, followed by Homer, tongue hanging out and desperate for a cold drink or a pacifier.

But that's not the kind of night it was; that's not the way it happened. And I'm trying to be honest here, so if you think a storm arriving that night is some big cymbal-crashing drama on my part, too bad. I can't make it different. Anyway, it's the truth of what happens in August on Parrish. You'll have this blazing, perfect eighty-two-degree day and suddenly the sky turns black as asphalt and the hail comes pelting down, as if there was only so much sun a Northwest town would be allowed before the rain stands up and waves its bratty arms singing, *Yoo hoo! Don't forget about me!* No one but that prune Cora Lee at the Theosophical Society would claim a storm that night had any deep meaning.

When you live in the Northwest, you know when a summer thunderstorm is coming. The air is so still and charged it's like watching an angry man hold his breath. The clouds started rolling in that evening, rolling, rolling, rolling, reminding the blue who was boss. Bad-guy clouds that all joined together finally to make one still smear of black. My father got up from the movie we were watching and began to shut the windows of the house.

"Should I pause the movie?" I asked.

"Nah."

I could hear the sliding of windows being closed, the clatter of blinds as he moved through the rooms upstairs. When the phone rang, I punched the button on the remote, making the image blur to wiggling lines. I took my feet off the coffee table, where they were propped. Then I eased up from the couch and went into the kitchen to answer it.

"Hey."

I could hear the open connection that meant my father too had picked up the phone. I covered the mouthpiece and shouted upstairs. "It's for me, Dad."

"Maybe he should just put a tape recorder on," Kale said after the click. "If he wants to hear what I say so bad."

"I thought I was supposed to call you," I said.

"Always so antagonistic. If I didn't know how much you like me, I'd have my feelings hurt."

"You should be thankful for your good looks, is all," I said truthfully.

"I'm giving you another chance. There's a party on the *Red Pearl*. I'll be messed up for work tomorrow, but hey, what the hell. I'll pick you up. Nobody should cross their legs for so long. Is it some kind of religious thing?"

"The *Red Pearl*, Kale?"

"A boat. It's a boat. What'd you think it was?"

"A skanky Chinese restaurant is what it sounds like."

"Wait'll you see it. A couple of divers in from Southern Cal. Fully equipped, if you know what I mean. Bunks and booze and hosts wasted enough not to give a shit. A perfect party."

I hated when people said things like "Southern Cal." I heard my father's steps coming down the stairs. "I don't think so, Kale. Dad and I are watching a movie. A religious movie. Nuns and Christ and crosses and Satan. The actor who plays him looks just like you."

"You gotta be kidding."

"Yeah, he looks like Clint Eastwood. And it's a western."

"You're actually gonna pass this up to watch a movie with Pops?"

"You're not that much fun, Kale. I don't even like westerns," I said.

"What do you think, I'm going to wait around forever? I'm not gonna wait around forever." From where I stood, I could see my father standing at the window looking at the sky. He'd been quiet since he came home from work with a couple of grocery bags full of dinner fixings. He had poured himself a drink while he cooked. Drinking was something he'd been doing every night lately. It didn't flatter him. The alcohol did nothing to improve his mood. Even from behind he looked edgy; his hands jammed in his pockets, his chin tilted slightly to the sky. It was Sunday night. Dad had always said Sundays were the days of unmet expectations.

The kitchen window was still open. I could hear the neighbor's wind chimes pick up speed, a jingly, giggly outburst.

"Fine, don't wait then," I said to Kale.

"I mean, you reach a point where you go forward or you break it off," he said. "You gotta fish or cut bait."

"You fish. I'm going to watch this western," I said. "I am against cross-denomination relationships."

"You call if you change your mind," Kale said, and hung up.

"Right," I said to the phone.

The television had stopped pausing and had gone on without us. My father had lost interest in cowboys chasing villains on black horses.

"Too many people washed their cars," I said about the darkening sky.

"I wish it would just rain and get it over with," he said.

"Maybe a few more people need to leave their sunroofs open first," I said.

My father didn't answer. Instead he went back into the kitchen and came out with another drink. He sat back on the couch and stared distractedly at the cowboys. His face was somewhere between morose and needing. That restless craving you get where you want some-thing—food? company? to be left alone?—but have no idea what.

"You don't have to baby-sit me," he said crossly.

"I'm not," I said.

"You could have gone out with that boy. He seems like a nice boy," he said.

"He's not," I said.

Dad looked at me. For a second I thought he truly saw me for the first time in weeks. I saw him in there, the real him, looking at me through all the complicated layers that had, over the last few months, clouded his eyes.

The phone rang again.

I often wonder what would have happened if we had just let it ring.

I got up to answer. Dad apparently wasn't expecting any calls that night. Or at least any he cared about.

I told him it was her. That's what I said. "Her." We both knew whom I meant. He ran upstairs to take the call in his room, actually ran with big bams up the stairs. The sound of her voice pissed me off. "Vince," she said into the phone just before I hung up. A thread of silvery anger shot through me. You can say a name and sound like you own it.

It was not a long conversation. A few min-utes at most before he came downstairs again, with a windbreaker on with something stuffed in the pockets. I don't like to remember that part, the pockets. You put something in your pocket and it means a plan. But that's the way it was, his pockets bulged out and puffy like the cheeks of a cartoon chipmunk.

"I've got to go," he said.

"It's going to rain," I said. "It's going to thunder."

His eyes looked swarmy from alcohol. He reeked a little, like that stupid plant giving off coffee fumes. "It doesn't matter," he said.

"You shouldn't drive," I said. His hands seemed shaky. I felt a bolt of fear. I could see him crashing into a telephone pole. He was not someone who should drink. He started to lean a bit, like a bad actor playing a drunk.

"It doesn't matter," he said. "I don't even care."

"Dad," I said. I put my hand on his arm.

"Forget it." He shook me off. He looked for his keys a really long time, rustling and banging around in the kitchen drawers. I pushed the stop button on the remote control, and the television gave off loud static. Dad walked out the front door and let it slam behind him.

"Goddamn dumb-shit asshole," I said. "You're stupid," I said to the door. "Stupid, stupid, dumb fuck." I paced around. Popped off the static of the television. I went upstairs, opened my bedroom window, which he had so recently shut. I wanted to see that he had at least made it down the street. I put my nose to the screen, which smelled that screen smell of dusty mesh and long-dead flies. It was eerie how still and warm it was despite the color of the sky. I wished my father's wish that it would rain and get it over with.

Dad's car was in the driveway. Both cars. The Ford, the one he usually drove, as well as the tarp-covered Triumph, which probably wouldn't start if you got down on your knees and asked for a miracle. I wondered if the alcohol had raced a good deal ahead of him; if he was passed out on the porch. I went downstairs, opened the front door. The air outside was the woolen, suffocating kind—the hug of a fat aunt who never really liked you and had bad breath besides. I didn't see my father.

I went inside the garage, preparing myself for whatever I might find. I wasn't sure what exactly I was preparing myself for. He wasn't in the garage either. But my bike was gone.

My bike. If it wasn't so distinctly unfunny, it might have been hysterical to think of him trying to maneuver my bike in his condition. Instead, seeing my bike gone filled me with new fury. It was as if he had taken a part of me and brought it along on whatever this horrible outing turned out to be. Not only that; the oddity of it scared me. It was so disturbingly strange, him taking my bike, that I ran outside to the street, looked again to see if I might find him rounding a corner. No Dad.

I walked back home, sweating from the anger and the murky heat. "Goddamn it, you stupid, stupid asshole," I said. I noticed he had left the garden hose on; a pool of water was gathering by the end of the nozzle, which lay in the grass. I turned the faucet off with a yank. I stood there with my feet in the soggy grass, trying to decide what to do.

My wet, dirty feet left nasty marks on the carpet. Marks my father would have been pissed about, if he cared about anything anymore, which I guessed he didn't. My legs were cold from wetness; I actually shivered when I got inside and picked up the telephone.

"Be there," I said to the ringing on the other end, said and felt with an urgency that scared me. Ring, ring, ring, ring. I almost hung up. If I'd have had to hang up, I might have flung the phone across the room.

"Yeah." His voice was out of breath when he finally answered.

"Kale?" I said. "It's me. I changed my mind."

# Chapter Twelve

I could hear Kale's car coming halfway down the street. It had the kind of roar that's a cheap knockoff of thunder. I just stood there, waiting for him on the porch. I didn't want to be inside that house anymore.

I opened the door of his car and got in. The fumes from a recently smoked cigarette hung around all slinky and victorious. Kale looked over at me and grinned. I noticed he could have used a booster seat to see properly out the windshield; his chin could have rested on the top of the steering wheel.

"Look who's here," he said. I slammed the car door shut. He grabbed a handful of denim from the pant leg of my shorts and pulled, telling me to scoot closer. He kissed me, running his hand up my bare leg. He eased away from me and released the parking brake. "You have lipstick"—he motioned to the edge of his own mouth—"right here."

I flipped down the visor and used my index finger to wipe the stray smear of Tango Red I had applied in the hall mirror before leaving the house. I looked like someone I didn't know. My eyes looked at me as if they were someone else's eyes. It was one of those times your body seems to be walking around and doing stuff without you while you watch.

I had nothing to say. Kale turned the radio on, loud, and rolled down his window. I guess he was making sure the cars that pulled up beside us would turn to look, although I'm not sure exactly what he thought it was they needed to see. That warm, electric air whipped through the window and blew my hair in front of my face, in my mouth. I tried to tuck it behind my ears, watched the trees sway and blow as my hair was. I could feel the pounding beat of Kale's radio through the soles of my feet.

Kale drove around Deception Loop, the water of the strait chill and steely looking below. Even visitors had enough sense to get off the open stretches of rocky beach where lightning was sure to strike, and where just offshore the whales and porpoises lay still so as not to provoke the violence of nature. It was one of the rare times of summer that the strips of beach would not be crowded with tourists tangled up with cameras and binoculars and the straps of knapsacks. Romantic Couples were now tucked safely in their B&B's, peeking over the tops of their books for a periodic gape at the show outside, a glass of red wine on the nightstand.

Kale parked in the lot of the Hotel Delgado, which was ablaze with lights. Curious faces peered outside from cozy tables in the restaurant. The staff had forgotten to move some of the outdoor tables in, and their plastic tablecloths flapped in the wind, held down only by wire baskets of sugar packets and bottles of catsup and red-netted candles.

The water of the Delgado Strait was blackturned-silvery from the lights of the hotel and the whitecaps of waves that were beginning to build. The dock was full of boats, a concert of nodding red bow lights. All the cautious sailors had pulled in. You hoped most of them had half a brain and had taken a room at the hotel for the night; sleep would be a wild, nauseous ride. Already you could hear the squeak of the rubber floats hanging from the boats' sides as they screeched and bobbed against the docks, and the complaining groans of the old wooden pier itself.

A few boats had their cabin lights on. Those

foolish couples would regret their cheapness in the morning, but for now were crammed down in their low beds. It was easy to guess which boat was the *Red Pearl*; the same thumping music Kale had played in his car was bumping across the water, sounding like a huge heart that had exercised too hard. Like one of the fat girls at True You just off the treadmill, or maybe Grandpa Eugene's heart the night it spun wildly out of control.

As my eyes got used to the dim light, I could see the people dotting the decks of the boat. They spotted us at the same time. A guy in a tank top and shorts waved his arm and shouted something our way which was lost in the wind. In reply Kale raised up the case of beer that he held at his side and shouted back.

"Party hearty!" he said stupidly, the wind throwing his words back in our faces. "I'm gonna get a boat like this someday," he said to me. "Ride where I please when I please, meet people."

I walked up the pier beside him. You could feel it sway a little underneath you. "Hey, say something," he said.

"What?" I said.

"You act like you're going to your grave." He stopped, took my chin in his hands, gave me a look that was supposed to be meaningful. "Be happy," he said.

"La, la, la," I said. God, my stomach was as rough and sickened as the churning water of the Sound.

"What are you waiting for?" Wendy Williams's voice shouted down from the boat. "You're gonna miss Martin slipping raw ones."

I didn't know what she was talking about and I wasn't sure I wanted to. If Wendy Williams was here, Jason Dale would be here too, and Andrew Leland. I wondered if Melissa would be pissed I didn't bring her along. At that moment I would have given anything to be where she probably was, in her bandanna decorated room with Boog lying at the foot of her bed and Mr. and Mrs. Beene downstairs watching a show about slavery on PBS.

I stepped up onto the deck of the boat behind Kale, who reached out his hand to help me. He handed me a beer and I cracked the top. Martin, one of the guys who apparently owned the boat, wiped the back of his mouth with his hand as people laughed. Oysters in a bowl sat on one of the boat's small Formica tables, all slippery like innards you should be hiding your eyes from.

"That is so dis-gusting!" a girl squealed, and he kissed her on the mouth as she tried to wiggle away.

Kale had already finished his beer and stuck his hand into the open case for another. From where I stood, on the lurching deck of the *Red Pearl*, I could see the ivy-covered wall of the Hotel Delgado and those peering faces sitting at the restaurant's window, which glowed yellow and comforting from the light inside.

"This is great," Kale said. I could hear the low roll of thunder off in the distance. It was too far away for the pelting rain to start yet. A summer storm could go on in the same way my mother said childbirth did—contractions and calmness, contractions and calmness, closer together until at last came the violent main event.

"Come on," Kale said.

He took my hand and maneuvered me through bursts of laughter, food and drink tossed into mouths, protests when the music stopped and then started again. The boat lurched. I lost my balance and grabbed onto Kale so I wouldn't fall on my butt.

"Oh yeah, I like that," he said, and grinned at me. A glass fell and shattered on the deck, and I heard someone curse.

I shivered. It was cold out there on the water. Kale held my wrist and guided me down a set of narrow stairs heading below deck. When we reached the bottom, he rubbed his hands up and down my arms to warm them.

"There," he said.

It was quieter in the cabin, the thumps of

the music muted and fuzzy around the edges. Dishes were piled in the tiny sink of the tiny galley. I nearly tripped over a grocery bag of empty cans someone had placed on the floor. An open jar of salsa on the counter was punctuated by half-drowned bits of chips. Several guys were jammed into the curved bench-seat of the galley's table, watching a miniature television and arguing about some tiny play of a tiny sporting event. I could see why Kale wanted a boat like this. Everything was just his size.

Kale opened a narrow door that led to a small cabin. A bedroom. In fact that's all it had room for, that bed. He shut the door behind us, and the compact space and Kale's presence made me suddenly claustrophobic.

"It's hot," I said.

"You're telling me," Kale said. He gave my chest a playful shove, with enough force, though, that I landed sitting on the bed. Suddenly, none of this seemed like such a good idea. Suddenly, I couldn't quite remember why it had felt so urgent to pick up that phone and call Kale, of all people.

"Oh yeah, worth the wait," Kale said. He lowered himself onto me, kissed me until I fell backward onto a foam pillow that stank like it had gotten wet once and had since mildewed.

"Relax," Kale said.

But I couldn't. The beer I had drunk started

to work around my knees, making them feel tingly and unstable. The unsteadiness, coupled with that closed-in place and Kale's body on mine, made my anger at my father rapidly disappear. It was a mental magic act; the horrible things I was sure my father was about to do changed instantly into more innocent possibilities. Maybe he wouldn't meet Gayle D'Angelo at all. Maybe he would be saved by the Second Chance Guy. Maybe he would do just a small thing and not one hideously life-changing; a bent fender, say, instead of a fatal crash.

Kale kissed me some more and pushed his pelvis into mine. I wanted him off me. Next to me on the bed was a sweatshirt rolled into a ball, a bottle of suntan lotion, and a pair of men's sandals worn into deep grooves at the heel so that the brand name had faded half off. I could smell the lotion; the kind that has that fake coconut odor stronger than any real coconut ever had. I didn't belong here. These were not my things, and this was not my place. I pushed at Kale's shoulder.

He took hold of my hand at the wrist. His face was down close into mine. His breath washed over me, warm as the air outside, steamy with beer. "You're acting like a baby," he said.

Something rose up in me when he said that. I'm not sure what it was; anger again, I guess. Anger at Kale, at my father, at the powerlessness

I'd been feeling lately. Kale was wrong. I was stronger than that, stronger than anything happening or about to happen around me. I was brave, and I wanted Kale to know it. "Anger is most dangerous," Big Mama says, "when it makes you want to prove yourself bigger than you are. Anger makes you stupid then, irrevocably so."

I pulled my shirt over my head. My bra seemed embarrassing. So white in the darkness, with its little bow between the cups. Why the little bow is necessary, I will never know. I could hear laughter outside. I imagined it was for me, for my silly white bra, but the short, pleated drape of the tiny porthole was pulled closed.

Kale took off his pants. I realized that at least one rumor about Kale wasn't true. There was no tattoo. The wind howled, both restless and pissed off.

My head felt sick and spinning. I thought about health class last year. Those pills in pink cases all lined up in an embarrassing oval. Those springy plastic diaphragms, trampoline fun for sperm. My heart beat crazily. Panicky. Sperm. Spermatozoa. So cheerful. Like a party hat with a tassel. My voice was squeaky and small.

"Wait," I said.

But Kale reached around from I don't know where, held up a square foil packet and waved it around as if he'd just found a dinner mint on his pillow.

"Don't worry. I come prepared," he said into my neck.

*Ha ha,* I thought. *A funny pun. That Kale.*

The boat lurched and my stomach did too, queasy from rocking and from beer I wasn't used to drinking. Down below, where we lay, you could hear water sloshing against the boat's side. A feeling began to work its way up sickeningly from my heart. Kale seemed to know what he was doing. That plastic thing he put on looked like it hurt. Like a person could snap it and really hurt someone. Now he looked ready for surgery or something. He gave me his sleepy, dreamy eyes.

He was hurting me, Jesus, but he didn't seem to notice. His face was sweaty. Turning red from somewhere inside the layers of tan. I turned my head. I didn't want to see him. I concentrated, concentrated on the worn-down inner soles of someone else's sandals. Concentrated on being away from there until Kale moaned the moan of something ripping away and laid his full weight on top of me.

I figured out what the sick feeling was. Betrayal. The horrible guilt of betrayal. And the one I had betrayed was myself.

Kale leaned away, finally off me, and reached to the floor where he'd set his can of beer. He took a long swallow.

"When my mom was having me," he said, "the doctor needed to be sobered up before I was born."

I wanted out of there, right then. My own nakedness seemed more humiliating than I could bear. I was so incredibly, unbelievably stupid. Stupid and foolish and hateful.

The handle of the cabin's door rattled. "Open up," some guy yelled.

"All right, all right," Kale said.

"Kale," I said. "Shit." I inched under damp, musty covers, hid my head. Kale rustled around, sat down on my leg as he pulled up his pants.

"Come on!" the guy pounded the door with his fist.

"Fuck, would you wait a minute?" Kale opened the door.

"I want my sweatshirt," the guy said. From under the covers, I could hear the guy snicker.

"Hey," Kale said, his voice swaggering.

I stayed there, flat and quiet. Cringing. Kale and the guy talked about boats. I wanted to change my name and disappear. I wanted to become someone else. I wondered how the hell I had gotten where I was. I wondered if I could die under there, from asphyxiation.

Finally the guy left. My face was hot and sweaty from hiding under the sheet. As much as I didn't want to lift my head and see Kale, and as much as I didn't want to have to come out of there and be me, the air felt good.

"What the hell were you doing?" Kale said.

"What do you think I'm going to do, let him see me?" My voice was back, but there was nothing behind it. No real strength to back up my words. I felt very tired. It seemed a long, long way back home.

"Yeah, let him see you. Jesus."

I had no smart remark for him. I wanted to cry. A feeling of loss and aloneness overtook me, and it seemed sudden and incurable and sad as a deadly disease. I wanted the smell of him off me. I couldn't forget what I had just done and how stupid I was until that smell was gone.

"Stay here and hide the whole fucking party," he said. He found his shirt on the floor, left through the tiny door. I didn't know what he was so mad at. I didn't know what to do. I waited to see if something might happen that would tell me what to do with the mess my life seemed to be, but nothing did. The music kept thumping, and the waves kept sloshing against the boat. I decided I would get dressed. I decided that I would have to get up and get Kale to take me home.

I went out the tiny door and into the tiny galley now empty except for a girl looking for something in the tiny refrigerator, maybe tiny food.

She ignored me, and I passed her as if it was

usual for me to emerge disheveled from bed-rooms during parties. As if it were usual for me to do stupid dumb-ass things I didn't even want to do in the first place. I held the rail and walked up the stairs to the upper deck. I wound my way through boozy strangers swaying to music that was now shouting loud again. It was amazing that the Tiny Policeman hadn't found that party yet. Thunder rolled and some stupid girl screamed, and the lurching of the boat made me feel like throwing up. I wanted to find Kale. Jason Dale was heaving over the side of the boat, forgetting to be a considerate neighbor and just vomiting away on the dock. I started to think that I would actually feel grateful when I finally found Kale.

But I did not feel grateful.

When I saw him, grateful would not be the word that comes to mind.

I heard his voice, laughing. I followed it, wound my way through bumping elbows and spilled puddles of sticky beer on the floor. I saw the back of his shirt. When I finally got to him, his tongue was trying to shove something down Wendy Williams's mouth. I'd always thought Wendy Williams rubbed Kale the wrong way. Judging from her hand on the crotch of his shorts I guessed I was mistaken.

I stared, caught between wanting to cry and wanting to grab at him and scream. People were looking at me as if I might be the half-time entertainment.

I turned and ran. As much as you can run on a pitching boat filled with people. I pushed my way through, to the love notes of "Hey, Bitch" and "Ex-*cuse* me!" and I stepped past the recovering Jason Dale, who stared at me like I was an apparition. I stepped off the boat and onto the dock, where my feet could run, run now, slapping on the wooden slats, the sound mixing with the beginning pelting of rain.

I got to the end of the dock. The rain had begun to wet my hair into thick ropy strands. A waiter and a waitress from the Hotel Delgado had finally dashed outside, doors slamming from the wind behind them, to gather the sugar packets and toppled Lucite frames describing desserts and the flapping plastic tablecloths. Inside, the golden light of the restaurant flickered off and was soon replaced with the bobbing lights of lanterns brought to the tables by shadowy waiters. The island still had magic, whether you wanted it or not.

I started to cry. The tears and rain made me blind. I gasped for air, started to walk. I didn't think about safety or lightning or darkness. I didn't dare think, I just walked stupidly, without plan. I would have to go back to my father's house. I would have to see what shambles were left there when morning came.

The rain turned into a furious hail, mean and stony balls of ice. They actually hurt as they struck the top of my head and my back, but I didn't care. It was only punishment for being such a fool. You could hear the wind come in a wave, the roar of it. Hailstones hurtled onto the hotel's stone path, the now-bare outdoor tables, the old roof.

I was listening to the weather be angry. I didn't hear the truck behind me, tires rolling on slick pavement. But I saw the double columns of headlights. I looked over my shoulder.

He opened the door of the truck. He was still in his waiter's uniform. Still had the white apron tied around his waist. Jackson Beene opened the door and then just stood there on the ground beside me, waiting patiently as I threw up.

He drove me home. Wordless again. But you can be silent and give a thousand gifts.

He pulled up in front of my house.

I do not know what craziness made me hop angrily out of the car and slam the door.

"Stop rescuing me," I said meanly.

# Chapter Thirteen

No, I did not see my father when he came home. Yes, I knew what time he came in: one forty-seven. Yes, I was sure. I saw the glowing numbers of my bedside clock when I heard the front door close. No, he did not take a shower, leave again, or run the washing machine. And for all the people who get into that mystical shit like that prune Cora Lee at the Theosophical Society, no, I did not experience a moment of horror, of knowing, near or around eleven fifteen. Near or around eleven fifteen I was only sitting in the passenger seat of Kale's car, driving toward the Delgado Strait with the music on too loudly and windows rolled down on a stormy, electric night. That would have been nice, wouldn't it? A warning, a flash of knowing at that very moment? But you can be peeling an orange or waiting for a light to change or looking for clean socks when your life is changing horribly and forever behind your back. Just sitting in a car and listening to a cruel boy say, "You have lipstick, right here."

My father didn't protect me the way he should have. He went to work that next morning knowing what was going to happen. He should have at least warned me. I'm angry about that. Instead he showered and dressed and put on a tie and aftershave. Put his cool, knowing hands against the cheekbones of his patients, shining his little flashlight into their eyes as if his own saw nothing different that day. He let me go to work, to True You, sullen and sick from the night before but most of all, unprepared. He let me go to measure the arms and waists of fat girls, who in only a matter of hours would be the ones measuring me in their thoughts. In a matter of hours they would shudder because my hands had been on them.

"Where were you last night? I tried to call after ten and you weren't there," Melissa said. She grabbed the metal ring of the projector screen in the conference room and pulled down, covering the chalkboard with a sudden square of white.

I walked the long snaky cord of the overhead projector to the outlet. "Kale," I said to the wall. "With Kale." I felt sick with the memory. It seemed both too close and far away and unreal, the way bad things do. My voice gathered up in my throat. I thought I might cry.

"Jordan?" Melissa said.

I was afraid to look at her. It was one of those times you know the smallest sympathy will do you in. I walked to the overhead projector, snapped it on. A goofy, misshapen square shined somewhere over by the coffee machine. I centered it on the screen. "A party," I said. "On a boat."

"A party on a boat," she said. "In last night's weather." She began to unstack the folding chairs, snapping them open and arranging them in rows.

"That's where I was," I said. My voice got high, stretched tight. I remembered myself, hiding underneath the sheets of someone else's bed.

Melissa stopped. "What?" she said. "Jordan, what?" She walked over to me, her head a big looming shadow on the screen. She actually took hold of my chin, turned it so I looked into her eyes. The white mustache she'd had a few weeks ago was gone now; she looked like herself again, her blonde hair frizzy and cut to her shoulders, her eyes the color of that blue china old ladies have. She looked so much like her mother; underneath all of her silliness, there was kindness in her eyes. I doubted if anything truly bad would ever happen to her.

"Oh God, what?" she said. My eyes filled with tears. Melissa reached out to hug me but was interrupted by Laylani bursting into the room and chirping in the annoying fashion of those overambitious springtime birds who wake you at five A.M.

"In this weather I want the air-conditioning on first thing, girls," she sang. She fanned herself with a manila folder. "Whewie." She rustled about in the folder, took out a plastic sheet, and placed it on the overhead. In big letters it said, A SETBACK IS A SPECIAL GIFT. She stepped back and admired the words on the screen. "Buddy's coming in today as a guest speaker. Here I was, thinking and thinking and thinking about how to talk to these girls about their episodes of backsliding, and *bam!* It came to me: Buddy."

Melissa looked at me in a way that said, *You and I aren't finished.* She said, "Buddy had a weight problem?"

Laylani looked brave. "Before he gave himself to the Lord he had another little problem. Gambling?" she said, as if she wasn't sure we'd heard of it before.

"What, like on football games and stuff?" Melissa asked.

"That's not exactly the point, *what* he lost so

much money on now is it? The *point* is that he Let Go and Let Lord. He fought back against his demons. He avoided tempting situations." Laylani was getting worked up now.

"Like what, the racetrack?" Melissa said.

"Craps tables," I guessed.

Laylani sighed. "I think it's wonderful what he's done. An inspiration. And I think the girls might be interested to see just who *is* married to Laylani Waddell. I want to introduce them to my rock. That's what I told Buddy. I've mentioned his name so many times, this way they can see a face. You two are welcome to stay and listen as long as the phones aren't busy."

Buddy arrived during the weigh-in and measurement and just stood in the back in his white suit. Where you get a white suit anymore, I have no idea. He got several suspicious looks from the girls, which he returned with a big smile. It would be easy to be suspicious of Buddy Waddell, broad and no-necked as he was. You'd think Laylani would have the thin guy with the shiny face and extra white teeth, but no. Looking at Buddy, you're not a bit surprised he had a gambling problem. You wouldn't be a bit surprised if he ran an illegal gambling operation or killed people while wearing that smile he was giving the fat girls. He was a big jewelry guy, even though he wore only a gold cross on his lapel. He was an extra-onions guy. Put-on-the-

Monster-Trucks-and-hand-me-a-beer-honey guy.

There were three new team members that day, or two if you discounted Marilynne Monroe, this girl who was close to a hundred pounds overweight and who kept leaving True You and coming back. Laylani insisted she be treated as a new team member each time so that she could have what Laylani called a "clean slate." And so she could pay the start-up fee every time. If you ask me, all Marilynne Monroe needed was to go by her middle name and most of her problem would be solved. The second new team member was a young woman returned home from college with more than a bag of dirty laundry, and the third, a sullen looking girl who I'd seen working the espresso cart at the Front Street Market. She had a tattoo on her bare arm, an eagle, and when I measured her, I made its talons sit on the tape as on a perch.

Laylani introduced Buddy and clapped for him, her manicured nails making little lightning-bolt flashes of red as they moved back and forth. They made me think of Gayle D'Angelo's hands. Buddy walked to the front and stood beside his wife. With Laylani in her bright pink suit and Buddy in his white, they looked like a pair of Good & Plentys.

Buddy gave his sobby tale. Seems he almost lost their house and actually watched his car being towed away by creditors. Laylani sniffed a lot during his speech. Then she stood up, patted her chest with her hand, and put up the overhead, which read, FIVE THINGS YOU CAN DO AFTER A SETBACK. She used a pointer to go down the list AVOID FURTHER TEMPTATIONS, GRASP HOLD OF THE SITUATION.

"Crap," I heard someone mumble. My eyes shot around the room. Laylani had not heard. She was moving toward the "Thin Person Screaming to Come Out" speech. Buddy hung around the front as though he was unsure whether to sit down or not.

"Everyone has a personal story of backsliding to tell," Laylani said. "I'd like to congratulate Marilynne for coming back and joining us." Laylani applauded, starting a lukewarm splattering of claps. Marilynne looked like she'd like to push Laylani off a cliff.

"I can't believe this crap." Louder now. The Espresso-cart woman with the eagle tattoo. This time Laylani heard.

"Something you want to share with the group?"

The woman stood. "I said this is crap," she said. Laylani blushed. The woman looked around the room. "Who are you all doing this for, *her*?" She pointed to Laylani. Her necked strained with anger.

"Well, certainly not for *me*." Laylani gave a half-laugh. "This is something you've got to do for your*self* . . ."

"Didn't you just hear the guy in the ice-cream suit?" With this Buddy lifted himself up as if he were getting out of a chair, despite the fact that he was still standing. "He just said he did all that because he wanted a nicer car, something to impress the neighbors . . ." She looked around. "Sheesh," she said. She scooted out of her row with a fury, upsetting her chair, which the lady behind her caught with her foot. She strode past me, creating a burst of air that made me shiver. Either that or Laylani had turned up the air-conditioning too high.

"Well," Laylani said. Her pink suit was turning dark under the armpits. "The need for change can be a difficult thing for people to accept," she said. That's what she said whenever we had a walk-out. She took a big breath. One she would call a "cleansing breath." "Maybe Mr. Waddell can take some questions." I wondered if she always did this, handed the ball to Buddy when the going got rough.

Marilynne Monroe raised her hand. "Mr. Waddell never said what kind of gambling problem he had," she said.

Laylani caught his eye, but it was too late.

"Bingo," Buddy said.

Because we had been asked to listen to Buddy Waddell's inspirational story in the conference room, I was not in the reception area as I would have normally been, answering phones and listening to Peppy Johnson on the radio. I did not hear what some already knew, that Wesley D'Angelo of Parrish Island was missing and presumed dead. I did not hear that his wife, Gayle D'Angelo, had gone to police saying she knew who had killed him. I did not hear that the suspect, Dr. Vincent MacKenzie, a local optometrist, had been taken from his office and brought into the Parrish station for questioning.

I also did not hear the two messages on True You's answering machine from my grandmother. It is another fact that your life can be falling apart and Mole Thurber from Boss Donuts can know it before you do.

"Ew, maybe he has like a crush on you," Melissa said as we walked home, me holding the waxed bag that Mel/Mole the Donut Man had run from his shop to give me. "Here," was all he had said, kindly, before running back in. I hadn't even had the time to say thank you. Later it would strike me as one of the strangest things about tragedy. Who would be there for you. Who wouldn't. How you couldn't even guess.

I didn't tell Melissa about what happened between me and Kale. I told her it had been an awful party, drinking, how I saw him with Wendy Williams. I needed the sympathy then, without the distance she'd have put between us if she knew what I'd really done. This way she said only nice things, "Women are from Earth, men are from Uranus if you ask me," and she gave my arm what she thought was a knowing squeeze before she went inside the Beene house. "Just think bingo," she said, pointing at the corner of her own smiling mouth.

I was surprised to see Grandma sitting on the front porch of our house. At first that was all it was, a surprise. That double-take you do when you see someone where you don't expect them, like seeing one of your teachers in the video store. When Grandma saw me she got up and came forward. But it was the way she came toward me, with her arms out. It was bad. I understood that. You don't go to someone like that, with your arms out, unless it's bad.

Dad. I knew it was Dad. She put her arms around me. *Dead*, I thought. I thought I'd lost him. I *had* lost him.

"Dear," she said. "Oh my dear." She started crying into my shoulder. I started crying too, even though I wasn't sure exactly why except that I knew my life had changed horribly. Sickness clutched at me. Dread was swimming so violently inside that I thought I might shatter.

Grandma pulled away from me. The space between us seemed very big and sudden. "I didn't know if you had a key somewhere, hidden under a flowerpot . . ."

"Is he . . ." I said. "Oh, Grandma . . ."

"At the police station now," she said.

"What?" I cried. Her words made no sense to me. She might as well have been moving her mouth without sound, that's how little I understood her. "What?"

"Questioning, you know, they're questioning him. I still don't believe it. There is no way on this earth . . . I *know* him. I know my own son."

"Grandma, Jesus, what? Is he dead?"

"Oh, sweetie, I'm so sorry. I'm so sorry. I'm not thinking. I thought you knew. I'm so sorry." She grabbed me and clutched me to her again, her hands pulling my head to her bony chest, her palm covering my ear as if she didn't want me to hear what she was telling me.

"They think he killed that man. Oh Lord, I can't believe I am saying those words. That D'Angelo man. They found blood . . ."

That's when I screamed. And screamed.

And, please, I can't stand to remember what I felt inside right then.

I begged God that Peppy Johnson was only getting carried away on the radio again. The police would only say that yes, my father was there. My father, whoever he was. I hated thinking of him in his white coat, sitting across from that creep, the Tiny Policeman. Nothing seemed real. I felt like I was faking the part, acting in some stupid TV movie; nothing like that happens in real life. Not to people like me, not to people like my dad, who changes the oil in his car and pays his bills on time and gives money to the Fire Fighters' Fund whenever they call. I mean, imagine it. Your father. Your *father*. I can tell you, though, it does happen. To people like me.

My mother wanted to come get me. She insisted. I said no. I said, "Don't you understand? I need to be here when he gets home." If he ever got home. Grandma was there with me anyway. It got later and later. Grandma called the station again. Yes, he was still there.

We were two baby birds, abandoned in their nest. Weak and lost and stuck, thinking only of who was not there. I could not understand what was happening. My body and I seemed separated from each other. The phone made us both jump as if it were a gun shot. Once it was my father's nurse, concerned. And then, someone selling carpet cleaning. The idea that someone was just out there, selling carpet cleaning, was ludicrous and thoughtlessly mean. Finally someone from Peppy Johnson's station called. My grandma slammed down the phone. I doubted she had ever slammed down a phone in her life.

Grandma had been organized enough to bring a small suitcase, which I lifted from her trunk and carried into the house. She put on her robe, her legs looking thin as a crane fly's underneath. All of her was thin, hands and legs and the skin on her face. Thin and veiny and too old to be dealing with something so large and evil. Grandma made us soup and toast, which neither one of us ate. Grandma just sat there, stirring and stirring. There was a knock at the door, which made us jump.

"Oh Lord, what next?" Grandma said.

We ignored it. Doesn't your heart beat like hell when someone is knocking at the door and you are hiding inside? But the knocker was persistent. I walked soft steps to the door. I peered through the peephole.

"It's Ms. Cassaday," I said.

"Jordan," my grandmother said when I turned the knob.

"My teacher," I said. "It's okay."

Ms. Cassaday pushed inside, hugged me. It was funny to be hugged by my teacher, to have her there standing inside my house. "Okay," Ms. Cassaday said. "The thing is, if he's there without a lawyer . . . Well, he needs one. Mrs. MacKenzie?" Ms. Cassaday asked Grandma.

"That's right," Grandma said. "Jordan's

grandmother. Pardon my attire . . ." Grandma patted the sleeve of her housecoat.

"Under the circumstances, I'm surprised you're even upright. Elaine, a friend of mine, suggested I bring this to you." She handed over a business card to Grandma. "Her brother is an attorney. We thought you might need his help." Grandma nodded. "He'll take good care of you. The radio said . . . Well, I got worried. Jordan's one of my best students. And this. I mean . . . *goddamn*."

Grandma smiled weakly. "I won't keep you," Ms. Cassaday said. "Call the lawyer, okay? So I can sleep tonight?"

She whispered to me on the way out the door. "Be strong." It made a lump start in my throat. But I didn't want that. Crying would mean it was real. The girl in my body pretending she was me didn't want that.

In the driveway I could see Ms. Cassaday's old car and the shape of someone waiting in the passenger seat, Elaine Blackstone, probably. I wondered why it was to our house they came, and not to the D'Angelo house to see Markus and Remington. That's where most people would have gone. That's where *I* would have gone. I pictured the two of them talking, Ms. Cassaday and Elaine Blackstone. Over the kitchen sink as they washed the smell of oyster off their hands, if they ever could get that smell off. I guess they probably knew something about where I was right then. About people thinking thoughts about you that had nothing to do with who you are.

Grandma sat on the couch. "You get old," she said. "And life gets increasingly filled with horror."

There was nothing I could say to that. Instead of answering, I went into the kitchen. I took that stupid plant Dad had been watering with coffee and I threw it away. I dumped it right in the garbage, pot and all. It was the strongest thing I could think to do.

The problem was, there was no body. No body, no witnesses, and my father was insisting he knew nothing about what happened to Wes D'Angelo.

And they believed him. Because he had never done anything like that before. Because he seemed to be telling the truth. So at first they believed him and he came home.

We were living in a house of cards. Our steps were careful, our words were careful, even our thoughts were careful. You can live like you're holding your breath, and that's what we did. I suppose we were the only ones on the island not talking about the murder. Peppy Johnson at the radio station took callers on the topic. Bill Raabe, my father's best friend and our neighbor down the street, was quoted in the newspaper "He was absolutely crazy about her. It reached a point where his friends were seriously concerned." A sign on the old oil tank said, GOOD THING MY WIFE'S GOT 20-20 VISION.

God.

Grandma stayed with us. My mother called three times a day, asking me to come home. I wanted to sleep. Sleep lured me, the way it does when you're upset, only to tease you viciously once you finally pull the covers up. Waking up has the meanest trick, that first moment before you remember.

I was questioned by some detective who had come in from Seattle and who had shoved the Tiny Policeman into the role of second fiddle now that he'd finally got his big chance. They asked me a bunch of stuff as Elaine Blackstone's brother sat by me with his hand on my shoulder. No, I'd said. I'd never seen a hat like that in the house.

But what I saw in my mind was those bulging pockets. Fat with intentions.

I said, "It looks like anyone's hat, the hat of thousands of people."

What I thought was, *He wore a hat?* This was my father we were talking about. Dad with his toe poking out from a hole in his sock. Dad, who used the eye chart with the cows and chickens and pigs for the little kids who couldn't read yet. Who pushed the phoropter gently to their face, saying so they wouldn't be scared, "Now look at this funny pair of glasses. These are the biggest, funniest pair of glasses ever, and you get to wear them!" He could be so embarrassingly corny, my father.

"I mean, the whole thing's ridiculous," Melissa said. "He probably got on a ferry and got the hell away from that woman. I can't believe that they're doing this to your father."

"He went out on my *bike* that night," I said. We stood in my driveway. I showed up for work at True You that morning, but Laylani said I could go home, the stress I must be under.

"I mean that just makes a ton of sense," Melissa said. "What, he lugged that man somewhere on your bike? I'm sure."

"Right, that bike can barely carry me," I said. It struck me how unbelievably odd it was that I was having that conversation. But it was good. To finally be able to speak about it. It was like air whooshing out a balloon.

"What do they think, he hid him in here?" She knocked on the hood of my father's old Triumph, hidden under the tarp. "Jeez, I can't believe any of this. I know your dad. Your dad wouldn't hurt a fly."

Isn't that what the neighbors on the evening news always said? The ones in too-tight pants and bad perms? He wouldn't hurt a fly?

"Jordan?" Grandma came outside, her purse over her arm. "I've called Mrs. Beene. They're expecting you. Your father has gone back to the station. Mr. Blackstone advised me to stay put, but I simply can't sit here and do nothing. I will sit *there* and do nothing if need be, but I won't have your father there all alone. He is still my son."

"How many times are they going to talk to him?" I said. "This is crazy."

"I don't want you alone. Will you do that?" she said. "Just stay at the Beenes' until I come get you."

"Okay," I said.

Melissa looked worried. Like she'd just been told she'd be holding that stick of dynamite a little longer. I had the feeling she'd have been relieved to go home alone. Hell, I bet she'd have given her right arm to be with Chantay West right then. She'd have been thrilled to join her in eating a meat-loaf sandwich, even.

I watched Grandma drive off, her head a small white puff over the steering wheel. Inside the house, I could hear the phone ring. Melissa glanced at the house anxiously. "Just ignore it," she advised. "See? Mom's looking for us. We're coming!" she yelled to Mrs. Beene, who had appeared in her front yard.

The phone started to ring again. I was worried it might be important. "Just a sec," I said.

"Ignore it, Jordan," Melissa said again. But I was already running toward the front door.

"I can't," I said. By the time I reached the phone it had stopped, but the message light was blinking. I pushed the play button.

"Jordan? It's Laylani. Laylani Waddell over at True You?" For a moment I smiled. I mean, there wasn't exactly more than one Laylani Waddell in my life. "I just wanted to tell you. Um, I think we'd all be more comfortable if you didn't come into True You anymore. You know, considering the circumstances."

Laylani paused. I listened to the sound of the tape whirring, watched the small reels going round. Finally her voice returned. "Buddy and I both talked and brought it to the Lord, and well, the girls at True You just have to come first." I pictured Him, their Lord, sitting across a big desk from Laylani and Buddy, nodding his head meanly in agreement with them.

Laylani was quiet again. When she spoke again, her voice was strong. "So what I'm saying is, Jordan, you're fired."

The click of the phone hanging up sounded guilty. It didn't sound guilty enough.

"What I was thinking," Mr. Beene said, "was that I could cook us up something on the grill. Sound good?"

"Doesn't that sound wonderful?" Mrs. Beene said. "I know I've got steaks."

It was pitiful how cheerful they were all being. And how nice Melissa was being to her parents. As if she was suddenly pretty grateful she had any mother and father but mine.

"I'll get the bag of briquettes, Dad," Melissa said.

"Great!" he said.

We all stood around on the back deck, watching the coals get hot. And let me tell you, that takes a long time. Mr. Beene talked about weather systems. About the weather in the east. About weather back in 1962. "I wonder if there is going to be much of an Indian summer this year," he said. He wiped a little sweat off the top of his shiny head. "Then again I don't know. And should we even be saying *Indian summer* anymore? Maybe we should say *Native American summer.*"

"By the time you say that, it'd be over," I said.

Everyone laughed. Too hard. Too long. Mrs. Beene slid open the screen door and stepped out onto the deck with raw steaks on a plate, which she handed to Mr. Beene.

Mr. Beene stabbed them with a long fork and laid them on the barbecue. "Ah, nothing like fresh kill," he said.

"Larry," Mrs. Beene said.

"Oh jeez," Larry turned red. Even the top of his head. "Hey, I'm sorry," he said. "What a stupid . . ."

"It's all right," I said. God, was this supposed to help? I didn't want to be with them, standing around that barbecue. "Excuse me," I said, and got up. Even *excuse me* was not the kind of thing I usually said when I left a room. That's something girls in the movies said. Ones whose fathers might have killed someone.

I went inside. Even from there, I could hear Mrs. Beene giving Mr. Beene a whispered lecture over the winding smoke of the grill. I disappeared into the shell bathroom with the shell soaps and towels that no one was supposed to use. I wished Jackson was home. I wished I could be in his room with the box of bagpipe pieces and the funny soccer statues. I wished I could be in his truck with him, riding to somewhere else. Jackson, with his strange eyes and streaked hair and way of knowing things; just driving anywhere with one arm out the window like the owner of that truck, Slim Wilkins, with that dashboard compass spinning as he rounded a corner.

I came out of the bathroom and looked up the stairs. I considered going up. Being in his room for a second, well, it sounded right then like oxygen.

"He's not home," Melissa said. She'd come inside. She leaned against the hall wall.

"I know he's not," I said.

"It's okay," she said, but I wasn't exactly sure what she meant. I wasn't sure what exactly was okay.

I picked up Boog, who was lying in the hall, and plunked him in front of the refrigerator for a little cooling off. Melissa and I went back on the deck where a chastised Mr. Beene was keeping his mouth shut. Mrs. Beene set the outdoor table for dinner, and we ate under this big flowered umbrella. Everyone kept sneaking looks at me. It was as if they were afraid I was going to escape or suddenly burst into flames.

"Damn bees," Mr. Beene said.

"Don't swat at them or you'll only make them mad," Mrs. Beene said.

"I heard this story of this guy who got stung like a thousand times," Melissa said. "Actually Matt Bennetson? It was him. They said his throat puffed up so big he had to go to the emergency room."

The phone rang inside. Mrs. Beene pushed her chair out so quickly, the Coke in all of our glasses made big surfer waves.

She stuck her head around the screen door. "Jordan?" she said. Her forehead was crinkled with worry. Her hand was over the mouthpiece of the phone as she handed it to me. You could never accuse Mrs. Beene of forgetting her manners.

I wiped my fingers on my napkin and came

to the phone. "Your mom," Mrs. Beene said. She went back out the screen door and sat back down. I could see all three faces looking at me anxiously through the mesh. I turned my back on them. I picked up that pitiful dog Boog and held him in my arms. He felt good, hard and solid with his fat chest breathing against my hand.

"Mom?" I said.

"Jordan, honey, I'm coming to get you. No, I don't want to hear it, this time it's a have-to. Your grandma just called. Just stay where you are and I'll be there in ten minutes."

"What happened?" I said.

"Honey, I don't want to do this on the phone."

"I want to know what happened. Tell me what happened."

She sighed. I waited. Just feeling Boog's heavy breathing, in and out, under his tight skin.

"I will not hang up until you tell me," I said.

"He confessed, Jordan. . . . He—"

"Oh no. No."

"Please just stay there. There might be police—"

"At our house? Why? Why at our house? They know where that man is, don't they? They know where he is. I know it. I can feel it."

"Jordan—"

"Tell me. I want you to tell me right now."

"Ten minutes. I'll be there in ten minutes."

"You tell me now," I said. "You tell me or I won't be here when you get here."

"Oh God, honey, don't do this."

"I'll leave," I said. My mother sighed. She didn't say anything for a long time. "I mean it, I'll leave."

"Daddy confessed." She hadn't called him *Daddy* since I was a small child. "He told them everything. The body . . . It's in the trunk. Of the Triumph. Okay? You see why I didn't . . . I need to get you out of there—"

I hung up the phone. I didn't want to hear her voice anymore. Frankly, I was tired of everyone's voices.

I popped my head out the screen door. "I'm just going to run home a minute," I said. I smiled for them, even. To let them know everything was A-okay.

"Your mom said she was coming to get you," Mrs. Beene said. She looked unsure.

"She wanted me to get a few things," I said. "At the house. I might, you know, be gone a while." I laughed. I felt a little crazy.

Mrs. Beene said, "Melissa can go with you." She glanced over at Melissa. Melissa looked like she'd been given a lesson in smiling but hadn't quite been listening to all the directions.

"No, really. I'll be fast. I'll be right back. I've got to be fast. Mom will be here any minute," I said.

"Okay, honey," Mrs. Beene said. Everyone was calling me *honey*. Maybe that's what people did when your father killed someone. "We'll be right here. You need a suitcase or anything?"

"No, no. You know, just underwear and stuff," I said. Mr. Beene looked down at the table. I still had Boog in my arms. I set him down. I patted his big round rump.

"Just a sec," I said, and pointed a finger in the air to let them know just how long I meant. I left out the front door. I ran past the Triumph, not looking at it, not successful either in blocking any image of what was inside. All I could think of was Melissa knocking on the hood. *What do they think, he hid him in here? What do they think, he hid him in here?* Melissa's voice sang in my head. *Well, wasn't it a good thing he kept that car running,* I thought. *You never know when you've got to jaunt back to the scene of a crime and pick up a dead body.*

I ran upstairs. *What do they think, he hid him in here?* Melissa sang and sang again. I shoved stuff in my backpack. Clothes, I'm not sure what. A wad of money from my work at True You, I remember that. Put some change in my pocket. A small photo album, I remember that too. Down the steps and through the living room and back again. I stopped at the coffee table. I grabbed one of my father's books. I don't know why I did it. The smallest on the stack: *Florentine Architecture of the Renaissance*. I shoved it in my pack.

I took my bike out of the garage. I was almost afraid to touch it at first. Was it some kind of evidence? Was there blood on it? Where exactly had Wes D'Angelo been killed? Lucky for Dad, I guess, that Crow Valley was rambling and full of hidden areas. I shuddered. The details were more than I wanted to know. All of it was more than I wanted to know. I looked down the street and made sure Mrs. Beene wasn't standing on the lawn or something, waiting for me.

And then I pushed off. Pushed off hard and pedaled hard. Even standing up on the pedals to go faster, the way I did when I was a kid. Warm wind hit my face. My face, whatever that meant at that moment, me, mine, my, I didn't really know. Where I was going, I didn't know that either.

I rode. I ended up at Point Perpetua. I stopped pedaling, let my bike coast. I stopped, straddled my bike. I looked out over the strait. Stood by the rock where Clyde Belle shot himself several years ago. I wondered why he didn't just jump. It would have been a whole lot less messy to destroy yourself that way.

Strange thing was, I actually started looking around for him. Not Clyde Belle and the pieces of his splattered body, but Jackson. Jackson

Beene. I expected him to be there. I expected to hear his truck. I listened for the sweet, mournful sound of bagpipes but heard only crows. The cawing of those nasty black crows in the tree branches overhead. I looked toward the light-house. That's where he'd be. I wondered if I waited if he might come. But I had told him to quit rescuing me. I had told him and he had done what I asked. And I didn't have time to wait.

I rode toward the ferry dock. I expected to see my mother pulling up behind me at any moment, so I rode hard. I realized I was an easy target, just a girl on her bike riding on the main roads. I realized I would not get very far very fast. I pulled into Eugene's Gas and Garage. The sign, ABARE'S, still spun slowly on its pole, but the store's lights were dimmed and the parking lot empty. I pulled out some change from my pocket and stepped into the telephone booth at the corner of the lot.

The coin rattled down the machine and the numbers beeped their song as I punched them. I was praying again. I hoped Laylani and Buddy Waddell's God wasn't the one listening. *Please be there. Please, please be there.*

"Yeah," he said.

"Kale?" I said.

"Yeah?"

"It's me. Jordan."

"Shit, you aren't kidding your dad's some murderer."

"Hey, I'm real sorry about the other night at the boat," I said.

"Jeez, you probably had a lot on your mind. I told you, you could have talked to me."

"Well, you know, I know that now. I just called because, well, I need you. Kale. I'm, uh, in some trouble. I want to get the hell away from here. With you."

He thought for a minute.

"Okay," he said.

"I need you to come and get me. In your car."

"Where are you?" he asked.

"My grandpa's gas station. You know that new one, Abare's? By the ferry dock?"

"I saw you there that time," he said.

"Oh, yeah."

"I'll be right there," he said. "Hey, cool. Road trip."

I dumped my bike behind the gas station. I stood by the phone booth and waited. I figured I was already in enough trouble, so what the hell. I picked up rocks and tried to hit the spinning Abare's sign. Most of the rocks were too small, making only a sad ping before bouncing off. The big ones were too heavy too throw that far.

I heard the rumble of Kale's car. He rolled down his window. "You trying to hit that sign?" He chuckled. "I saw you trying to hit that sign."

"I hate that thing," I said.

"Hand me that." He motioned to a big rock on the ground.

I did. Kale got out of the car, stepped back, and hurled the rock into the air. It sailed and struck the sign with a huge clatter of cracking plastic, leaving a large jagged hole. You'd be surprised how thin those things actually are. He bent and picked up another and threw it, hitting the bottom of the B.

"Come on," I said. "We'd better hurry."

But Kale wasn't done yet. When Kale set his mind on destroying things, he did a thorough job.

"Kale, come on. That's great. We've got to hurry and catch the ferry."

A few more rocks. More clatter. I was getting nervous. I was afraid someone might hear.

"There," he said.

Kale was finally satisfied. The sign, still spinning oh so slowly, now said only AHA.

# Chapter Fourteen

"So, are you like a fugitive from justice?" Kale asked.

"Jeez, Kale. *I* didn't hurt anyone," I said.

"This is cool, Bonnie and Clyde," he said. Kale liked this idea. He beeped his horn twice. The car was parked in the bottom deck of the moving ferry, and the horn reverberated loudly against the ferry's old iron sides. Some guy two cars ahead of us rolled his window down and stuck his middle finger out at us.

"I ought to blow you to pieces," Kale said.

"Kale, don't get carried away," I said.

"Goddamn tourists," he said.

We had gotten in the line of cars being shuffled onto the ferry by Joe and Jim Nevins in their orange vests. I ducked my head down into a magazine as we drove by. *Hot Rod*, which I found on the floor with an empty bag of Chee-tos and a crumpled pack of cigarettes and a few paper napkins with orange mouth-swipes on them. We were lucky it was a weekday; on a weekend the wait for a ferry was sometimes three boats long. I didn't know where the nuns were. They usually worked the weekdays unless there was a special nun event. In just a few weeks, Parrish would have the annual Thank-God-They're-Gone festival. The ferry traffic would be cut so drastically that most of the time you'd see Joe and Jim Nevins just sitting on the pilings, eating pastrami sandwiches and drinking Orange Crush out of cans.

"We can probably get out of the car," I said. "I doubt we have to sit in here the whole ride."

"Someone might see you," Kale said. He reached around the floor for that pack of cigarettes. Okay, it's bad enough sitting in the car on the bottom deck of the ferry, that loud whoosh in your ears, cars cramped together like toes in a pair of too-tight shoes and only a small rectangle where you can see the water of the Strait of Juan de Fuca rushing past. But having to sit there for nearly two hours getting lung cancer was another thing.

"I'm sure it's fine," I said. I tried another tack. "You can be the lookout. We can duck around a corner in the nick of time if anyone sees us."

Kale sat up again. "Okay," he said. We

inched sideways between the cars, the lower half of my body rumbling from the vibration of the ferry's engine. Wind took hold of my hair and lashed it in front of my face. Kale said something, but I couldn't hear him above the roar.

We reached the door leading up to the passenger deck, pulled on the handle, and walked up the steep stairs. "I hope he didn't see me," Kale said when we reached the top. His voice was loud in the sudden quiet of the ferry's cabin.

"Who?" I said.

"Mr. Wykowski? I just told you, I thought I saw him. Sitting in his car and having a toke. He's got that license plate. I'D RATHER BE AT A SPRINGSTEEN CONCERT."

"I wouldn't worry," I said.

Kale lurked around, walking a few steps ahead of me to make sure the coast was clear. Making us look more suspicious than if he walked around with a sign on him that read SHE RAN AWAY with an arrow pointing at me.

Kale decided the safest place for us to be was on one of the front outside decks; no one went out there except the little kids who wanted to swallow the wind blowing hard in their faces. It was cold as hell up there, with darkness beginning to fall. The waters of the strait were choppy as the ferry wound slowly through the islands of the San Juans. There are close to forty islands and knolls set in the Strait of Juan de Fuca, most uninhabited but some inhabited and accessible only by plane or private boat. On the ferry ride to the mainland city of Anacortes, you stream by these islands, sometimes close enough that it seems you could reach out and touch them. That night the islands were dark, forested mounds, small and large, occasionally dotted with pin-points of light from isolated houses or the ends of docks. But mostly they were just dark and spooky, like the lumps of a sea serpent's back.

"That's where I want to live," I said, pointing to a small island that appeared to be floating past. I pictured myself there on that island, fishing for my breakfast and cooking it up in a frying pan.

I've noticed that, about that ferry ride. You can forget almost anything when you're out there. It's as if there's this place in between the mainland and Parrish; this place where real life is on hold and you can't touch it even if you want to; this dreamy place that only the old white fer-ries and the drifting sailboats can enter. The deep watery smell and the cold air and the islands that play with your imagination when they pass all put you into such an unreal state that it is like waking up when the ferry slows and the engine quiets and you feel that bump of the boat into the pilings. The whole ride is like disappearing into a daydream. Sometimes you need to disappear into a daydream.

Kale had his hands shoved into his pockets. I

doubt if he even heard me through the wind. Goose bumps stood out along his orangey skin. He looked deep in thought, and I wondered if that might be possible. My fingers were so cold I wasn't sure if I would ever be able to uncurl them. I motioned for him to come inside the ferry's cabin. We sat down on one of the padded seats, behind a couple who looked tan and rested from their stay on Parrish, their backpacks thrown on the seat beside them. She was halfway through a thick book; his feet were propped on the seat across from him as he read a newspaper. For a moment it struck me. That he could actually be sitting there, reading about my father. This stranger with the beard gone unshaven for his vacation. But I didn't want to think about that. Jesus, I couldn't think about that, or I would see the Triumph covered by the tarp sitting in our driveway. I would see my father with his head in his hands. I would see those pockets of his jacket. . . .

Kale rested his head against the back of the seat. "You ever have those dreams where your teeth fall out?" he asked.

"Teeth? Jeez, Kale, I don't know. Not really," I said.

"I have this dream?" he said. "Where I'm chewing gum and someone comes along to talk to me, like the coach or someone? And I try to get the gum out but it doesn't come out all the way. And I keep trying and trying, and still there's more and more gum stuck in there. I just keep pulling more out." He demonstrated as if I needed assistance with this mental picture.

"It probably means you have deep psychological problems," I said.

He appeared to think about this. He put his hands behind his head, his armpits showing that fluff of hair and giving off a musty smell. A musty smell that made me think of that night on the boat. What we did together, or rather, what he did on his own. The thought made me feel sick. A cheese grater going against my insides. Kale seemed to be thinking for a real long time, too long even for him.

"Kale?" I said.

I nudged him. It was getting late, but sleeping was not on the agenda. I wasn't sure exactly what the agenda was, but I definitely knew it didn't include him sleeping. "You tired?" I said loudly. Kale's head popped up.

"Shit," he mumbled. He put his palms to his eyes and looked over at me. "Too much partying is detrimental to the health, I can attest. Plus, I worked all day. My boss? What an asshole. You miss a day and he docks your pay, no questions, doesn't ask why, nothing. I mean, Jesus."

"How unfair," I said. "Maybe we should get up and walk around."

"Nah, let's go back to the car." He rubbed his hand on my leg. "Hey, people are getting up," he said.

He was right. The guy in front of us was folding his newspaper, people were throwing out paper coffee cups and heading for the stairs. I looked out the wide window beside me and saw the lights of Anacortes a few minutes away. Disappointment fell heavy inside me. It always hits a little when the ferry is about to dock—back to real life—but this was worse; much, much worse. Dread. I remembered what I was doing. I was walking around in someone else's body again, and I had no idea who that someone was.

We followed the crowd back down to the car, inching our way sideways again, past Mr. Wykowski, who was sacked out against the driver's seat with his mouth hanging open. Kale made faces at him through the window until I nudged Kale's shoulder with my hand. We continued down the line to Kale's car, got in, and sat there a while until the ferry bumped into place and the car engines started up.

"Kale," I said. He still seemed groggy. He turned the ignition key at the sound of his name. "Let's get coffee," I said as we clunked over the metal ramp and headed into town.

"Hey, that's fine, but I want you to know right here I don't have any money with me. Hell,

I don't even have my *wallet*. You called and I was like, *bam*, out of there."

"I'm the fugitive, I'll pay," I said.

The funny thing about the Seattle area is that you see coffee stands everywhere—street corners and gas stations and banks and Laundromats. I spotted one right away. Kale pulled into the all-night drive-through espresso place, which sat in the empty parking lot of an animal hospital, closed down for the night. I bought us a couple of lattes from a girl with a pierced tongue.

"Shit, imagine Frenching that," Kale said. That's what I liked about Kale. Always full of insightful observations.

We sat in the parking lot under the sign ANACORTES VETERINARY CLINIC. WE CARE ABOUT YOUR PET with a big red cross, and sipped our coffee through tiny straws. "What I'd like to know here," Kale said, "is, like, what the plan is. I mean, I don't think I can drive around all night."

I looked out the window. I watched the girl with the pierced tongue serve up another cup of java and reach out her arm to hand back the change. I can't tell you if I knew where I was headed all along or if it only occurred to me at that moment. All I know is that right then, after Kale asked the question and began sucking the foam off the end of his straw, I knew where I was heading. Let me tell you, it can be such a relief to know where you're heading.

"Three hours, tops," I said. "Then we can stop. We'd better get far enough away so they won't find us."

"You have some idea where we're going to end up? I can do this maybe two days, then I gotta get back to work or I'll get fired."

"We'll head over Snoqualmie Pass tomorrow," I lied. "Eastern Washington? I've got friends who have a ranch there. I bet they'd even give you a job. You like horses? They're rodeo riders."

"No shit," Kale said.

"Yeah, shit," I said.

"Hey, as long as I finish school I could swing it with my folks. They won't care."

"Oh, you'd love it," I said. "The open range, riding horses all day long. You've got to have a lot of stamina though. It's not easy work, you know. People think rodeo riding is easy work."

"I got stamina," Kale said. Jeez, once you knew how, you could play him like a fiddle. Maybe more like a kazoo.

Kale got dreamy again. "Maybe we should put on some music or something," I said. "Kale?" I clapped my hands. "How about some music?"

All I needed was for him to get me to the town of Nine Mile Falls. I'd never been there, but I knew it was less than three hours off the ferry. I knew because that's what she always said. Just before she said, "Come and see me. Any time. I'll show you the salmon fingerlings."

"Sure, whatever," Kale said. I turned on the radio. Listened a while until Jimmie Dix came on. Which made me think of him in his mirrored suit, which made me think of my mother, which made me think of her driving up to the Beenes' house and finding me gone. Thoughts can be so spoiled, the way they insist on having their way. The less you want them, the more insistent they become. The more they stamp their feet and demand things.

"I hate that fag," Kale said. "Jimmie Sucks Dix is what he should be called."

I thought about Jimmie Dix in that video, where he's on the beach with that woman. I bet he already knew love wasn't that simple.

I pushed the search button on the radio, and it found the next clear channel. *It's too bad*, I thought, *that we all didn't have a search button*.

Kale turned onto the freeway. "I'm hungry," he said. Kale was getting cranky. His empty cup was rolling around by my foot, but the coffee didn't seem to have had the effect I was hoping for.

"I'll buy you a cheeseburger when we get closer," I said.

"I don't want a cheeseburger," Kale whined. "I gotta watch my cholesterol. My whole family's got high cholesterol. I don't want to just drop dead of a heart attack some day like Uncle Pete.

Thirty-five." He shook his head. Personally, I wouldn't have minded if Kale dropped dead of a heart attack right then, except for the fact that he was behind the wheel.

"I can see you're so concerned about it," I said. I rattled the Chee-tos bag with the tip of my shoe.

"What? Oh, fuck, never mind. You know, I'm just trying to talk to you about a legitimate worry of mine. Always gotta be the wise-ass. You watch it or I'll be the wise-ass and drop you off right here."

I shut my mouth. I'd forgotten that a kazoo still has to be played carefully, or that little piece of tissue paper breaks and it's all over. I just looked out the window at blackness, at the occasional sign—WAYNE'S WORLD OF CAMPING, MINI STORAGE 4-LESS—and the headlights of the other cars whipping past us. Kale's car seemed to be going awfully slow. I didn't know if it was just him, a tired foot on the gas pedal, or if something was wrong with the car. That's all we needed, to get stuck out there.

"You want me to drive?" I said.

"You don't know how to drive my car."

"You could tell me what to do," I said.

"Forget it. You're not driving my baby." He patted the dashboard. A huge truck whipped past us, making his baby shudder. "Shit!" Kale said. He beeped his horn at the driver. "Drive like an asshole. Oh man, look," he said.

Up ahead were the spinning red lights of police cars, parked at odd angles at the side of the road, and an ambulance, its back doors open. Traffic slowed, a congestion of red brake lights. We were stuck behind the huge truck that had sped past. Kale craned his neck, and I admit, I did too. The scene made me shudder. I saw a lumpy bag on a stretcher, two cars that looked like a pair of Coke cans squashed by some burly show-off.

I felt a dull ache start in my heart. Someone was dead here. Really and truly dead and gone. I thought about Remington and Markus D'Angelo. I thought about that picnic, and about Wes D'Angelo's hand on his son's shoulder. I thought about what my father caused and my throat got tight and my eyes hot and I tried not to, but I couldn't help it. I started to cry. Too much emotion washed over me at once, and a feeling of panic came in its place. I wanted to leap out of the car and run; I'd forgotten I was running already.

"A dead body," Kale said. "Mark that off on your Auto Bingo." He chuckled. Then he looked over at me. "Oh, shit," he said.

I guess I was sobbing. What I saw was Wes D'Angelo at his mailbox that day I rode my bike over there. Thinking he heard someone in his own bushes. Knowing something was wrong and not wanting to believe it. That startled look; the same look I imagined he wore when my father surprised him in his driveway with his own gun. Coming home that night and standing in his own driveway, coming home to his sons like every man had a right to do. My own shame overpowered me. I felt as if I killed Wes D'Angelo myself.

Your mind can accept only so much horror and then it starts to shudder and shut down; I found that out. I thought I might have to throw up. We inched past the scene, putting the spinning red lights and the street that looked shiny from wetness behind us. I rolled down my window, tried to gulp fresh air, but instead breathed the stinky exhaust from the truck in front of us. I gasped, wiped my eyes on my arm. "Oh boy," I breathed.

"You're not gonna puke in my car, are you? Let me know if you're gonna puke." Kale took quick side glances at me.

"I'm okay," I said. "I'm all right."

"You know, I'm getting a bad feeling here," Kale said. "Here, your dad just offs someone, there's a dead body on the side of the road, I don't know. I think we ought to stop or something."

"We're not that far," I said.

"Hey, I don't want to end up like that." He crooked his thumb over his shoulder. "Don't think I believe in any of that karma shit or anything because I don't. I saw all the money you've got. No reason we can't stop somewhere for the night."

The last thing I wanted was to be in a motel room alone with Kale, but he was already flicking on his turn signal, his car chugging off the exit ramp.

"Look here," Kale said. He turned into the parking lot of the Sunset Motel.

Just our luck, the sign said ACANCY. By the look of the place, that capital V had been burnt out a long, long time.

Kale was springing up and down on the bed, making all the candy bars we'd bought from the vending machine bounce about on the olive-and-brown-striped bedspread.

"This is great," he said. "Hand me a Baby Ruth. Hand me a baby, Ruth," he chuckled. *Now* he was perking up. I tossed him the candy bar, which he caught with a crackle in his palm. He patted the bed beside him. Shit.

"Hey, Bonnie," he said.

Okay, you know, whatever.

"Hey, Clyde," I said.

He leaned in, started kissing me. He tasted of that dark, ashy smell of old coffee. I probably did too. His tongue danced around with mine, and I let it. I wasn't sure how I was supposed to be acting, after my own father had done something so unbelievably awful. I had no idea what girls whose fathers killed people should act like.

Kale suddenly leapt up. Did this little jog to the bathroom. When he came out again, he was in only his underwear. Those white ones with the thin yellow-and-blue stripes at the top. From the open bathroom door, I could hear the toilet whooshing and gurgling with effort from the flush.

Kale did a dance in his underwear. "I'm your Boogie Man," he sang. "That's what I am. I give you. Whatever I am." I think he had the words wrong, not that I ever listen to that shit. Like my mother says, it was bad enough the first time around. Kale boogied toward the bed. I'm not kidding. Swiveled his tight butt around in that white underwear.

"Wow, Kale," I said. You'd be speechless too.

"This is something, isn't this something? Who'd have guessed when I woke up this morning I'd be here now with this girl that killed someone."

"I didn't kill anyone," I reminded him again.

"Well, you know what I mean." He yanked back the covers on the bed. I was a little worried to look down and see what he might have uncovered, but the sheets looked all right. He got in, stretched his body out so that I might admire it. He took hold of his crotch. "Look what I've got for you," he said.

"Look at that," I said. What I thought was, *Oh no, not again.*

He lay there, giving me that sleepy look and waiting until I could no longer resist. After a while, he realized he'd been waiting a long time. He reached over to me and circled my hips, scooted me down to him. He started to kiss me again, grabbed a handful of my butt like we were at the movies and it was the bucket of popcorn. My mind was spinning, reaching. And not working too well. I was more tired than I'd ever been in my life.

I ended the kiss. "Kale," I said. "You don't have your wallet."

He put his nose on my neck, nuzzled downward. "I'll be careful," he said. We kissed some more, the kisses getting sloppier, lazier, more dangerous.

"Kale," I said. I pulled away. I thought fast. "You know how much I want you." I gave the knot in his skivvies a little pat to prove my sincerity. "But this is so embarrassing. I've got my, you know . . ."

Kale shot up. "You're kidding," he said. "Oh man."

"It's okay with me, though," I said. "Really, I don't mind."

"Well, I'm not dealing with *that*," he said. "Forget that idea right now."

His arms were crossed. Who would have

thought periods, even fake ones, would come in so handy? Someday, I thought, some stupid girl would actually marry this guy.

"You could still . . ." He pulled down his underwear and his penis popped out with a *boing*. It didn't stay that way for long. It began to look half-hearted. He pulled his underwear back up. "Hell, you probably got a lot on your mind anyway."

"We'll have a lot of time alone when we get to the ranch," I said.

This cheered him up. "Maybe we should watch TV. Maybe your Dad will be on. How did he do it anyway? They said he used a gun. Bam! Bam! Two shots." Kale looked at me. "Hell, I'm sorry," he said.

"I'm just really tired, Kale," I said.

"That was insensitive of me," he said.

I stayed awake for a long time, pretending to be asleep as Kale watched some hockey game and ate candy bars. I was still awake when he finally shut off the television and the lights. When you're in a strange place, the darkness seems darker than usual. I could hear the sounds of the freeway, the whip of the cars back and forth. It was distracting to have someone sleeping next to me, his weight shifting my own on the mattress every time he moved. His face sometimes turned unnervingly my way, making me think we might both pop our eyes open at the same time. He started to snore, this low rumble in the back of his throat that sounded like one of the tools Nathan used to cut metal.

When I woke up I was alone. I had no idea what time it was. The dark green curtains of the motel room were lined with plastic, and only the thin slit of daylight between them told me it was morning. I wondered if Kale had left me, if he'd gone back home or decided to tell some small-town newspaper reporter about the night he spent with Vince MacKenzie's daughter. I didn't really care that he'd left. I could get where I was going on my own, though he'd make things easier. In some ways, I wished I could just stay in that ugly dark room. Just hiding and staying in that dimness.

I got up and peeked through the curtains. If Kale had left, he'd done it without his car, which was still parked outside our window. I went to the bathroom, cringing at the thought of my bare feet against the disgusting tile of that floor. I threw water on my face and decided against using the towel. I heard the knob of the room door rattling, the jiggling of a key. Either Kale was back or I would be the victim of some slasher. It occurred to me then, how many jokes would not seem very funny anymore.

"There was a little problem," Kale called. "But I've got it handled."

I came out of the bathroom. Except for wearing the same clothes as yesterday, the tank top with its small smear of dropped coffee-foam on the front, Kale looked amazingly fresh and rested. He had regained steam for the adventure. He was holding a brown bag at his side, and was bouncing on his heels.

"The thing is, we gotta hurry. I saw the guys through the window still looking at menus, but we better get out of here."

"What are you talking about?"

"I'm telling you, we gotta go," Kale said. "I've got the engine running."

"Okay, okay," I said. I don't know what I imagined. Maybe he'd seen Mr. Wykowski again, though that seemed unlikely. Or that his car was having problems. Anyway, he was obviously agitated. He grabbed my arm and pulled it.

"Can I get my pack at least?" I scooped my backpack off the room's one chair and followed Kale outside. It was bright and hot. Nearing the end of August, this would be the last good weather we in the Northwest would see until June. Normally at that time of year, the only complicated thoughts you have are if you should keep watering the lawn even though it's yellow, and if your white shorts look clean enough.

"Where are you going?" I asked. "I thought you said the car's running."

"Not *mine*," Kale said, as if I should have figured this out by now.

"What do you mean not yours?"

"I came out this morning to go get us some doughnuts. I didn't know how long you were going to sleep. One thing you need to know about me, I wake up starving." He was talking over his shoulder. He walked around the back of the building, where the Sunset Motel had a couple of Dumpsters and not much else. I was starting to get a bad feeling.

"I thought the car was acting funny last night, but it does that sometimes. I can't figure out if it gets overheated or the fuel pump is screwed or what. So, shit, what do I find but the goddamn thing won't start."

A couple of Dumpsters and not much else but this fancy-looking sports car. I'm not good with car names, but I can tell you this thing looked expensive. One of those that look like a cat about to pounce. The license plate holder said RETIRED AND LOVING IT.

"Oh no, Kale," I said.

"Get in," he said.

The engine was on. Barely audible. A purr.

"Kale, you *stole* this."

"Would you just get in? Jesus, it's not like I want to get caught here."

Kale got in. He reached over to the passenger door and opened it. "I said, get in."

"Kale, I'm not getting in a stolen car."

"Goddamn it, get *in*! The old fart's getting his pancakes by now, fuck! Do you always have to be so difficult?"

I got in. I nearly shot out of my chair when this woman's voice came out of nowhere.

"Buckle your seat belt," she said.

I reached for my seat belt and plugged it in. "Do you realize how stupid this is?" I said. "Do you realize how absolutely stupid this is?"

"Buckle your seat belt," she said again. Kale ignored her.

"What are you talking about? Do you want to get out of here or don't you? I saved our butts. I saw the car wasn't gonna start and I lit over to this Denny's across the street."

Kale pulled out into traffic. In another minute we were on the freeway. "Man, what a smooth ride. Feel that smooth ride? I always wanted a car like this. Those bunch of old farts in Denny's, they don't deserve this car. You wouldn't believe it. They had these fucking ridiculous hats with tassels hanging off the top."

"Shriners?" I said.

"How the hell am I supposed to know? I mean, if you're going to wear a stupid hat like that . . . You should have seen the parking lot. Those guys must have the bucks. I could have gotten us a Lincoln. Or motorcycles. You should have seen these motorcycles. Me, I like a sports car."

He tossed me the brown bag. Inside was a package of Hostess powdered-sugar doughnuts and a tube of toothpaste that Kale had already squeezed. Dental care was apparently high on Kale's list. I unscrewed the cap, put a dab of toothpaste on my tongue with my finger. Fresh breath can make you feel more capable, even in the worst of circumstances.

"Hand me one of those, will you?" Kale said. "Jesus, I cannot believe the way people drive. That guy cut right in front of me."

Kale beeped his horn. "We're in a stolen car, Kale," I said. It did not seem like an especially good idea to draw attention to ourselves. I mean, our license plate said RETIRED AND LOVING IT. I mentioned this to him.

"Maybe we should put mud on it," he said.

"This is not the movies, Kale!" I said. "You stole a car. I can't believe you stole a car! Those guys give money to hospitals!"

"You're not my mother, you know," Kale said.

I stared out the window and fumed.

"You know why it takes ten women with PMS to screw in a lightbulb?" Kale said. He waited, but I was trying to ignore him.

"I don't know, goddamn it, it just does, okay!" Kale said in a falsetto. He laughed away like he was the king of comedy.

"Your seat belt is still unbuckled," the woman said. She had a Japanese accent.

"That chick's beginning to piss me off," Kale said. He reached over and yanked his seat belt over him and clicked it into place. We drove along in quiet a while, until Kale turned the radio on. Frank Sinatra blasted out. Some old guy like that. Kale snapped his fingers, played at loving it, then turned the dial and settled into his usual thumping. Kale liked thumping.

The music improved my mood. I got thinking. I made a plan. I looked around the glove compartment for a pen and paper. I found a pad of paper that said AIR KING—*HEATING AND AIR CONDITIONING. NUMBER ONE IN SERVICE*, and a pen that was slow to work until I scribbled a few circles.

Kale looked over at me. "What are you writing?"

"I just thought I'd better write down the address of where we're going. You never know what might happen. Say I get caught. You'll still be able to go on to the ranch without me."

"You think they'd still take me?" he asked.

"Well, sure. You're my boyfriend," I said.

"That is so cool," Kale said. "I mean, I can *see* myself there."

I got creative with the pen, ripped the piece of paper off the pad and set it in one of the dashboard's handy compartments. Those expensive cars have a lot of handy compartments.

"Do you feel that?" Kale said a moment later.

"What?" I said.

"Chick's getting fresh. She's warming up my butt. Feel." He rubbed his hand on the seat. Now that he mentioned it, I could feel it too. The seat was getting hot.

"Jeez, these old people must have cold asses; it's eighty degrees out. Find out where to shut that off, will you?" He ran his hand along the side of the seat. "Hey, I want my ass warmed, I'll ask," he said to the Japanese woman. "You crossed the line now, babe," he told her.

I found a couple of switches by the parking brake, decorated with a picture of wavy lines. "Try this," I said.

We waited a few minutes. "Yeah, she's cooling down. Hey, didn't I say to hand me one of those doughnuts?"

I opened the container, took a white, powdery doughnut between my fingers. "Try not to get that shit on the seats," Kale said.

I licked my fingers, then took out one for me. We ate doughnuts and drove for a while. Kale told me a long story about this guy he knew who stole stereo equipment, which turned into a story about the sister, who apparently liked tight dresses and had a thing for Kale. "Not my type, no way," he was telling me. He had a small avalanche of powdered sugar on his upper lip, which was all I could concentrate on. "Her bra, shit! It was so big you could carry your basketballs in it when you go to the gym." He laughed at himself. "One of those chicks you look at and you say 'Ten years she'll look just like her mother,' and let me tell you, that wasn't a compliment in this case. Even Ronnie called her *Wide Load*, and that's her son talking. I said, 'Ronnie, that's your mother, show some respect.'"

I watched the road signs. I listened to another story about some friend of his who cracked his neck playing football, and heard how much alcohol Kale planned to consume when he went away to college next summer. My stomach leapt with nerves when Nine Mile Falls started to appear on the signs. Soon, I thought. I was listening to Kale tell me how disgusting it was that Jason Dale never cleaned underneath his fingernails "You watch him eat and it makes you sick. I don't care, there's no reason you got to walk around looking dirty when there's a thing called soap" when the Japanese woman piped in.

"Low on fuel," she said.

I loved that woman. The great thing was, it was her idea and not mine. See, I wasn't quite sure about that part yet. We were a little farther away than I wanted, just before the town of Nine Mile Falls, but close enough for me to walk.

"Oh man, we better pull off. That chick means what she says," Kale said.

Kale veered over two lanes, then flicked on

his turn signal as an afterthought. We had to look around a bit to find the gas station. We had driven through a couple of large Seattle suburbs, but now the towns were getting small again.

"There," I pointed. Kale turned into the Texaco. At the corner of the lot, a group of teenagers in shorts and tank tops were waving signs reading CAR WASH $5 and SUPPORT GIRLS SOFTBALL. A car sped past them, ignoring their waving signs.

"Fuck you!" one of the girls yelled. That was one way to deal with those pesky business rejections.

Kale parked at the pump. I looked around the lot. Damn. No phone booth.

"I'm going to go to the bathroom while we're here," I said.

"Jeez, we only left two hours ago," he said.

"You know us girls," I said.

"You're not kidding," he said. He eyed the softball team. "Maybe I'll get a car wash while I wait. It's a crying shame to have a car like this all dusty and shit."

"Why don't you do that first," I said.

I reached in my wallet and tossed him a five-dollar bill. It was the best five dollars I ever spent.

I slung my backpack over my shoulder and went inside the mini-mart. The man who popped his head around the coffee machine looked as reluctant to be there as Grandpa

Eugene would have. He had a big belly that looked used to sitting on swivel chairs across from a calendar of naked women, not to unpacking box after box of Corn Nuts and Mountain Dew and Big Red.

"Help you?" he said.

"I was wondering if you had a phone book I could use," I said.

He scratched his belly, then dropped a fat phone book on the counter, which fell open with a sloppy splat. "Charge you a quarter if you use the phone and no long distance."

"I don't need to use it," I said. "I just need an address."

With that, the man's voice became more friendly. "One thing or another with that phone. That GTE picked it up and took off with it. Whole damn booth like it was a fish on a line." He jiggled with laughter at the memory. I turned the pages quickly. I was afraid to look over my shoulder and see what Kale was doing. I knew I didn't have a lot of time.

I rolled my finger down the list of names. "Course now all anyone comes in here for is the phone," the man said. He rolled a pen across the counter without me even asking. I wrote the address on a napkin that he slid over next.

"Thank you," I said.

I saw the big map, pinned on the wall over the freezer case filled with Eskimo Pies and Dum

Dum's. I peeked out the window before going over and saw Kale eyeing the softball team as they soaped up the car. Even from across the parking lot, I could see the splotch of powdered sugar still on his upper lip. On the map, I found the red star showing where we were. I looked around the map for the street name. Black Nugget Road. Black Nugget Road. Black Nugget Road.

"You're kidding," I said aloud.

"What's that?" the man said.

I wanted to laugh. For the first time in days, I felt a tiny bit of joy. The possibility of joy. "This map," I said. "It says Bobcat Road."

"You want to get to Bobcat Road?" he said. "Just a couple blocks from here. Over by the old school."

"No, I'm actually . . . I'm looking for a place in Nine Mile Falls. I just can't believe there really is a Bobcat road."

"Bobcat Road, Cougar Mountain, Tiger Valley. You want a cat, we got it."

"That's great," I said. "That is so great." I laughed.

The man shrugged his shoulders as if to say *Whatever floats your boat.* "You find Nine Mile falls there? You got, what, maybe two, three miles. You need directions?"

I knew this trick. Ha ha, I knew this trick well. "No, I see it. I think I got it."

"That boyfriend of yours gonna get gas?

He's gotta pay first. I don't have none of that pump-first-pay-later business."

"Believe me, that guy out there is not my boyfriend," I said.

"Well, not to get personal, but it's a good thing, considering what his eyes are glued to over there," the man said.

I thought of Kale that night on the boat. I thought of the sound of that storm, of Kale on top of me. I remembered his thick tongue, poking into Wendy Williams's mouth. I let hatred fill me. Finally I let it fill me and it felt so good.

Felt good and also cleared my head. My plan had been to send Kale east of the mountains without me to some place that wasn't there. But running out of gas, Kale's interest in the softball team, and my new friend in the mini-mart gave me another idea. A better idea.

"He's not going to be getting gas," I said. I was sure about that. "And there's another thing you should probably know," I said to the man. "It's about that car he's driving."

"His Daddy's?"

I shook my head.

"Stolen?" His voice rose.

"I didn't know until after the fact, I promise you. And there's no way I'm getting back in it," I said.

The mini-mart man watched Kale out the window for a moment. Watched as this girl flicked a clump of soapsuds at Kale and he flicked some back. One big breath could pop the buttons of that mini-mart man's shirt right off and send them skittering along the floor.

His eyes traveled away from the window. He looked back at me. "I didn't see no girl with him, Officer," he said.

# Chapter Fifteen

I could have walked right up to Kale, stuck my thumbs in my ears, and waggled my fingers around, and he wouldn't have noticed me. Kale had become suddenly overheated and now had his shirt off. He'd lit a cigarette. Behind me, I could feel the mini-mart man pick up the phone. I could feel his voice speaking into the receiver. I walked around the back of the building where the bathrooms were. And then I ran.

*Maybe,* I thought for the first time, *my life isn't over.* That's the best part about joy. How you can think it's gone for good and then it sneaks up on you, just a small bit making you fill up and feel you are someone for whom things are possible. *Stupid dumb-ass Kale,* I sang in my head.

*What did your parents pay to get you in that gifted class? And what's your favorite book, Kale?* I sang. *Let me guess.* The Yellow Stream, *by I. P. Freely, right, Kale?*

I ran, my pack beating a rhythm on my back. I didn't know exactly where I was going. I just ran south, through neighborhoods of chain-link fences and little dogs and inflatable wading pools in the front yards. Past the gates of a forested park, from which I could see a peek of a small lake, dotted with lazy air-mattresses and kids running around in drippy bathing suits holding their flip-flops in their hands. I knew I was getting close when the traffic picked up and suddenly there were a few small stores and finally the main street of a town.

"And what's your favorite thing to do, Kale? Besides having sex with girls too stupid to say no?" I said to myself. "Oh, roll rubber cement boogers and kill helpless animals," I said in Kale's voice.

With that, the joy that had filled me disappeared. The game stopped being fun. I had thought of the rabbits. I thought again about the look that must have been on Wes D'Angelo's face that night. I quit running. I was tired, hot, thirsty. I needed a bath. Mostly, I had remembered again why I was out there, standing on the main street of a town that was a stranger to me. My pack felt heavy. I felt stupid that I had been so sentimental. My pack would have been a whole lot lighter without that architecture book.

You could put Nine Mile Falls in your pocket, it was so small. And it was either trying hard to be charming or it really was, I couldn't tell which. Flower baskets hung from the lampposts, although the flowers looked limp and thirsty, and the building-fronts were those of an old mining town. From the street you could see three forested mountains rising in an arc above the town, as if they held it like loving mothers in their laps. An old man crossed the street and raised a hand in greeting to the car that had stopped for him. A dog sat under the bus-stop sign.

I opened the door of a store—used books and records—making the bell bang against the glass. A guy with a long ponytail and tiny glasses looked up, and I asked him the way to Black Nugget Road. I followed the map the book guy drew on my hand with an ink pen. The streets in town were named for trees. After Alder there were houses again—small houses with low fences and mailboxes along the sidewalk—some painted in wild designs or shaped like birdhouses. I crossed a bridge with a shaded creek flowing underneath, and posted with a sign decorated with a leaping salmon. PLEASE KEEP THIS RIVER CLEAN, it said. I looked down, thinking I would see salmon swimming, but there was only the low rushing water and shoots of grass along the bank. The creek followed the street; as I looked back, it appeared to wind its way through town.

I walked past more leaping-fish signs; the sound of the creek, water burbling over smooth rocks, was a cool, peaceful sound. The map on my hand said I was close, and I knew it too. This looked like where Big Mama would live. My stomach was doing as much flopping around as the fish on those signs.

But I was relieved, too, when I saw the house. Two-seven-seven. A small white house that needed paint, with a few pots of geraniums on the porch and a cat lying in a shady spot of the grass. I pushed on the stuck gate, knocked on the door. I heard the yipping of a small dog inside, the brave barking of a creature who thought he was more than he was. I waited for the sound of Big Mama's heavy footsteps. I knocked again. Nothing.

I had to think about what day it was. It felt like years had passed since I was at the Beenes' house for dinner. *Big Mama is just at work,* I told myself. I told myself, *Calm down.* Fatigue and heat made all the nasty possibilities flash through my head. And truly they *were* all possible—because for all I knew Big Mama was in Oregon visiting her son Burke or in Montana staying with her daughter, Angela, or in

Arkansas checking on her aged mother. Two other sons lived in California. I was just so sure she was going to open that door. So sure she was going to open her arms so that I could disappear into them for a while.

Tears were starting to make their shaky way to my eyes. I sat down on the porch. I folded my arms, lay my head down on them. I was so very tired.

I thought the sound was in my head. I thought the long walk and the heat were doing things to my brain same as those guys you see in the movies who have been walking in the desert too long. But I wasn't sure if a mirage was something you could hear too. I figured the brain was an equal-opportunity trickster. The ears or the eyes, whichever was vulnerable enough to be fooled.

But damn it if I didn't keep hearing it. I thought a mirage was supposed to vanish once it'd been found out.

I lifted my head. I listened. My sudden movement made the cat get up and rub herself against my legs.

"Shh," I said to her. She hadn't made a peep, but her hot fur against my skin was distracting.

"Do you hear that?" I asked her.

She looked up at me. Her *mrow* was impatient and cranky from the heat.

"I think I'm going nuts," I said to the cat.

But I heard it. I did. I stood up, as if that might help my ears somehow. God, I felt so crazy, but I could have sworn I heard the sound of bagpipes coming from the direction of the creek. Sweet notes, lifting themselves on the smallest of breezes.

I pushed open the reluctant gate, and the cat followed me out, her tags jingling as she trotted behind me. I walked toward the creek. Stopped to listen.

"It is," I said. "It is." My heart started to fill. I could feel my own hot tears. I wasn't sure whether I was laughing or crying. It was all emotions at the same time, fighting for space. Overcome.

I followed the creek, faster, faster. The cat had given up and plopped down in a spot of shade somewhere behind me. I was almost running. But the music stayed slow and calling; he never played the jaunty, silly songs. No leprechaun jigs for him. Only measured, tender waltzes.

He stood on the bridge over the creek, leaning with his back against the rail. When he saw me, Jackson took the pipe from his mouth.

"I've been waiting for you," he said from across the bridge.

He set the instrument down with care. And then I went to him. He cradled my head against him as I cried. Cried with such gratitude and release that I understood—deep as my pain felt, endless as it seemed, the scraggly hair bent next to my cheek meant there was always healing.

We sat on Big Mama's porch. Jackson had parked his truck across the street, and the cat had discovered this new place, curling herself in the back of the pickup. The bagpipes lay across Jackson's knees. With Jackson, it was always as if we recognized each other.

The yapping dog inside had given up and accepted our presence on the porch. Earlier, Jackson had brought out a couple of bottles of water from his truck and a bag of nectarines. We ate them, licking the sticky juice that rolled down our arms; the fruit was warm and tasted like summer if summer could have a taste. Then Jackson rinsed his hands with a squirt of water. He was careful with that bagpipe.

"This is the chanter," Jackson said. "And the drones."

He held the pieces in his palm as he said their name.

"Sounds like the parts of an insect," I said.

Jackson smiled. "These here are the tenor," he said. "This long one, bass. And the blow-pipe."

Jackson talked about circular breathing and grace notes and calling troops from battle and lamenting the dead. I confess I wasn't listening much to his words but more to the sound of his voice, which was soothing. And I was looking at his face. It wasn't sadness that Jackson wore; more that his eyes seemed to show thoughts he was weighing deep inside.

"So the bagpipe"—Jackson laughed—"was played by either the village drunk or the shepherd. He was supposed to entertain, sure, but he also played to call in his animals and lead them home."

"But why do you play?" I asked.

"Same reasons," he said. And then, "I heard it when I got lost. . . ." I waited for more, but none came. This time I knew to keep my mouth shut. I had a feeling that more would come, someday. A mail truck came down the street. We watched as it stopped in front of Big Mama's house. The woman inside the truck opened the curved door of Big Mama's mailbox, slid in a thin slice of mail, and slammed shut the door, which protested with a squeak.

"Sometimes I think of it like this," he said. "A piano's keys are like an extension of the fingers that play it." He wiggled his fingers on an imaginary piano. "Right?"

"I guess so," I said.

"A violin is played with a bow, an extension of the arm." He curved his arm, put one cheek against his shoulder. "A horn is round like the mouth that plays it." Jackson looked at me to see if I was following. I nodded.

"But a bagpipe," he said. "What is it? This thing is weird." He patted the instrument on his lap and I laughed. "It's a jangle of bones, awkward insides. It's played by the mouth and fingers and held against here." Jackson moved his hand in a circle around his chest. His heart.

"Awkward but beautiful," I said. "It makes beautiful music."

"Right," Jackson said.

We watched the mail truck get smaller until it disappeared altogether around a corner. "Look, I think she's coming," Jackson said.

He was right. Though to this day, I have no idea *how* he was right. An old Volkswagen convertible bug, faded yellow with the top down, chugged toward us. I stood. Calm left and nerves filled me again. Needlessly, I realized soon enough.

Big Mama pulled up along the curb and slammed the Volkswagen door, causing the cat to leap out of the back of Jackson's truck. "I'm coming, I'm coming, get over here, you," she said. She lumbered down the walk, gave the gate a shove with the palm of her hand, and held out her arms.

"I told myself this morning, 'Louella, you ought not go to work today, in case she is coming your way.' But I listened to my mind instead of my soul." She thumped her chest, large and squishy as the arm of a sofa. "And my mind said

'Get yourself out of bed and go to work.'"

She gathered me up into a hug and said into my hair, "I figured you were in God's hands either way, and if you were coming to me, you'd get here."

"I got here," I said.

"And who is this?" she said. "Look what you've got there."

"This is Jackson Beene," I said.

"Louella Belle." She took his hand in both of hers.

"Nice to meet you," Jackson said. "But I'm gonna leave you two alone now."

"No, no. Don't go rushing off. You look hot and dusty. You can come in for a beer." Big Mama jiggled her keys in the lock. She opened the door and out sprang a tiny, scruffy dog. "Get in there now, Frankie," she said, poking him with her shoe. "Quit with the racket."

"I already made friends with your cat," I said.

"Oh, that cat is Rhonda and Jay's next door, but she thinks she's mine. You see her, you tell her to go home. Come on in, don't mind any mess you see."

Jackson stepped back, away from us. "I'm going to go now," Jackson said. "But thanks anyway."

"You sure?" Big Mama said. "We didn't even properly get to know each other."

I didn't want him to leave either. But Jackson, well, Jackson was someone who made up his own mind about things.

"I'm sure," Jackson said. "See you." He left out of the gate, did a jog toward his truck.

"Jackson!" I called. "Jackson!" But the truck door had already slammed with a clatter, and Jackson started the truck's engine.

"Thank you," I said.

He put his hand up in a wave, but if he'd heard me, I couldn't tell.

I took a bath in Big Mama's tub. You have to let the water run a bit first, to get the rust out, but it felt wonderful to be clean. And wonderful to be in one of Big Mama's terry-cloth robes so huge I had to gather it up behind me like a ball gown when I walked. Big Mama made me dinner. Chicken with fresh rosemary from a pot in her backyard and a tomato salad and crispy potatoes fried in oil in the oven. Cooking smells, terry cloth, soap, and linens taken from the cupboard and put on the bed in Angela's old room; Big Mama was treating me like I was sick, which I guess in a way I was. We ate dinner while that old scruffy dog Frankie, an afterthought of a dog, scurried under the table for scraps.

Then Big Mama tucked me in. She actually tucked me in, making the covers tight around me. Then she sat on the bed. The springs groaned from her weight. She smelled like dinner and outside air. Given the work she does, her hand was surprisingly soft on my forehead.

"Your mama knows you're here," she said. "Okay?" Her voice was quiet, as if I were already asleep and she was afraid to wake me.

"Okay," I said.

"It's good. You did good coming here. You don't want to be there now."

"Is my dad okay?" At the thought of him, the real him, not this other him, tears sprang into my eyes. I loved my father. He was my dad. I couldn't imagine, didn't want to imagine, the hell he was going through.

"Oh, darlin'," she said. "They're watching him. They thought he might . . . Well, he's more desperate than even my Clyde."

It was starting to get dark in the room. Just the warm glow from a table lamp that sat on a crocheted handkerchief. The sheets I lay in were soft from years of washing. I set my cheek on the pillow. Big Mama kept her hand on my head.

"I've lost him, haven't I?" I whispered.

"You'll have him different," she said.

"I lost him a long time ago," I said.

"Mmmm."

We were quiet a while. Somewhere outside my window I could hear the jangle of that cat's tags as she loped about on the grass, re-energized by the night, probably leaping to catch mosquitoes.

"How could he do something like that, Mama? I can't understand it. I just don't get it. I *know* him." Tears rolled down my cheeks, made my pillow damp.

"Another person's heart is a mysterious place," Big Mama said softly. "A mysterious place indeed."

"But how could he do something so awful? How?"

"To that man? And to you? And to himself and to his mother? You harm yourself, you harm someone else, same thing, isn't it? Just where you put your pain."

"It was just too much pain? Did he snap or something? Was that it?"

"All it needs is to feel important enough for one minute. Your father, my Clyde."

"My grandma says it never would have happened if Grandpa were still alive," I said.

"Well, we can't know that, can we? Maybe your grandpa's voice would have come stronger and clearer than the others, and maybe no. We can only guess, can't we, unless your father tells us himself?"

"I just don't understand why," I said. "Why do you think he did this, Big Mama?"

"Me too. I'd be only guessing."

"Guess then."

"Maybe he just *wanted* things without knowing exactly what they were."

"That's something my mom would say."

"Truth is worth hearing twice."

"I don't know," I said.

"Don't expect all the answers at once," she said. "It's going to take a long time."

"It was scary, Mama," I said. I cried.

"I know it was, darlin'."

She held me until I was quiet again. She kissed me on the top of the head, then turned out the light. I slept. I woke because I heard a horrible howling sound. Coyotes. A pack of coyotes sounding both tough and suffering, a frightening thing to wake to. I sat up in bed. I wondered about Jackson. Where he was for the night, if he'd made it home. I could feel by the temperature of the room that the weather had changed. In the Northwest, late summer can fall as definitely as the curtain in a play's last act, rising perhaps for a last applause, perhaps not—show's over. Get out the coat, which feels surprisingly heavy after its stay in the closet, and go fetch the beach towel, hung over a chair to dry and now flung across the yard by the wind.

I got out of the tight covers and walked to the window.

I smiled.

Jackson's truck was parked across the street a few houses down.

I worried about him, though, sleeping in that truck. I hoped he had a blanket. I told myself that someone who had been lost in the woods, to the point of near death, would have a blanket. Still. I thought about going out there, making him come inside.

What I did instead was, I went back to bed. And I slept well, knowing he was still near. When I woke it was late, I could tell. I'd slept better than I had in weeks. I got out of bed, went right to the window. Jackson's truck was still there, but I couldn't see him inside. I wondered if he had slept in the back, under the stars as Melissa said he did sometimes. I wondered if he was cold and horribly stiff or if he'd been abducted by the coyote pack.

But I shouldn't have worried. Because Big Mama *had* gone outside the night before and made Jackson come in. When I went into the kitchen, I saw him sitting with Big Mama at the kitchen table and drinking coffee. The two of them just as chummy as ham and eggs.

# Chapter Sixteen

"Well, here, you'd better take one of my sweaters," Big Mama said. "You take off somewhere next time, Jordan, make sure you've prepared yourself for every kind of weather."

"I'll remember that," I said.

"Yes, I know how much you'd like to come, Frankie. But today's your day to stay and guard the house." Big Mama gave the dog a nudge with her foot as she opened the door for us to go out. That sorry dog; he was a small rug that went through the wash when it was supposed to be Dry Clean Only.

"I'm not sure Frankie could guard an anthill," I said.

"Shh, now, we don't want him getting his

feelings hurt," she said. "He's sensitive." Frankie looked up at us with old watery eyes. You wouldn't hesitate to blame any bad smell on him.

Outside, the yard and the flowerpots and even the neighbors' painted mailboxes had lost their brightness. The sky just hung there, fuzzy and gray as a slab of laundry lint. I put Big Mama's sweater on. It hung down to my knees, and if I put my arms out, I looked like I had wings.

"You want me to help put the top up?" Jackson said. He walked around the Volkswagen and bent to look at it.

"There's a small problem with the top," Big Mama said. "It's called 'Stuck Open.'"

"You drive like this all the time? Even in the winter?" I said.

"This'll be my first winter. But on rainy days, well, we just use those." Big Mama pointed to the floor of the car. Jackson reached inside, picked up one of the umbrellas, and opened it up. It was a clear plastic bubble umbrella with a banana yellow handle. I'd had one like it when I was eight.

Jackson looked out from it. "You want to take my truck?" he asked.

"No need," Big Mama said. "I'm the one that knows where to go. We can stand a little cool air."

Big Mama could stand a little cool air, with her extra flesh and heart like a furnace, but I had to stick my arms down inside her sweater so the sleeves hung loose and empty, and I had to hunch low behind the windshield where the heater in Big Mama's Volkswagen was turned up high. Which, if you've been in a Volkswagen on a cold day, you know doesn't mean much. Jackson sat in the back. His chin was tucked down into his jean jacket, and his hair blew out behind him in a solid sheet. He looked afraid to move in case he might disrupt the workings of his circulatory system. I wanted to laugh. It occurred to me that I might love Jackson Beene.

Big Mama drove through town, leaving the quaint buildings and sidewalked streets behind. The winding back roads outside Nine Mile Falls passed farmlands garnished with backdrops of great snowy mountains before the roads curved and rose once again to enter shaded forests. She took the curves slow—you had to watch for deer, she explained, and for the logging trucks that sped too fast for their own good. At one point the road widened to include a strip of parking lot at the shoulder. Big Mama pulled over.

"Get out here a minute," she said. "You ever see this?" she asked. Jackson nodded, but I shook my head. I could hear the roar as we walked closer to the cliff's edge. Over it, I could see an enormous thundering waterfall with a lodge perched at the top. Looking down, I saw dots of people, hiking toward the misty bath at the bottom.

"Snoqualmie Falls," Big Mama said. She had to speak loudly to be heard over the rumble. Sprays of tiny water droplets rose up and wet my face. "Hundred feet higher than Niagara, though don't tell anyone. They can have the tourists, thank you."

We walked back to the car. The breezy ride and mist from the falls had turned Jackson's scraggly hair into Rastafarian ringlets. I smiled at him, and he grinned back. Home seemed far away. I felt like a kid on a field trip; that surge of happiness and energy at leaving school behind and forgotten for the day.

"Steelhead in there," Big Mama said, her voice quiet now that we were back in the car. "Tribes met for council by this riverbank. *Snoqualm* means 'moon.' White folks called them the 'Moon People.'" Big Mama pulled a wide arc of seat belt over herself and started the Volkswagen again.

A few more blowy, freezing minutes down a forested road and we were at the start of a dirt path closed to cars by a link of chain.

"I have the privilege of running this place, but it's really nature that's in charge," Big Mama said, and got out of the car. I watched the back of her lumber over to unhook the latch. The pockets of her flannel shirt looked wide enough to carry a picnic lunch, and her huge work jeans (bought in the men's department, she had complained) had to be rolled at the cuff.

"This is a homemade hatchery, funded with private donations, so don't expect all the fancy billboards and cement walkways," Big Mama said. We walked behind Big Mama, whose breathing was heavy but pace quick as she headed toward a small cabin built on the banks of the Snoqualmie River. Contraptions that looked like rows of low workbenches stuck up from the water, as did a trio of high, neck-breaking platforms. I hoped Big Mama didn't have to get up on those.

"Here, we worry. Only one or two of every thousand salmon survive the journey back. That is, of the ones that even get out of the gate. You got overfishing"—Big Mama counted off on her fingers—"you got dams, you got natural predators. And sure, you can grow some extras in a cement pool and give them chicken feed, but real baby salmon don't eat pellets. So here we aim to increase the salmon populations, but we do it their way, in their place."

She surveyed her surroundings, looked over the river. "Sure, you can take Mother Nature's arm and force it behind her back, you can use your science or what have you to make it go the way you want it to go. But we are talking about a creature with the most ancient of instincts. You mess with that, you don't *listen*, then you'd better not sit and wonder why you yourself can't find your own way home. Come here," she said.

But before we could follow her to the edge of the river, a guy dressed like Big Mama in flannel and jeans came out of the cabin.

"I thought you called in sick," he said to Big Mama.

"I've got visitors," she said.

The guy had a long ponytail and small glasses. I realized I knew him. He realized the same. "Hey," he said, pointing finger at me. "I know you."

I held up my palm, which still had the trace markings of the map he'd made for me to Black Nugget Road from the used book-and-record store. "He helped me find the way to your place," I told Big Mama.

"How about that," she said. "Tom Stone, these are my friends Jordan and Jackson."

"Pleased," he said. "I work at that other place so I can eat. Only the boss makes enough around here to live lavish."

"Ha," Big Mama said.

"I'd have warned you not to ride in her car, but it looks like you did already," he said.

"Never mind, you," Big Mama said. "Tom

takes his bike. Up that road we came? Imagine this big ass on a bike." She slapped her hips.

Jackson laughed. "What are you laughing at?" she said. And then to Tom, "I wanted to show them the chums. You want to come with us?"

"I've got to count in"—he checked his watch—"Six minutes."

"Okay then," Big Mama said. Tom waved good-bye, then took a clipboard from where it hung from a nail on the cabin wall. "For five minutes every half hour someone counts the chums coming through," Big Mama said. "You'll go calling us primitive if I don't tell you we also count with sonar. But there is nothing like the eyes God gave you. You get good at it, too."

We followed her down a path near the river; behind us I could see Tom climb the plywood steps of the platform, clipboard under his arm. Big Mama eased sideways down a slope where the river curved to a quiet inlet.

"There," she said.

I had never seen so many fish in one place. They were about a foot long and a deep red. They huddled together in thick groups or swam against the current, broad tails flapping, sometimes raising themselves and landing with a slap against the surface of the water.

I knew their story. I knew that they had finally returned after a ten-thousand-mile journey. Seeing them there, knowing that they had nearly done it, filled me with awe and joy. I know it sounds corny, but it was true. The wonder of it made me take Big Mama's hand.

"This is where they were born," Big Mama said.

"They look tired," I said. They did. The color they had earned from their ocean trek, a deep red, seemed to seep from them.

Jackson leaned over the riverbank, hands in the pockets of his jeans. "The scales are rotting," he said.

"Scales are being absorbed. To finish the trip. Four years in the ocean, and now they have only enough energy to get back home to spawn and die," Big Mama said. She released my hand. "They left here no bigger than my finger." She held it up. "And these are the ones that made it. So spent, they don't even eat. Don't even eat. Now, that *must* be tired." She laughed. Took my hand again. "But they're hurrying. Can you see it?"

You could. I found myself leaning forward. I wanted to help with the physical strain I almost felt myself as I watched the efforts of their ragged bodies.

"They've left home and had their adventure," Big Mama said. "But now it's time to go back and finish. This is where they're supposed to be. They know that home is the best place to love and die. And they gotta be strong to get there." She squeezed her big palm to mine.

"How do they know they're supposed to be *here*?" I asked. *"This* stream?"

I had heard it all before, sitting on the end of Big Mama's bed in her room at my mother's house years ago. And she had told me the story countless times again over the phone, and in her broad handwriting in the letters she sent. Still, watching the fish fight with their last strength, I was caught up. It was almost unbelievable that after a ten-thousand-mile adventure they were back.

"Exactly how is a mystery. Life is full of mysteries, isn't it? We just get used to them," she said. That's how Big Mama talked. She caught Jackson's eye and winked.

"Right," he said. They'd had this talk before. My heart felt full knowing that Jackson and Big Mama saw things the same way.

"I tend to think it's the same way you'd know your own mama's kitchen," she said.

We watched the salmon for a while. They were ugly and wonderful. I was proud of them.

"Okay?" Big Mama said, breaking the silence. Back at the cabin, Big Mama showed us the barrels that in a month or two would hold almost fifty thousand eggs taken from twenty-five wild chums. The barrels would roll about in their home waters, a protected nursery, and be checked every day until almost April.

"The eggs," Big Mama said. "They're all eye when you look at them. All sight. At least all the sight they need. Thousands of years of memories."

When it was time to leave, we waved goodbye to Tom, whose five minutes of counting were up, but who was eating lunch out of a brown bag on the rickety platform above the river. I looked over this peaceful place. The entire time I was there, I thought not once of my father or Gayle D'Angelo or the scary tatters of my life that were waiting for me back on Parrish.

"I want to stay here forever," I said. "I'll come and work for you, Big Mama. I'll count fish."

Big Mama caught Jackson's eye. They exchanged a look. Big Mama sighed.

"What?" I asked.

"Oh, Jordan," she said.

It rained on the way home. All three of us clutched the stems of our bubble umbrellas as they lifted and fought the wind.

We stayed four more days. We went back to the hatchery with Big Mama, and Jackson and I walked the length of the creek from one end of Nine Mile Falls to the other. We bought some old paperbacks from Tom Stone at the used book-and-record place. In the mornings I would sleep late and wake to find Jackson and Big Mama at the kitchen table. At night we ate dinner, and Big Mama tried to teach us to play hearts.

That particular night Jackson had cooked. A frittata all yellowy brown, and biscuits with butter and honey. The smell of onions and peppers and frying butter still hung in the air as Jackson washed dishes at the sink with his sleeves rolled up to the elbow, darkness coming earlier than it had been to the small kitchen window where he stood. I waited for Big Mama to get the pack of cards out of her junk drawer, but instead she went to the living room and opened the lid of an old chest with a doily on top. She bent over the chest, moved around a couple of afghans as she kept the heavy wooden top propped open with one hand.

"What are you looking for?" I asked.

"Something I want to show you," she said. "Ah." She pulled out a photo album and held it in the air. "Here it is. Sit down," she said.

I sat cross-legged on the couch, and Big Mama eased down beside me, placing the book with one cover on each of our thighs. I wondered what she was going to show me. I was expecting to see baby pictures of her kids maybe, but when she opened the cover I was surprised to see a picture of my parents. They were standing with their arms around each other's waists in front of a small yellow house.

Below that was another picture of my mother and father, this time with Big Mama and Clyde Belle and Angela when she was about ten. This photo was all shoulders and heads, sloping downhill at such an angle that they looked like they should have rolled off the page years ago.

"Whoa," I said. "Hang on."

"We let Burke take that one," Big Mama said.

I leaned in for a closer look. The strange thing was, my parents looked in love. The strange thing was, Clyde Belle looked happy. It gave me the creeps to look at his picture, knowing what came after. It occurred to me that people would feel the same when they saw photos of my father. They would look and try to find in his face the seed of what he'd done.

"They came to visit us once when we were still in Chicago. Your mother was seeing her folks, I think. Before you were even born. Do you notice what I notice?"

"I don't know," I said. I didn't want to hurt her feelings and say what I noticed about Clyde Belle, in case that wasn't it.

"She looks just like you," Big Mama said.

"Who?" I said.

Big Mama laughed. Her huge chest heaved up and down. She poked the picture with her finger. "What other female in this picture could possibly look like you?"

"Oh, please," I said. "She does not. I've always looked just like Dad."

"You think so," she said. Big Mama flipped through pages. Burke blowing out candles on a cake. Big Mama graduating from college. Angela with one arm around Big Mama in her black gown, Clyde wearing the mortarboard on his head and a goofy smile on his face.

"Burke took a good one that time," I said. "You don't even have to turn your head sideways."

"Everything with practice," Big Mama said. She flipped through more pages, came back to the front again. She stopped at a photo of my dad, with sideburns and a young face, and my mother with her long brown hair, looking pretty. "I've known your mother a long time," Big Mama said. "You know that story?"

I nodded. "She met Clyde when she worked at the post office."

"She met Clyde when they worked at the post office," Big Mama repeated. "And after we were introduced, well, Clyde was barely part of the scene. Poor old Clyde." She shook her head.

"When we got the chance to move here, I thought I'd have the chance to see a lot of Claire, but it didn't work out that way until I got that job on Parrish."

Big Mama heaved herself up from the soft couch. She brought the album back to the chest and dug around inside again, unearthing another one. She sat back on the couch again. "Who'd have thought I'd have wanted pictures of that time in my life? But your mother, she knows how to take care, that woman. She sent them to me later. She said it'd help me remember how much I was loved."

These I recognized. A younger me with Big Mama, our cheeks together as if we were dancing. Big Mama sitting in our living-room chair, one of Miss Poe's needlepoint pillows at her back and Nathan standing next to her, wearing an apron that said KISS THE CHEF. Big Mama and my mother in their pajamas at the kitchen table, Nathan serving them a plate of muffins with a flourish. Big Mama and Hugh Prince sitting in a pair of slatted wood chairs out in the front yard, Hugh Prince with a pair of binoculars in his lap from a bout of whale watching. The yard, I noticed, looked bare and wide. This was before Nathan and Mom were married, before his sculptures hung from the trees. And then there was a picture of all of us, standing in front of Asher House. Big Mama had a suitcase at her feet. We had our arms around her. She held a pillow that Miss Poe had made for her: HE WHO LAUGHS, LASTS.

"Look at that," I said. I flipped through the pages. "Nathan's got an apron on in every one of those pictures. Sometimes I swear my mother treats him like a slave."

"Oh, hogwash," Big Mama said. "And what's that boy doing in there for you, huh?" She nodded her head toward the kitchen where the clinking of dishes against one another sounded suddenly very loud. "You can give love, you can give labor. Someone who gives both . . ." She raised her eyebrows to say, *Now* that *is something*. "Your mother gives both too. I know it. She helped me through the hardest point in my life so far."

"I'm very different from my mother," I said.

"Oh, you are, are you? Do you realize how much time you spend pointing out those differences? Too different is what people say when they are too alike and it makes them uneasy."

"No." I laughed. "I've always been more like Dad. *He* used to be the normal one."

"Normal?" she said. "Is that how you see yourself?" She took my chin in her hands. "You are not *normal*. You are not *conventional*, girl. You are *unique*. And a little scared to be who you really are."

I laughed. Took my chin back.

"You'll see," she said.

That same night I woke up again. I couldn't go back to sleep. I was thinking about my parents in the picture in Big Mama's album. It made me miss them. I was thinking about the things Big Mama had said about my mother and me. I went to the window and saw that the moon was out, the stars too, which meant that the nice weather would be returning for a little more attention.

I got back in bed again and put my face against the soft sheets, but I was too awake. I tip-toed through the house, turned the back door-knob slowly so that no one would hear. I sat in one of the lawn chairs Big Mama had in the backyard, one of those aluminum ones with the squishy cushions in alarming floral patterns. The kind that, after a rain, collect pools of water in the gathered dips of each button, as I discovered when I sat. I pulled the nightshirt Big Mama had given me over my knees and rested my head against the chair, just looking up. The night smelled of wet earth, and the moon gave the grass a white glow. There were no coyotes that night, but I could hear the jingle of the tags of the cat next door again. I was getting used to the night sounds at Big Mama's house. Even the refrigerator and the furnace when they came on in the night.

His presence, walking along the grass in his bare feet, startled me. He sat in the lawn chair beside mine, circled his arms around legs that looked skinny in his jeans. He wore his jean jack-et over the plain white T-shirt I now knew he slept in. His jacket was faded and soft, through wear, you could tell, and not bought that way. Earned softness.

He looked up at the sky, too, the way I did. "In the woods, when I was lost? When I first heard the noise, I thought a festival was going on," Jackson said. I knew this about Jackson by now, that he often began speaking as if the time since we last spoke was only one long pause. Jackson was someone you had to think with, be aware with. What he said might be a question about what you wanted to eat or the description of the most important experience of his life.

I said nothing. Just looked at the stars.

"I was sure when I got to the source of the sound there would be guys in plaid skirts and knee socks and little kids with balloons and booths selling cheap T-shirts. Some Scottish thing. One of those corny festivals."

"But it wasn't," I said.

"No," he said. "It wasn't."

"What then?"

"I was saved by some kind of spirit. I know it. I don't care how crazy it sounds. It's the truth. And you know what the newspaper said? This park ranger was quoted saying 'When people are lost and without food they frequently see and hear things.' They called what happened a hallucination. Said I was delirious. What a load of crap. I *heard* it."

"I believe you," I said.

"I knew you would. I could tell that right away."

I smiled. I hoped I could be all of the things he seemed to see in me.

"After I saw that article, I went to the library," Jackson said. "I thought, okay, maybe this *does* happen all the time. I mean, I almost *died*. I had a couple of tortillas in my pack, some cheese. After that, only water from streams, drunk from my hand. I could actually feel myself getting weaker. Like I was fading."

His voice wobbled. He took a large gulp of night air. "Oh, man," he breathed. "This is not stuff I talk about."

I didn't say anything. I had learned that too. I just sat and looked at the stars some more and waited. I wondered if Big Mama was right about all the stuff she said about God. I wondered if Grandpa Eugene was looking down at us with his halo. Except that Grandpa wouldn't have a halo. He'd refuse it. Maybe he'd compromise with some glowing baseball cap. There were things in my life now, I realized, that even Grandpa Eugene couldn't fix if he were alive.

I surprised myself. I leaned over the arm of my chair and took Jackson's hand. It was cold from the night air. I put it near my mouth and blew warm air on it. He smiled.

"You," he said.

And then, "I went to the library. I looked up every hiking accident, every disappearance until the place closed down. There was nothing. No one else hearing music that led right to a ranger station. I didn't know what to do with this, this information. This *absence* of information. I kept playing the situation over and over in my head. Had I heard it? But I knew I had. I followed it once, even passed out from exhaustion, and when I woke, it was there again."

He brought our clenched hands to his own mouth, ran the back of my hand over his lips softly. His eyes peered at me in the darkness. "I heard it. It was real. I had to say the hell with park rangers."

Jackson held my hand next to his cheek, like I was something treasured. I *felt* treasured with him.

"What I'm saying I guess, Jordan, is, when you need help, there is always something to bring you home."

The next morning Jackson was not sitting with Big Mama at the kitchen table when I got up. The house was quiet. I wondered if they were both still asleep. But Big Mama never slept late. It was as beautiful a morning as I thought it would be, and I looked out the back door, expecting to see the two of them out there, sipping from their mugs. But the two lawn chairs we had sat in the night before were empty. Frankie lay under the kitchen table.

"Where are they?" I said. Which excited him

unnecessarily, causing him to scurry out and leap around at my feet. I parted the curtains over the kitchen sink. Jackson and Big Mama stood to the side of Jackson's truck. I watched them talk a while, then Big Mama gave Jackson a hug, thumping him on the back. It pleased me to see them together. They walked up the path and I ducked behind the curtains again. The door opened, and I heard the scuff of Jackson's shoes as he wiped them on the mat.

"Where were you two?" I called.

"Packing up," Jackson said.

I walked to the hall where they stood. "Are you going somewhere?" I asked.

"We," he said. "We are."

"Where are we going?" I asked.

"Home," he said.

Big Mama just stood behind Jackson, her arms folded across her chest, smiling a small smile.

I thought about this. "But I haven't even had breakfast," I said.

"We weren't planning on sending you off hungry," Big Mama said.

We had breakfast. Big Mama was pleased because Jackson had gotten her convertible top to close. "It's good to let God pick a man for you," she whispered to me as we were leaving. "We don't do so well when we pick them ourselves. They end up like lipsticks in a drawer, all those wrong colors you thought looked so good in the package."

Outside, Big Mama propped her camera on the gatepost and we all hunched together next to Jackson's car as the shutter clicked. "You will want this," she said. "Later."

I was ready to go. And not just because the two of them had been working on me.

I was ready because I saw a glimpse of him. The Second Chance Guy. In a Hawaiian shirt and a straw hat with a flower in the brim. He looked good. Tan. His arms hairy and brown, his nose a happy pink. He was giving me a sideways glance, a little wink. I guess I was ready to find out what was going to happen next in my life.

"I want to hear the bagpipes," I said to Jackson.

And so he played.

"Okay," I said.

# Chapter Seventeen

**Yes, I crossed the sea on the** way home, but it was not a treacherous voyage of ten thousand miles, but a slow easy ride on a ferry called the *Whidbey*. I did not have to fight currents or the hungry mouths of swordfish and seals; I only had to hold the hand of the strange young man who loved me. And when I arrived, I did not have to leap a ladder or fight the stream with my last strength, but was gently pulled into port by a trio of Franciscan nuns yanking on a thick rope while trying not to step on the hems of their habits.

Just the same, I came home.

I was sick with nerves when we landed, don't get me wrong. But I felt like a different me was arriving back there, on Parrish Island. I felt as if for a long time I had been just standing out-side one of those photo booths where you sit on a swivel chair and get four poses for a dollar, just waiting for the smelly strip still wet with chemicals to slide down. And now it had, and the person there was not who I was expecting.

Jackson's truck clanked over the metal ramp of the ferry. I did not look down the street where Eugene's Gas and Garage had turned into Abare's. I would not look for a long time. We passed Randall and Stein Booksellers, turned onto the Horseshoe Highway. Even the forces of nature seemed to be working to shake my shoulders and make me sit up to take notice of what I had around me, because the island looked especially beautiful that day. The maples and the dogwoods and the alders were begin-ning to turn orange at the tips of their leaves, and the waters of the strait glittered around the sailboats taking a few last spins before winter. Cliff Barton had his biplane parked, and so the skies were quiet except for the rich sounds of the thrushes and sea birds. If you went down to the university research center on a day like that, Grant Manning would let you put on his head-phones to hear the hums and whistles and clicks of the orcas gliding in the coves of the Strait of Juan de Fuca.

I loved that place.

That crazed energy that begins in early June

with the first smell of spring was beginning to quiet; now would be the quick drop into a gray and drowsy winter of thick socks and looking down to keep the rain from your face. It was catch-your-breath time, the last big sigh before the weather changed. The island had been busy showing off its beauty and aliveness, and now, like a wild summer girl in an open convertible for whom the show was temporarily over, it had an air of resignation and calm.

The signs on the oil tank had gone back to the mundane. HAPPY SWEET SIXTEEN, KRISTEN! and VITAMIN E FOR LONG LIFE with the number for that prune Cora Lee at the Theosophical Society. When we curved onto Deception Loop, Jackson took my hand. Probably because he heard how loud my heart was beating.

I started to swallow hard when Jackson's tires first crunched along the gravel driveway, when I saw the door fling open and my mother run down the steps, her braid flying out behind her. My throat closed tight when I saw Nathan standing in the doorway, holding Max's hand, Max squirming to get loose; and when I saw the curtains fold back and caught Miss Poe trying to peek outside without being noticed. But I couldn't hold back the tears when Jackson squeezed my hand and said, "They're waiting for you. All the people who love you." And then the wind picked up, and all the crazy sculptures went spinning and jangling, and my mother's arms were around me as I sobbed into her shoulder. And I was so grateful for her.

Luckily Max got loose and lifted his bangs, showing me the banana-peel sticker he'd put there, and Nathan explained that they'd just looked through a *National Geographic* on India, and we all laughed. Homer came around the corner, jingling prettily from the pair of finger cymbals hanging from his mouth that he'd snitched from the marimba school next door. Finally, Miss Poe could stand it no longer and clunked down the steps in her new clogs, which she showed off to me by holding up one pant leg.

And I can't tell you why, but this made me cry too. Everything that day made me cry.

You will want to know that I saw my father shortly after. That I brought him his architecture book that I'd carried in my backpack. I was afraid it might make him sad, but he seemed happy when he saw it. I asked him why he did it. Of course I asked him why. He just shook his head. "I don't know," he said. His hands trembled when he said it. "I don't understand it myself. I stepped out of my life. I killed a man I didn't even know. . . . And I don't know why." He says he still loves her.

I am trying to get used to having him different, as Big Mama says. To see him when there is always something between us. I am trying to get used to the sadness of his life. Bonnie Randall sees him frequently. They write almost every day.

You will want to know about Gayle D'Angelo. She sold her house right after the murder and moved to the mainland. Gayle D'Angelo tried to sue for my father's assets. "I can't even date, I'm so terrified," she told the newspaper. She said she hoped no man ever loved her that much again.

Melissa heard from someone that Remington tried to run away from home. I couldn't help but think that maybe he knew the truth about his mother's role in his father's death. I heard later that Markus got a scholarship to some fancy college. People tell you these things, as if it is information you should have. I still wonder about Remington and Markus, what they thought and felt through all of this, how they are doing now. It's like there's a weird bond between us. I hurt for them.

My grandmother tried to have Gayle D'Angelo investigated. "She put the gun in his hand," Grandma said. "She put the idea in his heart. He only thought she needed protecting," Grandma said. The only new thing the investigator discovered was that before the D'Angelos married, Wes had followed the advice of his wealthy businessman father and had gotten a prenuptial agreement. Divorcing Wes would have left Gayle with a lot less money than the way things turned out. Unfortunately, although Grandma and I didn't know this before, my father's attorney did. It would not have changed the outcome much, he'd told us. My father had pled guilty.

Because of where my father is, Gayle D'Angelo will never be gone from our lives.

When I first came home, my mother wanted me to see a counselor. Her friend Bea Martinson, the one who tried to be a lesbian but couldn't, did that sort of thing. I refused but finally compromised and let her take me back to Dr. Mary, who, with the help of Nurse Larry pronounced me the picture of health. Despite her cheery prognosis, I had some getting well to do. I didn't go back to school for my last year at Parrish High, though Melissa tried her best to get me to go. I didn't want to see Kale again, who after stealing the car got let off with a few hours of community service. According to Melissa, he'd had to pick up litter along the Horseshoe Highway, with Jason Dale and the gang driving by every few minutes to honk and yell and throw gum wrappers, and now he wore his notoriety with the same pride he used to wear that stupid flowered hat.

Seeing Kale, though, would have been nothing compared to dealing with the crap I knew I would get from the other kids. I didn't feel strong enough for that. I couldn't be the person they thought I was now. I imagined my empty seat. People would look at it and claim they'd seen tragedy coming.

I just needed to be home. I needed to figure out how to make sense of something that made no sense. I needed to be where I could see the photo Big Mama sent later, which I had propped up on my dresser. The three of us in front of Jackson's car in Nine Mile Falls.

Ms. Cassaday started bringing me books. I was too smart, she said, not to get my diploma and go on to college. Ms. Cassaday understood what it was like having other people thinking about the most private things in your life. She came every week. I read a lot of books, books about plants and nature and people and Renaissance architecture. She told me I ought to write out my story.

I used to think it was stupid, those people who talked about finding themselves. But I got lost enough myself once, to need that. I wandered away from myself one day and ended up in a small town. At last I pulled up beside myself and said, *Hey Jordan, glad I found you! What the hell are you doing here?*

I do not measure fat girls anymore. People measure me. They wonder about what kind of person I am, his child. They ask their questions, and I try as hard as I can not to give them what they want. Those things are mine. I keep them locked away. I picture them folded up in velvet, hidden in a case; it looks like the Baptistry in Florence my dad used to show me in his book. The one that looks like a rich lady's jewelry box, the one with the doors so beautiful they are called the Gates of Paradise. My father will never get his wish to see those doors.

I work at the Hotel Delgado, at my favorite part of the island. Every now and then I walk the path to the McKinnon family plot. Sometimes I even sit in one of the stone chairs. I hope the McKinnons don't mind. I like it there. I like that family table made of stone. That group of people who always have a place with one another.

Mostly, the things in my life are broken but still whole. At my mother's house this is literally true. The screen door will come off its hinges one week, the freezer will drip an ocean of water onto the floor the next. The dryer has been broken for more than a month.

So I ride to work with my wet waitress uniform on my handlebars. I wave to the nuns at the ferry terminal, who have gotten used to seeing me pass. By the time I get to where I'm going, my uniform is dry.

And sometimes Jackson gets there before me. He stands on the hill behind the hotel, playing his bagpipe. The tender notes drift over the choppy waves of the strait. They settle upon the stones and in the folds of the old roses. They carry along a breeze and find me, riding my bike his way. Always, the music sounds like a welcome.

# About the Author

Deb Caletti grew up in the San Francisco Bay Area, and now lives with her family in the Pacific Northwest. She steals her best lines from her mother, her kids, and the dog, who doesn't seem to mind. When she is not writing or reading books, Deb is a painter, a lyricist, and a 2001 recipient of the Artist Trust/Washington State Arts Commission Fellowship for literature.